# COUNTRY ROAD ROMANCE

# COUNTRY ROAD ROMANCE

TJ WEST

ISBN 979-8-9986231-0-3 (ebook)

ISBN 979-8-9986231-1-0 (trade paperback)

*To Aaron, for everything.*

# CHAPTER 1

"Ugh, this guy is the *worst*," Jared muttered to himself. "No one should get to be that handsome and successful and also be gay and be from West Virginia. It just isn't fair."

"Who are you talking to?"

He turned around to face Rebecca Oggleson, the director of the Mountain State Queer Film Festival, his boss and, not coincidentally, his best friend. In an earlier time and place, she would have been called a lipstick lesbian. Her honey-blonde hair was styled into a variety of tight curls, and her full lips pushed out in a bright-red pout. Though she was just over five feet tall, her pointed high heels gave her another couple of inches and, with her sleek pantsuit, she looked like she was about ready to run for office.

"Um," he stammered, "no one." He knew it was too late to try to cover up who he'd been looking at on his computer, but he was still tempted.

Rebecca narrowed her eyes and then, when she saw what was on the screen, actually smirked.

"You've been internet stalking Charlie Garrett again, haven't you?"

He sighed and thought about disputing that claim, but it would be a waste of time. "Fine, yes, I've been internet stalking Charlie Garrett," he said, throwing up his hands in mock exasperation. "You got me. Are you happy now?"

"I don't know why you have such a hang-up about him," Rebecca said. "He's handsome and successful and also gay and from our state. And, perhaps most importantly, he happens to be a pretty good actor. What's not to love?"

Jared snorted at that. "I guess that's true, *if* you count being in cheesy romance movies for the Romance Network being a good actor."

"Don't be a film snob."

"I'm not," he insisted. "It's just that I think there have to be some standards where movie acting is concerned. He's handsome enough, but that doesn't mean he's *good*."

"Well," she said, "are you sure that you're not being hypercritical of him because you have a little bit of a crush?"

"Absolutely not," he said. "There's no way I would ever have a crush on someone like that, and let me tell you why. Not only is he a subpar actor; he also does literally nothing for West Virginia or the LGBTQ community, either here or elsewhere. He made it out, and he's never looked back, which is apparently good enough for him. As if *that* weren't enough, he's also one of those 'straight-acting gays' who thinks they're better than those of us who are more explicitly queer." He snorted to show just what he thought of such self-hating gays.

As he went on, the look on Rebecca's face became more and more concerned, and he started to have a dark suspicion about what she was going to say next.

"What?" he said, interrupting his own diatribe.

"Well, you know how we've been struggling to put the film festival together?"

Jared nodded. It was no secret that there were some members of the Huntington City Council that would have liked nothing better than to see the Mountain State Queer Film Festival canceled altogether, and Rebecca had had to make do with both a very small staff and a very skinny budget. He admired her abilities in that regard, and he'd been open with her about that fact. Her next words, though, made him rethink all of that.

"It turns out that we were very fortunate in our timing, because your celebrity boyfriend has a new movie coming out, *The Gentleman Usher,* and as part of the promotion for it he's volunteered to headline our festival. Surprise!"

Jared couldn't believe what he was hearing. Oh, sure, he'd read the rumors about this new project of Garrett's and how it would elevate the erstwhile TV star into the realm of movie stardom, but he'd never imagined it would premiere in Huntington, let alone that Charlie Garrett himself would be here.

Ugh," he groaned, "that's just great. Didn't you hear what I just said? We're going to have a straight-acting gay headlining our *queer* film festival and, as if that weren't enough, now the whole city is going to make a nuisance of itself, with middle-aged wine moms beating down the door to get a sight of him."

Rebecca wagged a finger at him. "They're going to buy tickets, and that's the important thing. And it wouldn't hurt you to be a bit more positive about this. This is a big get for us, and it's gone a long way toward convincing City Council, particularly Councilman Rhodes, that this festival has the ability to be a genuine draw for the city. The paperwork is all signed, sealed, and delivered. This is going to be our crowning achievement."

Jared could tell from the way that she was talking there was something she wasn't telling him, and he knew it was going to be something he didn't like. He narrowed his eyes at her and was rewarded with a faint blush.

"I know you're hiding something from me," he said. "Out with it."

"Well," she said, dragging out the word, "it turns out that one of the conditions for him coming here was that he have someone to show him around town. You know that he did his degree at WVU, and amazingly enough he hasn't ever been to our little corner of the state. So I kind of...volunteered you to do it."

"You did not."

She shrugged sheepishly. "I'm sorry, Jared, but you were the only other member of the board who was going to be available. Besides, you know Huntington like the back of your hand. If there's anyone who can show him the best points of interest it'd be you."

He snorted. "You're actually a native of the city, you know. I'm just a transplant who's been here too long."

"Yes, but I'm also the chair of the board and the one handling all of the rest of the planning." She batted her eyes at him. "Surely you'd love to be a key part of the festival's success?"

"Okay fine," he said. "I'll do it. But I'm not going to be happy about it, and I can't guarantee that I'm going to be very nice to the guy." He huffed. "I'm sure you knew I'd cave the moment you asked."

"I did, in fact," she said.

"When does he get here?"

"Well," she said, "the festival is in a few days, and he's slated to arrive the first day of it so...Thursday."

Jared sighed. A few days wasn't that long to prepare for what he knew was going to be a very unpleasant experience dealing with a Hollywood diva, but he supposed it was better than nothing.

"Okay, fine. I just hope that Mr. Hollywood is content

with riding in my old Ford pickup truck, because I'm not going to rent a car for him."

Rebecca gave him a mischievous smile. "Actually, that's perfect. If you happen to run into any reporters, and you most certainly will at some point, it'll be good for his image to be seen driving around in a truck just like regular people. It'll help give them the impression that he really is the humble guy that he says he is."

Jared didn't even bother hiding his eye roll. "What are you, his publicist now?"

"No, but there's always hope."

"So what time should I be at the airport?"

Rebecca tapped her chin. "He's set to land very early in the morning. So I'd say that you want to be there at eight at the latest. They're hoping that they can get him into town without a lot of reporters noticing. I'm sure they'll start hounding him later on, anyway, but at least he can have a bit of time out of the spotlight."

"You have got to be kidding, right?"

Before Rebecca could say anything her phone started buzzing, and she gestured at him to stay there while she answered it.

"Hello? Yes, this is Rebecca. Oh, hello Councilman. Yes, we have someone already lined up to go pick up Charlie Garrett. Yes, everything's in hand, I promise, and everything is going to go smoothly. You don't have to worry about anything." There was an ominous pause. "Yes, it is Jared, why do you ask? Oh, well, you don't have to worry about that, either. He's promised to be on his very best behavior. Okay, fine, yes. Goodbye, Councilman."

"That," she said, "as you might have guessed, was Councilman Rhodes."

Jared hated just hearing that name. He'd had more than his fair share of run-ins with him, largely during meetings of the Council, when Jared had pointed out his many deficiencies when it came to protecting the rights of the queer community. In fact, he could distinctly remember the time when he'd called the man an idiot to his face, to conspicuous laughter from the gathered crowd and even from some of the other members of the Huntington City Council.

Clearly, he wasn't one to forgive such a slight.

"And what did he have to say?" he asked innocently.

"He said that if you did anything to embarrass this city or himself again that he'd see to it that you were run out of town on a rail. At least, I think those were his words."

That did sound like something the prickly Rhodes would say. He was as blue-blooded as they came, but he always liked to make it sound like he was one of the common people, hence his earthy little sayings that sounded like they came from some 1950s western.

"I'm glad you told him that I would be on my best behavior," Jared said. "Though I suspect that his definition of what that means is probably different than ours."

"I'm sure," she said. "Ugh. I wish that Councilman Tate would hurry up and find a good reason to get rid of him." She lowered her voice. "Confidentially, she told me that she's been investigating him for some financial irregularities in his accounting, but so far she hasn't been able to find anything. When she does, though, that'll be the end of him. He'll be out of our hair for good."

"That day can't come soon enough," Jared said. "And now, if you'll excuse me, I've got to go. I have lots of good behavior to demonstrate."

Before Rebecca could say anything to that he was out the door, a satisfied smirk plastered across his face.

. . .

THE NEXT FEW days passed in something of a blur, as preparations for the film festival finally heated up, and everyone put their heads down and got to work. It was exhausting and exhilarating at the same time, but Jared loved every minute of it, not least because it helped him put Charlie Garrett out of his mind, at least until Thursday.

When the day arrived he got up early, had some coffee and, yawning so big he thought for sure he was going to dislocate his jaw, went out to get his truck started.

Once outside, he paused for a minute to admire his old Ford F150. It was a deep burgundy color, and it had been a gift from his father when he'd graduated college years ago. He smiled wistfully thinking about how proud his parents had been of him, and how they'd always shown him unequivocal support, even after he'd come out as gay during his first semester at college.

*I should go see them soon,* he thought. Even though he tried to go home as often as possible, the fact that they lived in the northern part of the state meant that it sometimes took longer than he would have liked. They always told him that they understood, that he had his own life to lead and shouldn't worry so much about them but, well, they weren't getting any younger, and it weighed on his mind.

*Standing here fretting about something that hasn't happened yet isn't going to get you to the airport any faster,* he thought.

He got in and started the engine, savoring the way that it still purred and giving the wheel an affectionate pat. "That's a good girl," he said. "I treat you right, and you treat me right. And don't let this Hollywood bigshot make you feel bad about yourself."

Jared smiled to himself as he started driving toward the airport, for once actually enjoying being up before the sun. It was rather exciting, to think that he was up and about and starting his day, when a lot of people were still waking up and having their coffee.

*Way to go Charlie Garrett,* he thought. *We haven't even met yet and already you're turning me into a morning person.*

It had been quite a while since he'd been out this way, and it was like revisiting old friends. Despite what he'd said to Rebecca, in the years since he'd moved to Huntington he'd really taken the town to his heart, and he basically felt like a native son. He liked to think that the city felt the same way about him, though there were times when he had his doubts. People like Councilman Rhodes had made their animosity toward queer people abundantly clear but, so far at least, the allies were standing firm.

Off to the right Jared saw Camden Park, complete with its clown sign. He'd always thought that it looked a bit demented–like something out of a horror movie–but he was always smart enough not to say that where anyone from the town could actually hear him. He'd never managed to make it to this little amusement park, despite the fact that his friends had ribbed him mercilessly about missing out on such a quin-tessential piece of city life.

*One of these days,* he thought.

He kept on driving, through the small towns of Ceredo and Kenova, and then at last he turned onto the road that wound up to the airport, rolling down the windows to let the clear, crisp autumn air inside. Already the leaves were showing their autumn hues, luxuriating in the first rays of the sun, and Jared felt that pinch in his chest that always came with fall. It was his favorite season, and he couldn't imagine being anywhere other than West Virginia.

*No one does fall like the Mountain State,* he thought, and he was glad that they were having the film festival at this time of the year, when his beloved state was at its finest.

At last the airport came into view, and Jared sighed. There

was no mistaking the hulking private jet that took up one of the airport's few runways. He grimaced, thinking of how much this whole situation was going to disrupt air traffic. It wasn't as if the Huntington Airport was *that* busy, but still, couldn't Mr. Hollywood have taken a commercial flight?

*I just hope that having Charlie Garrett as a headliner is enough to get people to come to the festival,* Jared thought grouchily.

Jared pulled into the parking lot, got out, and began walking toward the airport entrance. He wasn't sure just what he was supposed to do or where he was supposed to go, one more disadvantage of being awake before everyone else, including Rebecca, who might at least have given him some guidance as to what he was supposed to be doing. Then again, he probably should have asked for said information rather than being so committed to being a smartass.

*That wasn't very smart of me,* he thought.

Fortunately, a smartly-dressed woman who must have been Charlie's publicist came out of the airport and stalked toward him, stiletto heels clicking on the asphalt.

"You," she said, pointing at him. "I recognize you from the photo that Rebecca sent. You've been sent to take Charlie to his hotel, right?"

The woman's tone rubbed him the wrong way, but he wasn't going to start a fight right off the bat. So, instead, he just plastered on that plastic smile that he always used whenever he confronted people he didn't like and who clearly thought they were better than he was.

"Why yes, I am," he said, adding just a bit of a twang to his voice. It was all part of the act–since he was from the northern part of the state he usually sounded more like he was from Pittsburgh than West Virginia–but she ate it up.

"Where's the limo parked?" she asked, and Jared almost laughed at her.

"No limo I'm afraid, ma'am," he said, jerking his thumb at his truck. "All we had was the truck."

She frowned, but she clearly knew that this wasn't going to be an argument she was going to win. Besides, the sooner they got Charlie Garrett away from the airport–and any particularly intrepid reporters–the better. From what Jared had been able to learn about him, he was prone to saying things that got him into trouble and caused his communications and public relations team no small amount of headaches. While Jared would have been just as happy to let him spout off, he didn't want an off-color comment to torpedo the good-will they'd managed to get for the festival.

"I suppose that'll have to do," she said. "Just try to keep him out of trouble, okay?"

He gave her one of his best fake smiles. "Of course, ma'am. It would be my pleasure."

If she sensed that he was being disingenuous she didn't show it. Instead she just turned back and gestured toward the airport entrance. A moment later Charlie Garrett came bounding out–annoyingly chipper for it being so early in the day–and Jared got his first sight of the man who was going to be his charge for the next hour or so.

*He's like a golden retriever in human form,* Jared thought.

Charlie's California blonde hair was swept back from a face that looked like it belonged on an Abercrombie & Fitch model, and his tight-fitting T-shirt and jeans left little to the imagination. Broad shoulders rippled with muscle and, as he jogged over his shirt rode up a little, baring his midriff. Jared spent a fair amount of time in the gym, and even he couldn't help feeling a bit jealous.

*I guess I would be able to have a body like that too if I had all the money in the world,* he thought grumpily, even as he also felt more than a little stirring of desire. He'd seen quite a few pictures of Charlie Garrett, but none of them had really conveyed the man's raw, almost incandescent, sex appeal.

Charlie stepped forward and gave him a wide smile that was so familiar from his various movie appearances. Jared fought down the urge to roll his eyes, but even he had to admit that there was something almost magical about it.

*Maybe Rebecca was right,* he thought. *Maybe I do have a little crush on him.*

"Hi!" he said, sticking out his hand, "I'm Charlie Garrett. And you must be Jared Russell. It's so nice to meet you in person!"

Even though it was clear that Charlie had gone to a great deal of effort to sand away the edges of his southern West Virginia accent, Jared still heard it, and it almost made him like him a little more.

"Yes, I'm Jared," he said, a little stiffly, offering his own hand to shake. When their skin touched, he felt a little flutter in his chest.

*Don't be an idiot,* he reprimanded himself. *This is Charlie Garrett. He gets paid to be charming. None of this is natural.*

At the same time as he thought this, however, Jared also couldn't help but acknowledge that there was something effortless about the way that Charlie moved through the world, as if this was just the way that he was, nothing more and nothing less.

A brief moment of uncomfortable silence ensued, and then the publicist–whose name Jared still didn't know–broke in.

"Are you two going to just stand there making goo goo eyes at each other, or are we going to get to the hotel? We don't have all day, you know." She gestured at the largely empty airport parking lot. "And it's not going to be too much longer before this place starts up and the reporters show up."

TJ WEST

"Of course, of course," Jared said. "That was really rude of me. Right this way."

"Don't worry about your luggage," the publicist said. "I'll make sure that it gets to the hotel right after you do." She gave the bed of the truck a very dismissive look. "I wouldn't want to see any of it get...damaged."

Jared felt a momentary bit of embarrassment, because it was true that he hadn't cleaned it out before coming out here.

"Thanks, Sheri," Charlie said. "I knew I could count on you."

The next minute the two of them were getting into the truck. Jared noted with approval that Charlie didn't need any help getting in; in fact, he looked like he'd been doing it his whole life. Before Sheri could make any more sarcastic comments they were barrelling down the hill and toward the city.

*I just hope this ride goes quickly,* Jared thought. *Because I don't want to spend the rest of my day babysitting.*

"Thanks for coming out to get me," Charlie said, his voice a deep rumble. "I'm sure that you had other things that you'd rather be doing than going out of your way to come up here."

Jared was a bit taken aback by this offering of gratitude, but he managed to stammer out something that he thought was at least somewhat gracious.

"You don't like me very much, do you?" Charlie asked.

The blunt honesty of the question took Jared aback, and he couldn't think of anything to say. Instead he just kept his eyes on the road ahead.

"It's okay, you know," Charlie went on. "I'm used to it. There are a lot of people around here who kind of don't like it that I went and made something of myself, got out of my little podunk town." Out of the corner of his eye Jared saw Charlie shrug. "I guess I can understand where they're coming from. And then, of course, there are the ones who don't like it that one of the most famous people to come out of West Virginia is a queer. That rubs some of them the wrong way, believe me."

"I'm not one of those, you can be sure," Jared said, gritting his teeth. "But as it happens you're right. I'm not a big fan. You talk a big game about being proud of where you came from, and yet you almost never come back here, and when you do it's just to helicopter in, do a good deed or two, and then leave. Not exactly what one would expect of a proud son of the Mountain State, is it?"

Even though he didn't look to see what the effects of his words were, he was conscious of Charlie stiffening beside him. He waited for a Hollywood-sized explosion or tantrum, but none came. Instead, the star just sighed.

"I guess you're right," he said defeatedly. "I'm just another big shot celebrity without much substance."

Jared was so surprised by the fact that Charlie didn't even put up a fight that he could think of nothing further to say, and the rest of the ride proceeded in a tense silence. When they got to the hotel Charlie got out, his face still an expressionless mask. There was no sign of the gregarious guy of a half hour before. In fact, he almost acted like a robot.

*Well, what did you expect?* Jared thought. *You treated him like he was dirt, and he responded accordingly. You can't really blame him for that.*

What really surprised Jared, however, was how guilty Charlie looked, almost as if he was hiding something. There was no time to ask him about what it might be, however, because before Jared could even offer anything resembling an apology, Charlie was gone.

*That definitely could have gone better,* Jared thought. *Rebecca is not going to be happy about this. At all.*

# CHAPTER 2

*Well, that could certainly have gone better,* Charlie thought to himself as he walked into the hotel and went up to the front desk. *Of course, I can't really blame the guy. From his point of view I'm just another arrogant celebrity who cut and ran as soon as I could and never looked back. If I was in his shoes, I'd hate me.*

Charlie had wanted to tell Jared about all of the times that he'd tried to start various projects in one part of the state or another, only to be stymied by either recalcitrant leaders reluctant to be seen taking money or joining up with a gay celebrity, no matter how famous or successful they were. Or about all of the times that a project had fallen through because a bunch of protesters showed up, and Sheri, bless her heart, had said that it was just too damaging to his brand to be associated with it.

"Remember, Charlie," she'd said. "Your fanbase is Midwest moms. They don't want their golden boy to get caught up in a lot of drama. They don't care that you're gay. Just don't make a big deal out of it."

She'd made sure that all of those efforts, and all of Charlie's snarky comments about them in interviews, were swept safely under the rug and that the only image anyone saw of Charlie Garrett was one that had been carefully curated and approved by the executives of the Romance Network and by Sheri herself. These days it really took some digging to get to some of his more indiscrete moments, and Sheri and the other powers-that-be kept him on a very tight leash.

But, of course, he hadn't said any of that to Jared, had he? Instead, he'd just sat there and let him say those things, and now here they were. It was a frustrating position to be in, but he was used to it by now. Or as used to it as he was likely to be.

He walked up to the front desk, hoping in a distant way that the receptionist wouldn't recognize him and that he could enjoy a moment of anonymity. Unfortunately that hope was immediately dashed, and he wasn't surprised at this, either. It was just the way his day was going.

"Oh my God!" she said with that southern West Virginia twang that immediately made him feel at home. "You're Charlie Garrett. They said that you were going to be arriving sometime today, but I had no idea it was going to be while I was on shift." There was such transparent joy in her face that he couldn't bring himself to feel aggrieved, not even when she asked for a selfie (even though, as she confided to him, that was against the hotel rules).

Fortunately, she didn't belabor the whole thing, for which he was grateful. He was already quite tired, and he really just wanted to get into his room as quickly as possible, so that he could have a little bit of peace and quiet before the real chaos started. The Mountain State Queer Film Festival was only slated to take place during the weekend, and he knew that he was going to be busy almost the entire time.

It would have been nice to have some time to explore Huntington and the surrounding area, but when he'd proposed this to Sheri, she'd let him know in no uncertain terms that he must *not* go off on his own for any reason.

Doing so would only risk things going off the rails, and that was to be avoided at all costs.

"Remember," she'd said, "this whole festival is a chance for you to burnish your reputation and take the next step forward. Focus on that and nothing else."

All of this was how he found himself in his room, scrolling aimlessly on his phone. He thought about sending an update out on Instagram or TikTok, but resisted the urge. He knew all too well that anything like that had to get Sheri's approval before it went live. Since he'd already managed to alienate his handler for this whole adventure, the last thing he needed was to piss her off, too.

Charlie had to admit, though, that his handler was *very* attractive, which wasn't something that he'd expected. On the surface he looked like your typical country boy–with his plain white T-shirt, tight jeans, and boots–but he also had something classy and even a little nerdy about him, too. Maybe it was his chilly attitude, or maybe it was the way that his shoulders and thighs threatened to burst out of those same T-shirt and jeans but something made Charlie's heart beat a little faster.

*You just think that because he reminds you of all of the hot guys you went to high school with but didn't have the guts to approach.* That was definitely true, but back then he'd been plain old Charlie Slaughter and not Charlie Garrett, jewel in the crown of the Romance Network.

*You shouldn't even be thinking about him in that way at all,* he reminded himself. *You're here to do a job, so let it go at that. The fewer entanglements you get into while you're here, the better.*

Charlie laid down on the bed and closed his eyes. He slipped down into sleep much faster than he'd expected.

Suddenly his phone buzzed, waking him up. Seeing that it was Sheri, he swallowed a groan. He was sure she was going to give him a hard time, even though he had no idea what he could have possibly done wrong.

Sure enough, as soon as he answered it she was letting him have it.

"What did I tell you about taking selfies with people who haven't been vetted yet?" she snapped. "I specifically said to leave all of that to me, and what did you do? You went and got a selfie with the first person you ran into that wasn't that redneck who picked you up at the airport. Honestly, Charlie, why do you even keep me on your payroll if you're just going to ignore everything I have to say?"

He let her go on for several more minutes like this, until she finally ran out of steam.

"Are you done?"

"Yes, for now," she said. It was the same pattern that they always got into. He would do something that she didn't like, she would give him an endless hard time about it, he would apologize, and then the cycle would repeat. It was charming, in its own way, if also a bit irritating.

"Good," he said. "So what else do you have planned for me while I'm here? I really don't want to stay holed up in my hotel room for the entire trip."

"I guess that depends on you. Do you think you can stay out of trouble if I schedule you a ride around town with your handler later tonight?"

He looked out the window. It was still rather early in the morning, and he hated the thought of staying in his room for several more hours until Sheri decided that it was okay for him to come out.

"Can we bump it up a few hours? I haven't been to Huntington before, and I'd like to explore town a bit before all of the craziness starts."

Charlie didn't mention that he thought the handler hated him. He'd deal with that in a bit.

There was a pause on the other end of the line as Sheri thought about it.

"Okay, fine. You can go out on the town for the day, but I want you back in your hotel room by eleven tonight. Sharp. Is that clear?" They both knew that was hardly enough time to really get an evening going, but Charlie knew that this was the best he was going to get.

"Yes, mom," he said sulkily.

"Don't pout," she said, sounding uncomfortably like his actual mother. "And you should call her, you know. She hasn't heard from you in a couple of weeks, and she's been sending me vaguely passive aggressive text messages. I know I've said this before, Charlie, but I don't know why you bothered moving her out to California if you weren't going to spend more time with her. You might as well have left her here."

"I'll try," he said. "Um...I think I forgot to get my handler's number. Do you have it?"

Sheri sighed. "Yes, I have it. I'll give him a call and tell him to be there in fifteen minutes."

*He's going to just love that,* Charlie thought. *As if he didn't hate me enough already.*

"If that's everything for now, I'm going to leave you to your own devices," she said. "Remember. Behave yourself."

Before Charlie could say anything in response the phone beeped to tell him she'd hung up.

Fifteen minutes wasn't that much time, so he just did a routine check to make sure that he didn't look too rumpled from the flight, popped a couple of Altoids in his mouth, and made his way back downstairs. Someone upstairs must have been looking out for him, because he managed to get to the lobby without being seen by anyone. Even the fangirl at the front desk just gave him a knowing wink as he stepped through the revolving door.

And then the mob hit him.

There were the reporters, of course, and they were joined by at least a couple of hundred fans–many of them middle-aged women–and they swarmed him as soon as he stepped outside into the midday sunshine. No matter how many times this happened, and it happened a lot, he'd never really gotten used to it. Every time he found himself looking out at all of those faces looking rapturously at him he'd feel his heart start to beat faster and faster, his palms would get sweaty, and little spots would dance in his vision.

*Calm down, Charlie,* he said over and over. *You can get through this just like you always have.*

Suddenly an ugly voice broke through the crowd.

"Go back to California with the rest of the sinners, faggot!"

All of a sudden the adoring crowd turned as one, everyone looking either angry or horrified. For his part, Charlie's anxiety had suddenly turned into the scalding anger that he knew too well, the part of himself that he worked very hard to keep buried so that it didn't get him into trouble.

*Don't do it, Charlie,* he thought. *Don't pick a fight with this asshole, because it's just going to get you into trouble that you can't afford.*

Then the crowd parted to reveal the guy who'd shouted the slur, and whatever inclination Charlie might have had to be restrained flew right out the window. He'd half-expected the guy to be some kind of redneck but, to his surprise, he was dressed in a pair of khakis and a dress shirt and tie. A pair of brown loafers completed the whole getup, and the sign he was carrying–with the words "Go back to Sodom and Gomorrah" on it–was just the icing on the cake.

*I'm surprised that he doesn't have a whole gaggle of religious bigots behind him,* he thought.

Even though that little voice in the back of his head kept screaming at him not to give this asshole any encouragement by engaging with him, he knew that he was too far gone. He'd put up with guys like this his whole life, and now that he had the privilege and the money and the status, he'd be damned if he'd let him say that kind of stuff and get away with it.

*Not while I'm in West Virginia,* he thought. *I let assholes like this get in my way too many other times, but not this time.*

Just as he started to walk toward him, though, conscious all the while of the eyes of his fans and reporters locked on his every move, he heard the sound of an engine roaring and tires squealing, and then Jared was there, his hand resting gently on his arm.

"This guy isn't worth it," he whispered, somehow both urgent and reassuring. "Trust me. I've seen him at events like this, and he's trying to get you to do something stupid. Don't give in."

Something about Jared's calming tone seemed to bring Charlie back to himself, and he gave himself a little shake, thinking about how close he'd come to doing something colossally stupid.

"How did you know what I was getting ready to do?"

Jared gave him a level look. " I could see that you were about to deck the guy, and the last thing I want is for the festival to have to bail you out of jail."

Suddenly the brief feeling of euphoria that Charlie had felt at Jared potentially doing something to help him for his own sake evaporated. He should have known that he'd only been thinking about the festival and its well-being.

*So much for that,* he thought bitterly.

When Charlie didn't make any move to go to Jared's truck, the other man started guiding him, one hand on the small of his back. Even just that little bit of a touch was enough to send a flood of warmth through Charlie's body, reminding him that it had been way too long since anyone had touched him in a romantic way.

"I'm not an invalid," he snapped under his breath.

"Then stop acting like one," Jared snapped back. "I'm supposed to show you around the city, and that's what I'm going to do, whether you like it or not."

"You're really pushy and obnoxious, you know that?"

"Yeah, well, you've let fame go to your head, so I guess we're even."

They continued bickering like this as they made their way to Jared's truck, and all the while the gathered fans and reporters just kept looking at them and clicking their phones and the bigot kept shouting at them and waving his sign.

*I can just imagine what Sheri is going to say about this,* Charlie thought dismally. *She told me not to get into trouble, and the first thing I do when I walk outside the hotel is almost get into a fistfight with someone.*

As he got into Jared's truck, he started to wonder whether it was a good idea to have come to this festival at all, or whether he should have just stayed out in LA. It might have been at least a little bit easier if Jared had shown any signs of warming up to him, but if anything he looked even more hostile. As he started the truck back up he kept his eyes fixed straight ahead of him, staring at the road as he drove around town.

After about ten minutes of this, Charlie decided to try to ease the tension a bit.

"You know, if your job is to show me around and let me see the sights of your fair city, the least you could do is, you know, actually *talk* to me."

Jared just grunted and kept staring out the window.

Charlie sighed, but he was also starting to feel a bit annoyed about this whole thing.

"Thank you for coming back to get me," he tried. "Sheri said she was going to get in touch with you." He thought briefly about pushing Jared to try to get him to say more about why he didn't like him but decided against it. He'd probably get around to doing so in his own time, anyway.

Just then Jared sighed.

"I guess you're right," he said. "I know that you haven't been here before, and that kind of surprises me. I mean, it's the second largest city in the state, after all. And I know you've been to Charleston and Morgantown. So what gives?"

Charlie debated for a moment about just how much to tell Jared about his past and why it was that he'd avoided many parts of the state.

*Well, if you want him to warm up to you, you're going to have to open up at least a little bit.* Even now, Charlie still wasn't quite sure why it was that he was so invested in getting Jared to pay more attention to him. Maybe it was because there was something about him that went beyond appearances. Or maybe it was just the fact that by this point Charlie was so used to being adored by anyone he came into contact with that meeting with such hostility, particularly from someone who should have been starstruck, made him want to impress him all the more. Or maybe it was the opposite, and it was actually refreshing to have someone not be impressed.

*Or maybe you're just horny,* he thought.

Whatever the case, he was going to get underneath that hard carapace to the sensitive guy he thought he could see beneath it.

Taking a deep breath, he decided to reveal at least a little bit about his life. Not a whole lot, of course, just enough to get Jared to see him as a person rather than as some sort of entitled prick who'd forgotten about his roots.

*You're going to get yourself in trouble,* he thought. *But what the hell. Here goes.*

# CHAPTER 3

*J*ared hadn't been pleased to be called back to pick up Charlie a few hours after dropping him off at the hotel–he'd been looking forward to having some downtime–but now that they were together, he supposed that he would just have to make the best of things.

*I am not going to let anything this guy says convince me that he isn't just another shallow celebrity,* Jared thought as Charlie started speaking. *He may think that he's going to be able to use that charm on me, but he's got another thing coming.*

As Charlie started speaking, however, Jared couldn't help but look at him every now and then. After all, this was Charlie Garrett they were talking about, and there were some very good reasons that he'd managed to become a major star. There was no denying that he was beautiful, the kind of guy that Jared would have dashed his heart against again and again in high school and beyond. It was more than that, though: there was something kind about his eyes, some inner niceness that seemed out of place on someone famous.

There had to be something about himself that he wasn't revealing. His public image, as Jared knew all too well, was far too squeaky clean, but his digging, and that near blow-up outside the hotel, suggested that there was more to him than met the eye, that there was a darker side to the golden boy. Now was his chance to get to the bottom of things. All he had to do was let Charlie keep talking.

"I guess the first thing you should know about me is that I was born in a shithole little town up near Morgantown," he began. "I know I shouldn't talk about it like that, but that's what it was. Wedged up in this little holler, with a tiny school and a cluster of churches." He sighed, as if just thinking about the place caused him some pain. "It wasn't that bad, I guess, but it wasn't the best place to grow up if you wanted to get into the arts, and I always liked acting. I enjoyed watching old movies with my grandma, and as soon as I was old enough to drive I'd go up to Morgantown to go to the movies, even if it meant going by myself."

He paused, as if he was gathering his thoughts. Jared snuck another look at him, to see whether he could tell what he was thinking, but Charlie looked like he was a thousand miles and a hundred years away.

*Don't do it, Jared. Don't fall for his sob story.*

While Charlie was trying to think of what he wanted to say next, Jared turned his attention back to the road. He wasn't quite sure where he intended for them to end up, but somehow he'd brought them close to Ritter Park, without a doubt the nicest part of Huntington. It was the kid of place that you brought people when you wanted to give them a good impression of the city–with its historic buildings, its towering trees, its fountain, and its posh-looking people running and walking their dogs–but he was rather disappointed to see that Charlie was too wrapped up in his own story to be bothered to look around him.

*Typical,* Jared thought uncharitably. *I guess I shouldn't have expected anything else.*

He thought briefly of taking Charlie up to the rose garden–maybe that at least would impress him–but then the other man started talking again and he put it aside for the moment

*There's time to do that later, if you still want to do it,* he thought. *Besides, you don't want to give him the wrong idea. The rose garden might be a bit too...romantic.*

Even so, there was a strange little part of him that didn't think that would be such a bad thing.

"My parents weren't quite sure what to make of their shy little boy who wasn't interested in the same kinds of things as the other members of the family. I mean, I liked going outside and stuff, but I always felt like a fish out of water. They did the best they could for me, but I could always tell that they didn't understand me, at least not in the way that I wanted them to." There was a great deal of pain there, Jared thought, but he didn't want to interrupt.

"Finally, when I was in high school my parents enrolled me in some acting classes up in Morgantown, and it was like I'd finally discovered the meaning of life. I wasn't just the kid that everyone called 'faggot' on the playground. Now I was appreciated for who I really was." His voice turned a little wistful. "I had my first gay kiss while I was there, and that changed my life, too, even though it took me even longer to come out."

Suddenly he paused. Jared looked over, to see why he'd stopped speaking. It took him a second to realize that Charlie was waiting for him to say something in response to his story. Jared wasn't sure what possessed him, but before he could think better of it he blurted out: "I have a very hard time imagining you being shy."

There was a split second where he thought he'd really put his foot in it and managed to deeply offend their headliner–*again*–but then Charlie's face broke into that radiant smile, and he actually laughed.

"You have me there. What can I say? It took me a while to come out of my shell...and the closet. Once I did, though, there was no shutting me up, as I'm sure you've already noticed."

"Who, you? The great Charlie Garrett? Never." Jared hadn't meant it to come out quite as jagged as it did, but he could tell from the flicker of hurt in Charlie's eyes that he might have gone too far.

"Do you...do you think we could go to the rose garden?" Charlie asked. He was clearly trying to change the subject, and Jared was more than happy to let him, even if it meant that they were going to end up in precisely the romantic location that he'd been trying to avoid.

*Does this guy know how to read minds?*

"Um, I guess, sure?" he managed to stammer out, still flummoxed that Charlie was asking to go to the very place he'd been thinking about just a few minutes ago. "I'm kind of surprised that you've heard of it."

Charlie gave him a level look. "I know that you think I'm some sort of vapid star who doesn't have time to do his own research, but I do have an iPhone, and I am a little bit curious when the mood strikes me. All of which is a way of saying that yes, I have in fact heard of it. It's one of the things that made me decide to come here."

"Wait, really?" Jared didn't mean for it to come out quite so incredulously, but it just seemed so incredible to him that an actor of Charlie's stature would come to the city of Huntington just for the flowers, no matter how pretty they were.

"I'm starting to think that you have this idea of what celebrities are like, that they're just...some sort of heavenly beings that forget what it's like to be on Earth once they hit it big, but I can assure you that that's not the case at all," Charlie said. For a brief moment, Jared almost felt bad at how he'd been treating the other man, particularly since he'd given him no reason to be like that. Then he remembered all of the reasons he'd never liked Charlie Garrett to start with. The way that he seemed to only helicopter into West Virginia when it was convenient, the way that he'd try to say something meaningful about LGBTQ+ rights in the country before stepping back from any controversy, the way he didn't seem to have an investment in the place that gave birth to him.

He also hadn't forgotten that the entire reason he was letting Charlie go on like this was because he wanted to find out the truth about him. So far, he hadn't heard anything that outlandish or unexpected, which just made him want to find out more.

"I guess I just got used to the idea that some people do seem to separate themselves from their birthplace."

"I think you'll find that people contain multitudes."

"So you're both a philosopher and an actor? That's quite impressive."

Again there was that little bit of an edge to his voice that he couldn't quite control, but fortunately Charlie seemed to take it in stride.

Jared found a parking space close to the garden–it wasn't hard, considering it was fairly early on a Thursday and the park wasn't yet swarmed with its afternoon visitors–and they got out of the truck. Jared closed his eyes and took a deep breath of the clear fall air. As he did almost every time he came here, he marveled that there was this little oasis of calm and nature in the middle of a fairly big city. For a minute he could almost imagine that he was back in the country where he always wanted to be.

"Um...are you okay?"

Jared shook himself out of his reverie. "Yeah, I'm fine. I...," he stopped, not sure what he was going to say or whether he wanted to be honest with this guy. Then, shrugging, he went on. "I was just thinking about how lucky we are to have a park like this in the middle of the city. It makes me feel like I'm back in the country."

"You can take the boy out of the country, but you can't take the country out of the boy?"

It was an undeniably cheesy thing to say, but for some reason coming from Charlie Garrett—who had that earnest look in his eyes again—it felt just right.

"I guess you could say that. I've lived in Huntington for the better part of two decades, but there's always a part of me that wants to just move back to the country in a nice little cottage with a flock of chickens and forget the rest of the world."

"I gotta say I didn't peg you for the type of guy who would like chickens. You strike me more as the turkey sort of man."

Jared couldn't resist a laugh at that.

"You know what, Charlie Garrett? You're not so bad."

"That's quite a compliment coming from you."

Jared narrowed his eyes. "If you keep that up, I might just take it back."

"I'll take my chances."

Jared just shook his head and led them over to the small creek that ran through the edge of the park. As they walked up the stairs leading to the garden, Jared couldn't help but think how he would like to be doing this with someone that he was dating. It had been quite a while since he'd brought anyone here on a date—most guys he'd been with were far too cynical for that sort of thing—and it was actually quite refreshing to see how genuinely invested Charlie seemed to be. He almost seemed like a great big kid, so caught up in the adventure that he forgot to be on his dignity.

Jared wasn't ready just yet to give Charlie the benefit of the doubt, but he was definitely softening.

*You're getting sentimental in your old age,* he thought.

It certainly helped that the roses were in the full flush of their bloom. Even though it was early October, there were still blooms on almost every bush, and as they walked the brick pathways the air was filled with heady scents. This was, Jared thought, the most magical place in all of Huntington and, as absurd as it sounded even to himself, he was glad that he'd brought Charlie here.

"You know," he said, "this is the place that made me first fall in love with Huntington when I first came here back in the early 2000s. It was just...so magical, and so unlike anything I'd ever encountered. I almost couldn't believe I was lucky enough to be in a city that had something like this."

Charlie gave him a little smile. "You really were a little country boy brought to the big city of Huntington, weren't you?"

Jared knew that Charlie was gently kidding him, but he'd put up with so much teasing about being a country boy (and for being a gay country boy at that), that it always put his back up a bit when someone said something like that.

Charlie, however, with that sixth sense that so many actors seemed to have, immediately recognized his mistake.

"I didn't mean anything by that, you know. In case you've forgotten already, I'm a country boy too, and there's nothing wrong with that."

*Then why do you spend so much of your time trying to convince people to forget that about you?* Jared almost said. Instead he just gave him a weak smile.

They spent the next few minutes just ambling through the roses, pausing every now and again to lean down and sniff a particularly beautiful specimen. Jared was particularly impressed by the one suitably called "Perfume Factory," which was perhaps the most fragrant and intensely aromatic rose he'd ever encountered. When Charlie bent down to give it a whiff, he got such a look of pleasure on his face that Jared couldn't help but wonder what it would be like to be the one to cause it.

*Behave yourself,* he reminded himself. *You definitely do not have that kind of relationship with Charlie Garrett and you're not going to.*

Finally they took a seat on one of the stone benches, each of them content to sit in silence for a few minutes. Sitting there in peaceful quiet was his idea of a good time, and while he wasn't sure what had possessed him to share this particular location with someone that he barely knew, he was glad he'd done it.

"Thank you for bringing me here, Jared," Charlie said softly. "It means a lot to me that you'd share this with me, even though you don't like me that much."

Something about the raw vulnerability in Charlie's voice caused a tiny little knot to start twining itself together in Jared's chest, and he knew that he had to nip this in the bud before it got any worse. He wasn't going to start falling for this movie star, no matter how charming and handsome he was, and no matter how vulnerable he was.

*You know you have a crush on him, so why don't you just admit it?* That little voice in his head sounded irritatingly like Rebecca, and he pushed it away.

"Do you want to go to the Stonewall?" The words had popped out of his mouth before he could really think about what he was saying, and he kind of regretted puncturing the softly intimate mood that Charlie's gratitude had created.

Charlie looked hesitant, and Jared immediately regretted asking him. He should have known that he wouldn't want to go to some busy bar, particularly not after that little altercation in the front of the hotel. While the bar was usually free from protesters these days, things had been getting a little tense of late. What if that same guy showed up with his little sign once he found out that Charlie was going to be there?

"Before you answer that, I have another question" he said, to give Charlie a bit of an out from having to decline going to the bar.

"Hit me," Charlie said, taking it.

"How is it that we haven't had paparazzi tailing us all day? I thought that was one of the things that went along with being a star. I mean, there were some of them at the hotel when I picked you up, but they haven't been swarming after you every second of the day."

Charlie barked out a laugh.

"Well, I'm not exactly *that* kind of star, you know? I'm more of a grannies and wine moms kind of star. The press is usually just interested when I'm out doing something official, like arriving at the hotel. Of course, part of the reason there were so many of them there was because Sheri made sure of it. It's the same reason I came in on a private jet. She wants everyone to know that this is a big deal. She wants to make sure that I make the next big leap in my career."

He hesitated. "The reporters also tend to show up when I say something that I shouldn't."

Charlie rushed on, as if he didn't want to dwell on his past indiscretions. "If everything goes as planned while I'm here, I might finally get to be a real star, not just a made-for-TV movie wannabe."

"Are you kidding me?" Jared almost couldn't believe what he was hearing. "You're one of the most famous people to have come out of West Virginia, and you're going to say that you're not the right kind of star?"

Charlie shook his head.

"You don't understand. There are TV movie stars and then there are *real* movie stars. As I said, the only time the press really gets worked up about us is if our publicists do a lot of heavy lifting to make us a big deal or we do something stupid or controversial."

"You mean like punching a homophobe?" Jared asked. "Or saying something that ruffles a few feathers?"

Charlie looked sheepish. "Yes, exactly. Then my face would be splashed across every news website in the country, and I don't think I need to tell you that that would be very bad. In fact, it would probably torpedo whatever chance I had of actually making it big."

*Now we're getting somewhere,* Jared thought. *Now I get to see the* real *Charlie Garrett.* Unfortunately, however, he'd moved on from that bit of confession into safer territory.

"Don't get me wrong. I'm really happy with what I've managed to accomplish in my career, and I love my fans but, well, I've always wanted to become the kind of star that might even get an Academy Award. I know that sounds dumb, but that's the way it is."

In fact, it did sound a little silly–he was *Charlie Garrett,* for goodness's sake–but Jared also had to admit that there was something kind of sweet about Charlie's desires, too. Even if he'd never known what it was like to be a star of any kind, he did know what it was like to end up not quite where you expected to. When he was young he'd wanted to become a famous writer, someone who the world could look at admire but, though he'd managed to get a few pieces placed here and there, and he was occasionally asked to write press releases and other material for the Council, the truth was that his dreams hadn't worked out the way he'd planned. He loved the work he did for the Council and for the city of Huntington, doing what he could to make life better for the queer folks living there, particularly the young ones, but there were a lot of times when he wished that he'd been more adventurous when he was young.

"What are you thinking about?" Charlie asked.

Jared was so taken aback by the question, banal as it was, that he couldn't think of anything to say right away.

"Uh, I guess you could say that I was thinking about dreams, and about how sometimes life doesn't work out like you think it will."

"That's very deep for a country boy."

"You know, it's not just movie stars and people like them who get to think about big things," he said. "But yeah, it's just...well, I grew up wanting to be a writer, to see my stuff in print, to have everyone know my name, but I'm afraid it hasn't quite worked out like I wanted it to."

"It's never too late to do something about that, you know."

Jared decided to let that one go by without a sarcastic comment. Of all people, Charlie should know how hard it was to break into the creative industries, particularly when you didn't have any connections or know anyone.

*But then, Charlie was able to do it, so why can't you?*

That was a line of thought that he didn't want to pursue too closely, in part because it made him wonder whether his resentment of one Charlie Garrett was due more to his own jealousy and sense of failure than anything Charlie himself had done.

"I know it isn't," he said. "But it's also not as easy as you might think to get ahead in the writing business. No matter how hard you try, you get knocked down, and it can take a lot to get back on your feet after that."

Charlie barked out a little laugh. "I think that rejection is just a key part of being a creative. You have to develop a thick skin about these things."

Jared wanted to tell him that he knew all of that already, which was why he was content to just...not deal with it. It wasn't that he couldn't handle rejection–he could, or at least he thought he could–it was just that, having dealt with so many disappointments and rejections in his personal life, he would just rather avoid having to deal with them in his professional life.

*Don't go there, Jared,* he thought. *Just keep it light and smooth and let it go at that.*

Charlie seemed to sense that he might have overstepped a boundary because he made an abrupt change of direction in their conversation.

"You know what," he said. "Let's go to the Stonewall tonight." Again he got that rather sheepish look on his face. "I'll admit that I did a little bit of research on that place, too. I still can't quite believe a place like Huntington has a gay bar."

"It used to have three," Jared said matter-of-factly. "But, well, times change, I guess, and it's gotten harder to keep gay bars open."

Charlie shook his head. "You know, it's a shame. I don't think people these days realize how important gay bars were to guys our age." He snorted an indelicate laugh. "I guess we're being called geriatric millennials."

"Funny that you would make an assumption that I'm *also* a geriatric millennial," Jared said even though, of course, he was very much a geriatric millennial.

"Well," Charlie said with a smirk, "you do have quite a lot of gray hair, so unless you started going gray at an early age, I'd say that you're at least in your mid-thirties."

"Not all of us are lucky enough to be blonde," he said. "You're never going to really go gray. It'll just gradually turn white, until you look like a distinguished older gentleman.

"Or an English lawyer."

They both shared a laugh and, just like that, something seemed to change between them, for a while at least.

"You're just lucky that the Stonewall is open tonight at all," Jared said. "They're normally closed on weeknights, but they decided to have a special night since the film festival is in town."

Just then Charlie's stomach growled, and so did Jared's.

"Uh, would you like to get something to eat?" Jared asked. He glanced at his watch. "It's gonna be quite a while before the Stonewall opens, so we have some time to kill."

Charlie beamed that smile at him.

"I'd love that."

THEY GOT SOME MCDONALD'S–"IT'S my favorite cheat food," Charlie explained with a blush–and somehow managed to spend the next several hours just driving around Huntington and its environs. Jared found it strangely to show off this city that he'd come to love. By the end of the day they were at Harris Riverfront Park. It might have seen better days, but Jared had always thought it had its unique faded beauty.

The sun was already starting to set and, if Jared was being honest with himself, he wasn't quite ready to go to the bar yet. He couldn't quite define why, but he knew there was something magical going on here, something that he wouldn't be able to recapture once it went away.

*You really are a hopeless romantic.*

"I'm not quite ready to go yet, though," Charlie said, seeming to read his mind. "I just kind of enjoy sitting here in peace and quiet."

And that's just what they did, until the last sliver of the sun slipped below the horizon, leaving them bathed in the gloom of evening.

Jared sighed, because it was starting to get chilly, and he just felt that it was time for them to get going, before this little rendezvous could get any more romantic.

*You could kiss him right now and no one would be any the wiser,* a little voice in his head said. *You know you want to.*

He shook his head to clear it of that troubling little

thought. His life was messy and complicated enough without kissing Charlie Garrett and opening that whole can of worms.

"Shall we go?"

The words sounded abrupt and a little rude to his own ears, but if Charlie thought the same thing he didn't say it. Instead he just flashed that dazzling smile, and Jared found himself glad he was sitting down, because his knees felt a little wobbly.

*Good Lord, pull yourself together.*

"Yes, let's," he said instead.

# CHAPTER 4

The Stonewall, like so many other gay bars of its time, was situated in a little alley. There was a certain irony about the fact that it was *also* located right next to a Baptist church, and this made Charlie smile.

*I bet the little old ladies just love that their church is right next to a gay bar,* he thought, and then frowned. *But maybe I'm not being generous enough,* he thought. *Maybe they are more okay with it than they're willing to admit.*

Even though it was still early they could already hear (and feel) the thumping of the bass from where they were standing on the sidewalk.

"You know, I've been coming to this place for years, and no matter how many times I do, I can't help but think it's a bit of a miracle that it still manages to stay open." There was something earnest about the way that Jared said those words that made Charlie look at him and made him wonder whether, beneath that cynical and jaded surface, there was really a softer side to him.

"I know what you mean," Charlie said. "The minute I turned eighteen I started to go to the gay bar in Morgantown, and it was like...a whole new world. For the first time I was around gay people, and I guess quite a few straight people, too. I didn't really know what to do with myself, but I had a lot of fun."

"I came here my first week of undergrad, still a shy little kid from the middle of nowhere, and it was life-changing. I finally felt like I was among my own kind, even as I also sometimes felt a little out of place."

The bar was largely deserted at this time of night, except for a few older guys at the bar and scattered at a few tables here and there. Charlie sighed inwardly, because he'd been afraid that the place would be crowded if anyone got even an inkling that he was going to be there. The Stonewall wasn't exactly the type of place that his fans would frequent, of course, but he'd been in the business long enough to know that there would still be people who would want to come and gawk at the celebrity just for the chance of being close to fame.

Even so, he was glad that Jared had recommended this, even if Sheri would frown at him for taking a risk. He hadn't bothered checking his phone for the past several hours, because he knew that she was probably frantically texting him to make sure he hadn't managed to get himself into any trouble.

They sidled up to the bar and ordered a couple of drinks—a gin and tonic for Jared and a Long Island iced tea for Charlie—and then turned to survey the rest of the place.

"When was the last time that you were here?" he asked. He had to lean in and almost shout in order to be heard above the music.

"I gotta be honest," Jared said, shouting in his turn. "I don't really like coming to the bars anymore. I'd rather just spend the evening at home."

*I'd like to spend an evening at home with you,* Charlie thought but didn't say.

"It's okay," he said, draping an arm around Jared's shoulders, once again relishing the chance to touch the other man, "I don't really like to go to bars very much, either. They're always so crowded and full of vapid people, at least they are out in California. Not sure how it is around here, though."

"It's okay," Jared said noncommittally. "Though sometimes you end up running into people that you'd rather avoid."

He was looking at something else in the bar, and Charlie looked in the same direction. A tall guy in his thirties was standing there, sipping on some sort of purple confection and looking in their direction.

"Who is he?" Charlie asked.

"He's my ex."

Charlie knew rationally that he had no right or reason to feel jealous of Jared's ex-boyfriend, but for some reason the idea of someone else being close to him in a romantic way made him feel all nauseous and fluttery. More than that, he was also confused about how someone could let Jared slip through their grasp.

"Do you want me to bump into him so he drops his drink?"

"I...don't think that would be a very good idea. He's one of those people who's chronically plugged into social media, so unless you want everyone thinking that you're some kind of rude asshole, I wouldn't recommend getting on his bad side."

"Oh." Charlie shrugged.

So that's how it was, was it? He felt even more tempted to go bump into the guy.

For a few more minutes they just stood there drinking in private, but it wasn't long before the ex started wending his way over. Charlie felt his stomach starting to clench, because he knew this was probably going to get really ugly really fast.

"Well, well, well, who do we have here?"

When someone like Leslie Jordan said, "Well, well, well," in that southern drawl it was charming. When this guy did it, it was like nails on a chalkboard.

"Hello, Paul," Jared said without looking up from his drink.

"It's good to see you too, Jared," Paul said without missing a beat. "And who is this?" He took a very noticeable sip of his drink, and gave Charlie a look up and down. "Unless I'm very much mistaken, it's Charlie Garrett, Romance Network star."

Charlie took a deep breath through his nose and let it out through his mouth.

*Stay calm, Charlie. You've dealt with assholes like this a dozen times before. This isn't any different.*

"Paul, knock it off," Jared said quietly.

Paul actually laughed a little at that, as if he found it funny that Jared was actually challenging him.

"Someone's certainly changed their tune about Charlie Garrett. I've lost count of the number of times you've said something negative about West Virginia's golden boy. What was it that you said about him that one time? 'He's just a hack actor that no one would give two shits about if he wasn't blonde and muscular and looks like he stepped out of an Abercrombie and Fitch catalog?' It was something like that."

"I know that Jared has had a rather dubious attitude about my professional output," Charlie said, "so unless you have something else you'd like to add to our conversation, I think there are a lot of other places in this bar you could be."

Charlie felt a little warmth in his chest when he saw the admiring look that Jared gave him.

*See? I can be selfless, too.*

Paul, however, was one of those people who wasn't easily discouraged from being an asshole.

"Let me give you a piece of advice, Charlie Garrett," he said. "This guy right here is one of the most depressing people you'll ever meet. He's so busy finding reasons to be unhappy that he never bothers to look up and enjoy the world around him." He gave a bitter little laugh. "Trust me. I spent a good amount of my time trying to get him to snap out of his misery, and he just didn't want to do it."

And with that he was gone.

"Don't pay attention to what that asshole has to say," Charlie said. "He was clearly just trying to get under your skin."

If the strained look on Jared's face was anything to go by, it had worked, and Charlie gave Paul what he hoped was a particularly venomous look.

*Just try that again,* he tried to say with just his eyes.

"I don't want to talk about him, if that's okay," Jared said. "I didn't come to the Stonewall to deal with my past."

Charlie shrugged. He might have just met Jared today, but he could already tell that Jared wasn't going to do anything he didn't want to.

As the night wore on more and more people came into the bar, and Charlie loved the feeling of being among other queer folks. Even as his eyes wandered across the room, however, his eyes kept finding their way back to Jared sitting beside him. He seemed to be withdrawing more and more into himself, and Charlie's protective urge was getting stronger by the minute.

*You've got to make your move, Charlie,* he thought. *If you don't, the rest of this evening is going to be a bust, and neither you or Jared is going to be happy about that.*

"I assume that they have drag shows here?" he asked.

Jared gave him a look that told him plainly that that was a very stupid (and very straight) question to ask.

"Charlie, it's a gay bar. What do you think?"

"I don't know. You've sort of clammed up, so I figured I had to break the ice somehow."

That managed to get a little bit of a smile out of Jared. Charlie felt a tightening in the region somewhere behind his heart.

"And what time is this drag show?" he asked.

Jared rolled his eyes but still looked at his watch.

"In fact, it's about ready to start." He jerked his head to the side. "It's in that room over there."

"Are we going to go, or are we just going to sit here drinking alone the whole night like a couple of sad old drunks?"

"I don't know about you, but I sort of always saw myself as one of the old queens nursing a Manhattan at the bar in my old age."

"Well, you're not going to be nursing a drink tonight. You brought me here to have fun, and that's just what we're going to do. We're going to have *fun*."

A few minutes later they were right in front of the stage waiting for the show to start. All of a sudden the lights went down, the music went quiet, and then the most stunning drag queen that Charlie had ever seen came strutting out onto the stage.

"Hellooooo, Stonewall!" she shouted into the mic, her voice blaring out. "How y'all doin' tonight?"

There were some cheers throughout the room, but that wasn't good enough.

"I *said* how y'all doin' tonight?" she said louder, holding the mic out. This time the shouting was more exuberant. Charlie felt himself buoyed up by the sounds of so much queer joy.

"Boy do we have a show for you tonight," the drag queen continued. "And we hope you have as much fun as we do!"

And with that the show began. The queens at the Stonewall might not be as elaborate in their costuming as the ones in LA, but Charlie still admired their acrobatics and their commitment. He smiled and walked up to the stage several times with tips, and once or twice he thought that one of them recognized him (though fortunately they didn't say anything).

Jared cheered right along with the rest of them each time a new song came on, but he was clearly too shy to actually go up and tip the queens, no matter how excited he was to see them. He even let out a little squeal of glee when the last of the performers did a rendition of Shania Twain's "Man, I Feel Like a Woman!" It was clear that, for him at least, it was just like being back in college all over again.

After one of the final performances, Charlie turned around and saw that Jared had disappeared. He had an irrational thought that he'd gone home, but a quick perusal of the room revealed Jared sitting in a booth by himself, a guarded look on his face. Charlie looked around to see if Paul was lurking nearby, but there was no one. With a shrug, he walked over and slid into the booth next to him. "It wouldn't hurt you to get out there and dance, you know," he said. "Though you don't strike me as the dancing type."

Jared gave him a level look. "You're right about that. I've never liked dancing, even when I was a young gay."

Charlie let the music wash over him again, savoring the feeling of being just another gay at the bar, not "Charlie Garrett: Star."

"Is there anything I can do to convince you to get out there and cut a rug?" he asked. He wasn't sure why he wanted to get Jared out on the dance floor, other than that he genuinely wanted to see how he would look, out there being a little vulnerable for once. He'd managed to get him to soften up a little, but he knew that there was still a lot the other man was holding back.

"Well, you could start by not saying 'cut a rug.' That's a bit much, even for a geriatric millennial."

Charlie nudged him gently. "Come on. Do it for me?

Please?" He flashed his smile and was satisfied when he saw Jared's resistance beginning to crumble.

"Ugh, fine," Jared said. "Just don't blame me if I end up making both of us look foolish."

They both made their way to the dance floor, swaying along to Dua Lipa's "Dance the Night." Soon they were dancing next to one another, their bodies growing hotter and hotter by the moment. Whatever Jared might say, he had a natural sort of rhythm that, strangely enough, seemed to perfectly complement Charlie's own.

Charlie knew that he shouldn't be thinking like this, knew that this weekend was going to go by far too quickly, knew that Jared was probably not even thinking about anything remotely romantic, but he couldn't help himself. He wore his heart on his sleeve and he fell hard and fast. It didn't hurt that Jared was very attractive and, at this exact moment, grinding up against him, the friction of their two bodies producing the expected results.

He wrapped his hands around Jared's waist, and felt that familiar thrum of pleasure and desire race up his arms and settle into his chest.

For a second he just lost himself to the rhythm of the music and their bodies, but then he looked up and his heart froze.

For a moment, he couldn't quite believe what, or rather who, he was seeing: it was the guy with the protest sign from earlier in the day. He was dressed in the same clothes as earlier, though fortunately he didn't have his sign. He was trouble, though, of that there was no doubt.

Charlie tried taking a few deep breaths to calm himself and get the anger to go back down, and to an extent he succeeded. However, he couldn't help but be aware of the protester moving through the crowd. He couldn't tell whether the guy had come here deliberately to resume their quarrel or if it was just an accident, but he knew which one *he* was interested in. He wanted to teach the guy a lesson.

*Don't do it, Charlie,* he said to himself over and over. *Sheri told you to stay out of trouble.*

However, the guy came over to him, and all caution went right out the window.

"So, it's you again," Charlie said, pushing Jared gently behind him. "What are you doing here?'

The man cocked his head to the side, almost as if he was really considering what Charlie was asking.

"You know, I wasn't sure that I'd find you here, but I know that you people always tend to gather at the same place, so I figured it was a good bet."

"Do you want to take this outside?" Charlie snarled, acting like a total dude-bro and not even caring.

The other guy just shrugged. "Why bother going outside?"

It was at that moment that Jared decided to be a hero.

"Look, I don't want to get in the middle of anything," he said, pulling away from Charlie and striding up to the other guy. "But you've been making a nuisance of yourself this whole day, and I think it's time that you get out of here and find something better to do."

Charlie almost admired Jared for this, until he saw the ugly light that flickered in the man's eyes.

Before he could say anything, he gave Jared a shove that was just this side of rough.

In that moment all of Charlie's training at keeping his emotions in check, all of the admonitions from Sheri and the powers-that-be at the Romance Network to be on his best behavior and not to let his anger and frustration run away with him, went right out the window. Suddenly this guy was every homophobe that had disrupted his efforts to do something good for West Virginia, every hater who'd left a nasty message on social media, every executive that had said something vaguely (or not so vaguely) homophobic.

He didn't think about what he was going to do; all he could do was feel irrational anger that this asshole would lay a hand on Jared. Before he knew it, his fist was connecting with the guy's face, sending him crashing to the floor.

Suddenly the entire bar went quiet: there was no music, no chatter, nothing. Everyone was looking at them, and Charlie felt his anger draining away, leaving behind a sick feeling in his stomach.

"What did you just do?" Jared hissed. "What did you just *do*?"

Charlie looked at where the homophobe lay sprawled out on the floor. There was no denying the look of vicious glee on his face as he rubbed his jaw. He'd set the trap and Charlie, always willing to look before he leaped, had fallen right into it.

"I'm...I'm sorry," he managed to stammer out, even though he wasn't.

Jared rolled his eyes, but Charlie could have sworn that he also looked like he was a little impressed, too.

*This is going to get very ugly, very quickly,* he thought.

In fact, the several patrons were already fleeing toward the exits, while others were holding up their phones. This included Paul, because of course he wasn't going to let this opportunity go by. He had his camera up and was recording every horrible second of this, his eyes alight with malicious glee.

*Great, just what I needed. A jealous ex making this situation even worse.*

"Don't worry, bigshot. I'm not going to press charges," the homophobe said as he got to his feet. He gestured at all of the phones held up in their direction. "I think you've done enough damage to yourself."

*Well,* he thought, *fuck.*

46

# CHAPTER 5

*D*ancing with Charlie had been everything that Jared could have imagined and then some, which meant that it was very dangerous. It had been a long time since he'd felt that physically close to someone, and the fact that it was Charlie Garrett of all people...well, that was a complication, but he pushed it away for the moment.

Then the homophobe had come up to them, had shoved Jared just a bit too hard, and everything had turned to shit when Charlie decided to take a swing at him, leading to a stampede toward the exits, to say nothing of the people who'd caught the whole thing on camera.

*Oh come on people, calm down, it's just a little physical altercation, not a bomb threat,* Jared thought.

Even though he'd been short with Charlie right after the punch, truth be told he was more than a little impressed with him right then. That guy had been making a nuisance of himself, and he'd basically been asking for it. Then he thought about the impact this would almost certainly have on the film festival, and his mind started racing with thoughts about how Rebecca was going to respond to this. He'd had one job–to keep Charlie Garrett out of trouble–and insead he'd led him right into it.

At least he was doing it for something worthwhile, though. That was the part that made Jared feel conflicted. It also made him wonder whether there was something more to Charlie Garrett than he'd been willing to let himself acknowledge. Beneath the movie star good looks and charm and gloss, he thought he saw something else, some shadow, perhaps, of the lonely little boy that he'd once been, growing up in a holler with a family who didn't really understand him and didn't seem to want to.

"Well, your boyfriend certainly put his foot in it, didn't he?" Paul said, disrupting his troubled thoughts.

Of all the people to be in the bar tonight, why did it have to be him?

"Paul, do you mind?" he asked, turning to face his ex. "I know you don't have any reason to do me any favors, but please, knock off the recording?"

Unsurprisingly, Paul didn't even stop what he was doing as Jared was talking. He only stopped once the homophobe got to his feet and left the bar, and Jared had no doubt that he was sending this video to his own social media followers.

"You don't have to be such an asshole all the time, you know," he said, "even though I know it's kind of your brand."

Paul raised one immaculately-sculpted eyebrow, as if he found all of this immensely funny. Which he almost certainly did, because he was *that* kind of gay.

"It's so like you to want to make everything about you," he said in that lazy drawl that Jared had once found incredibly sexy but which was now excruciating. "First you drag this two-bit TV star here so everyone will look at you, and then you act like a whiny little girl whenever it all goes south." He clicked his tongue. "It's all so tediously predictable."

"You know, Charlie's not the only one who can throw a

punch," he grated out, even though they both knew it was an empty threat.

"Oh Jared, don't ever change," Paul said. "Enjoy your time with your new boyfriend, and I'll enjoy the social media clout this will give me. Who knows? Maybe I'll even get an article out of it. That way at least one of us will end up being a success as a writer."

Just this once Jared decided to take the high road.

"Just try to be less of an asshole," he said and turned back to Charlie, who looked like a deer caught in the headlights.

*How did this guy ever make it in an industry like Hollywood?* Jared thought. *He always seems so innocent.*

"Charlie, we've got to get you out of here," he said.

"That guy...he's, uh, not going to press charges. He thinks I've already done enough damage without that."

Jared snorted. "Yeah, I would say that's a bit of an understatement."

Somehow, they managed to get out of the Stonewall without causing any more difficulties or scenes, and even though the hotel was close enough to walk, he still decided to drive Charlie there.

*Better safe than sorry,* he thought wryly.

When they got to the hotel, Charlie turned to Jared.

"Do you...do you want to come up for a little bit?" he asked, voice quivering with vulnerability.

*In for a penny, in for a pound,* Jared thought, and nodded. "Sure, why not?"

They walked slowly through the lobby, trying to appear as inconspicuous as possible. The young woman working at the front desk gave them both a knowing–and, unless Jared was mistaken, slightly disapproving look–as they made their way to the elevator.

"I think she thinks that I'm your trick," Jared whispered.

"That's not such a bad thing, is it?" Charlie asked with a very obvious wink.

Jared didn't have anything smart to say, so he didn't say anything.

The elevator ride up to Charlie's floor was uneventful, and neither of them looked at each other.

*I feel like I'm trapped in one of those awful movies that Charlie's always starring in,* Jared thought. *It's like a meet cute, except we've already met, and this isn't cute.*

"It almost feels like we're in the middle of *Trapped in Love*" Charlie said, seeming to read his mind. "Though I don't suppose a sophisticated cinephile like you would have seen it."

In fact, he *had* seen it, though he would never admit to Charlie that he'd deliberately sought it out. He did have to admit that Charlie...wasn't bad, though the movie itself was so trite and saccharine that he had trouble sitting through it.

"I've...I've actually watched it. Once."

Charlie turned to look at him then, his trademark smile more of a smirk now. "I thought you'd already decided that none of my movies were worth watching?"

Jared felt trapped, but there was nothing for it.

"You were good, by the way," he said. "Better than you had a right to be given how...predictable...the rest of the movie ended up being."

"It is a romantic comedy, you know that, right? One of the things that people like about the genre is that it follows a certain set of rules that everyone knows and adheres to. That way, viewers don't have to contend with any unfortunate surprises."

"And don't you think that your viewers deserve something a little bit better than that?"

Jared regretted the words as soon as he'd said them, but Charlie just took them in stride, shrugging nonchalantly.

"You're probably right, but in the TV business you have to

go where the people are. And people want certain things from romance, and it's my job to give it to them."

Jared was going to say something to that, but at just that moment the elevator doors dinged and they stepped out into the hallway and walked toward his room. Of course, the organizers of the festival had put out a lot of money to make sure that the famous Charlie Garrett was put up in the finest room that the hotel had to offer, and Jared tried not to be jealous about that. After all, for all that he had lived in Huntington for years—and stayed at the hotel for a few helpings of afternoon delight—he'd certainly never had enough money, and never hooked up with anyone with enough money, to be able to come to this part of it.

The furnishings were simple but elegant, and with every step he took Jared began to feel more and more out of place.

Charlie, with that instinct he seemed to have for sensing when other people were uncomfortable, reached out and put an arm around Jared, who had to fight the urge to pull away.

"I know you're probably a little nervous being in a hotel like this one, but trust me, you get used to the fancy stuff pretty quickly. At least, I did."

"And what makes you think that I haven't been in a fancy hotel like this one before?"

Charlie sighed but didn't take his arm away, and Jared wasn't sure how he felt about that. "Do you have to be so prickly about everything?"

"I think I do, when people make assumptions about me that they have no business making."

"You got me there," Charlie said. "You're right. I shouldn't have assumed that." He paused. "But I'm also right, aren't I?"

"You're a real smartass, you know that?"

"I'll take that as a yes."

"You can take it however you want."

By this point they'd reached Charlie's room and come to a stop, neither of them quite ready to take the plunge.

Jared turned to Charlie, getting out from under his arm in the process, and raised an eyebrow. "So...are we going to stand here in the hallway all night, or are we going to go inside?"

"Come on in and be my guest," Charlie said.

"Okay, Lumiere."

"See, this is why we're great geriatric millennial gays. We both understand a reference to the original *Beauty and the Beast* when we hear it."

"There is only one true *Beauty and the Beast*," Jared said primly as he stepped into Charlie's room. "And anyone who says otherwise is guilty of Disney heresy."

"What's the punishment for Disney heresy?" Charlie asked, stepping inside and closing the door behind him. "Are you forced to watch *The Black Cauldron*?"

"You take that back," Jared said. "*The Black Cauldron* is a misunderstood masterpiece, and I won't hear another word against it."

"*The Black Cauldron* might have been a masterpiece before Katzenberg got his hands on it and literally cut up the footage that would have made it one of the great animated films of the 1980s. Unfortunately, as it is, it's just sort of a testament to how some people just can't resist the urge to destroy good art."

"You know, Charlie Garrett, I'm starting to think that you might have the makings of a film critic."

"When you've acted in enough of them, you start to understand a bit of how the business side of it works," he responded.

Despite himself, Jared found himself enjoying this playful little bit of banter. Strangely enough, Charlie didn't make him feel stupid or uneducated or childish just because he still liked Disney movies.

Now that they were in his room, Charlie was doing every-thing he could to make Jared feel comfortable. Jared wasn't sure where to sit, so he just sort of slumped in the nearest chair.

"I think we both know that this is going to be all over the news tomorrow," Charlie said, pouring them both a glass of wine. "I...I really don't know how I could let myself lose control like that."

Jared quirked an eyebrow at him. "I must say that it's not the type of behavior that I would have expected from Charlie Garrett. I don't think that punching a homophobe, no matter how much he probably deserved it, is going to go over very well with middle America."

Charlie sighed and, sitting his own glass on the nightstand, threw himself on the bed, his arms outstretched. His shirt rode up a bit, revealing his tight stomach and his nature trail. Jared couldn't help but think of what it would be like to run his hands along it, following it down lower, lower, lower...

*Keep your mind out of the gutter, Jared,* he reprimanded himself.

"Don't tell anyone I said this," he said, "but I'm actually kind of impressed by what you did tonight. I don't condone violence, and I know it's going to cause all kinds of complica-tions, but that guy *did* follow you all the way to the Stonewall, knowing that he was going to force you into a fight. And, well, he *did* also shove me, so part of me thinks that he had it coming. Y'know what I mean?"

He was flailing, and he knew it, but he really did want to make Charlie feel better about what had happened.

Charlie, for his part, seemed to appreciate it.

"Thank you for that, Jared," he said, pushing himself up to his elbows and holding him in a disconcertingly direct gaze. "You know, you might seem like a bit of an asshole at first, but deep down it seems like you're not so bad after all."

"I...guess I'll take that as a compliment." He laughed a little. "And you have every right to call me an asshole. I wasn't very nice to you when we first met, was I?"

"It was just a few hours ago, you know. Not like, a thousand years ago."

"You really are a very exasperating person, do you know that?"

Charlie flashed a smile. "I get that a lot, particularly from Sheri." At the mention of his publicist's name a shadow passed across his face, and the air seemed to go out of the room. "She's really not going to be happy when she finds out about tonight."

Jared sighed. "I don't think that Rebecca is going to be very happy with me either. She specifically told me that my job was to help keep you out of trouble, and that's exactly what I didn't do. And I can just imagine how the City Council is going to react to all of this. They weren't very friendly to the idea of having a gay movie festival in the town to begin with, and this...well, it's not going to be pretty."

Charlie levered himself off of the bed and came over, a genuinely concerned look in his beautiful blue eyes. "I'm really sorry, Jared," he said. "I hope you know that I didn't mean to cause you any kind of trouble."

For a split second Jared thought that Charlie was going to kiss him, and then the moment passed, and they were both just awkwardly looking at each other.

"It sure seems like Rebecca has a strong hold on your career," Charlie said at last. "I know how that feels. Sheri has something similar to me. I know that she's hard on me because she wants the best for me and my career, but sometimes I get the feeling she looks at me like someone she's babysitting. It's not the best feeling in the world. And then she recruited you to do the same thing."

"I mean, sure, when looked at in a certain light it does

seem like I was asked to be your babysitter," Jared said, feeling like he was groping his way blindly forward. "But I've actually sort of enjoyed it."

*Now why did I say that?*

Once again there was a moment of tension between them when everything–from a kiss to something else–was on the table, and then there came a knock at the door.

*Damn it,* Jared thought. *Of course someone would have to show up just before the good stuff happened.*

"Um...should I get it or should you?" he asked Charlie.

Charlie sighed, his shoulders slumping. "I guess I should get it. It's almost certainly Sheri."

Before Charlie could get to his feet, however, there came the familiar beep of a key card, and then Sheri was striding into the room. Her heels click-click-clicked ominously on the floor.

It was her face, though, which made his stomach turn to ice. If looks could kill, both he and Charlie would be dead.

"You," she said, fixing him in her hard gaze, "out." She jerked her head, and he seemed to be moving before he even realized that was what he was doing. He tried to give Charlie a reassuring look, but the actor's eyes were fixed on Sheri.

*This isn't going to be good for either of us,* he thought as he scuttled toward the door like a particularly awkward crab. *I just hope that Charlie doesn't let his temper get the better of him this time.*

Judging from how terrified Charlie looked, however, he didn't think that was very likely.

Jared opened the door as quickly as he could–managing to knock the "Do Not Disturb" sign on the floor in the process–and then he was outside, leaning against it. He briefly thought about eavesdropping, but immediately decided against it. It wouldn't just be a violation of Charlie's privacy; he also knew that it wasn't going to be long before he was getting his own earful from Rebecca.

In fact, as soon as he looked down at his phone he could see that she'd sent him a text.

MEET ME IN THE HOTEL BAR. NOW.

*Great. I love it when she uses all caps.*

However, there was no getting out of what was to come and so, a few minutes later, he was sitting across from Rebecca who, despite the late hour, looked immaculately put-together. She shook her head and took a long sip of her martini.

"I swear, Jared, sometimes I just don't know about you. I gave you one job, and you managed to not only not keep Charlie out of trouble, you let him get into a fistfight. What were you thinking?"

Jared shrugged, because that was basically the only thing he could think of to do.

That wasn't going to be good enough for Rebecca, however.

"You're going to have to do better than just the patented Jared shrug," she said. "You really messed up, J, and now we're all going to have to pitch in to dig Charlie out of the shit."

He knew it was serious when she referred to him only as "J." It was one of those things she liked to do when she was really upset with him.

"I don't know what I was supposed to do," he said defensively. "He was just defending me, you know. Seriously. The guy was asking for it, Rebecca. He'd been harassing Charlie all day, and then he came to the bar and was pulling the same shit. He even shoved me and...well, I guess that was just too much for Charlie." He tried to hide how much pleasure he got out of the idea of Charlie defending him, but he didn't think he was entirely successful.

She sighed and took an even longer sip. "If it's the guy I'm thinking of, I'm not surprised that things ended up this way.

He's always making an ass of himself. I kind of suspect that Councilman Rhodes puts him up to it."

"Are you really suggesting that Rhodes is some sort of secret manipulator? The man has the intelligence of a sack of potatoes."

"Don't underestimate him, Jared. That's your problem," she said, wagging the toothpick at him, "you always think you're the smartest person in the room, and that makes you careless."

"You got me there," he said. "But in my defense, it's not always easy to be the smartest person in the room."

"I really don't think you're taking this with the seriousness it deserves," she said. "Charlie's career could be on the line here."

She was acting as if he didn't know that.

"What are we going to do then?"

Rebecca rolled her eyes.

"How is it that I always end up getting called in to get gays out of the scrapes that they get into? What I want you to do right now is go home and get some sleep. Leave the rest to me and Sheri."

Jared didn't like the sound of that, but he really had no options at the moment. So, he did as she said and went home.

*I have a feeling this is all going to get much more complicated,* he thought as he snuggled into bed, faintly wishing that Charlie was there. *I just know it.*

# CHAPTER 6

*C*harlie knew that he was in trouble the minute Sheri stepped in the door. He'd seen her in a number of emotional states, but he'd only rarely seen her truly angry with him. This, though...well, this was clearly going to get very unpleasant.

For several minutes she just stood there, eyes closed, nostrils flared, and that made him more frightened than if she'd come in screaming her head off.

*She must be really,* really *mad at me,* he thought.

Finally, she opened her eyes.

"Charlie, what the *hell* were you thinking?"

She started pacing in front of him, her heels clicking on the hardwood floor of the hotel room. "I specifically told you not to get into trouble, to avoid getting into any sort of ugly confrontations, and what did you do? You got into a very ugly confrontation. You had to know that that guy was just looking for trouble, setting a trap for you, and you walked right into it." She huffed. "Just tell me something," Sheri said. "Why did you do it?"

How to answer this question in a way that would make

Sheri understand? She was an undeniable ally, and while she was always trying to get him to be less outspoken about queer issues and politics, Charlie liked to think that was because she was looking out for his career and not because she had any kind of discomfort with who he was as a person. Even so, no ally could really understand what it was like to hear that kind of word hurled in their direction, a word designed to hurt and to wound. And, growing up in California in a nice, liberal family, she'd never known what it was like to have religion wielded as a weapon against her, either.

She also didn't know what it was like to have a person like that go after someone that she cared about.

He took a deep breath and tried to gather his thoughts.

"Look, it's like this. Growing up, I had to put up with men like that, calling me names and telling me that I was going to Hell for being gay. They didn't even have to know that I was gay in order to say those things, because I wasn't like the other kids in my high school. Back then I was afraid to do anything about it, and ever since I've become famous and had the power to do and say something about it, I've wanted to push back." He took another breath. "And he also started to come after Jared, and that just pushed me over the edge. If you expect me to be sorry, I'm not. I did the right thing."

"Yeah, well, that comes with complications too, doesn't it?"

He sighed. She was right. It did come with a hell of a lot of complications, many of which were staring him right in the face. This was supposed to be a weekend in which he burnished his image and showed that he was worth taking seriously as an actor, not just someone who happened to be in a bunch of made-for-TV movies. This was also supposed to be the weekend in which he showed that he was responsible and that he could be trusted with a big press tour.

And now all of that was at risk because he'd let his principles get in the way again.

"You know, Charlie, sometimes I don't think you want to be helped. Sometimes, I think that you just want to do what you want to do and let other people pick up the pieces. I don't think I need to tell you that that isn't fair, to either me or to the people that end up having to do the picking up."

She took a deep breath to calm herself.

"But that's all water under the bridge. The only thing that we have to figure out now is what to do with you. We're just going to have to go into damage control mode." She huffed. Couldn't you have just chewed the guy out rather than punching him?"

"What would you have done if you'd seen someone pushing someone that you cared about?"

He hadn't really meant to ask the question so bluntly, but now that it was out in the air, he was glad that he had. He loved Sheri dearly, but she didn't always see her own blindspots when it came to what homophobia was like in the real world.

"Well," she said, "I probably wouldn't have punched him, if only because I wouldn't want to set my career on fire."

She looked like she was going to keep on in this vein, but then her phone rang. She looked down at her phone and frowned.

"This is just fantastic. It's Rebecca. I'm guessing she's already heard about what's happened and wants to talk about what we're going to do about it. About you. Give me a sec."

Without waiting for permission she stepped out into the hallway. He could only dimly hear what she was saying, but it was enough to tell him that things were getting a bit heated.

"And just what would you propose that I do with the headliner for your little festival?" Sheri almost shouted. Charlie cringed, not just because he hated the thought of her and Rebecca getting into but also because he didn't like the idea of Sheri making a scene in the hotel. He'd already made enough of a fuss for both of them.

"You know, that's actually not a bad idea, not a bad idea at all. Okay. That's what we'll do then."

Her voice faded away again, and it was another moment or two before she came back into the room, her face set in a resolute expression, the type of expression that said very clearly that she was going to ask him to do something he didn't like.

She once again took up a position right in front of him, looking him up and down as if she still couldn't quite decide what to make of him.

"There's only one way we're going to be able to manage this. Rebecca and I agree that we've got to get you out of Huntington for a day or two, just until this has time to blow over. We'll make sure that you're back here for your big premiere."

She sighed. "We're lucky that it's almost the weekend and that the news cycle will move on pretty quickly." She frowned. "Unfortunately, there are some voices in the City Council who are making noise about potentially pulling the funding for the festival and banning it from the City Hall. I don't think I need to tell you how devastating that would be, not just for the Festival, but also for your personal brand. This whole trip is supposed to be proving to the studios that you can be on your best behavior and that you won't be a liability."

"And all of this ruckus is because I got into a fight with some guy at a bar?"

"Once again, Charlie. Damage control. That's the most important thing right now."

"So where are you shipping me off to?"

"Rebecca and I have decided that you're going to stay with Jared's parents until Sunday."

"And he's okay with that?"

"Since he was supposed to be keeping an eye on you and yet he let this happen anyway, I don't see that he has much choice in the matter."

"I don't think he likes me very much."

Charlie supposed that wasn't entirely true, particularly now that they'd managed to have at least one semi-intimate moment together. His mind wandered back to the moment when he'd been so close to kissing Jared, and he could almost forget what was happening around him. Until, of course, Sheri snapped her fingers.

"Charlie, snap out of it," she said. "One, I don't think that's true, and two, it doesn't really matter. We need to make sure that you're not in town for a while to cool things down. Do you think you can manage to stay out of trouble while you're off the grid?"

Charlie knew he should be focusing on what she was saying, but he wasn't quite able to get around the fact that she'd said that she thought Jared actually liked him. That couldn't be true, could it?

"Charlie, where are you?" Sheri asked. "You've got that look on your face like you're a mile away." She huffed and pinched the bridge of her nose. "You're thinking about Jared, aren't you?"

He could feel himself blushing, but he didn't care. "And what if I am?"

"Charles, you hardly know the guy."

How could he tell her that there was something rich and uncomplicated about Jared, something that reminded him of all of the things that he'd always liked about the guys he'd grown up with, without all of the annoying baggage and toxic masculinity bullshit. Jared was in fact just the kind of gay that he could never seem to find in California, the type that drove a truck, wore a backwards baseball cap, and yet still wasn't afraid to have a rainbow flag on the back windshield.

He was, in other words, perfect.

He didn't say any of that to Sheri, of course, both because that wasn't the nature of their relationship and because he could already tell that she would just call him an idiot.

"Look, you can do whatever you want with this boy while you're with him, but at least try not to punch anyone else, okay? This is your chance to get your big break. If you don't straighten up and fly right, I'm not going to keep picking up after you. Spend the weekend getting your head on straight, and then come back here and give your big speech, and we'll go back to LA and forget this ever happened. Do you think you can do that?"

He actually wasn't at all sure that he could, or that he wanted to, but Charlie knew that this wasn't the answer she was looking for. He could tell from the set of her shoulders and the hard glitter in her eyes that she wasn't messing around, and that if he didn't do a quick course-correction that his career as he'd known it would be over.

*Would that be such a bad thing?* He asked himself. *Maybe I've been going about this whole thing the wrong way since the beginning. Maybe I should have stood up to the studios earlier...*

But no, he knew that he couldn't do that. He had his mother to look after. And, much as she frustrated him sometimes, he wasn't going to leave her out in the cold.

"Okay, fine," he said. "I'll do whatever you tell me to do."

"One last word of warning," she said. "Don't let yourself get too involved with this Jared guy. I know you think I don't care about you, that I only see you as a paycheck, but I do care about you as a person. I think that you deserve happiness, but I don't think you're going to find it here. Remember that there was a reason that you got out of this state in the first place. Don't let it suck you back in."

"I think I'm more than capable of making my own decisions when it comes to my love life. Or lack thereof."

Sheri rubbed her temples.

"You are without a doubt the most rebellious client that I have ever had, and considering the types of people that I've had to deal with, that's really saying something. It's a good thing for you that I see a lot of potential in your career and that I happen to like you. Otherwise I'd toss you to the curb and let someone else take care of you."

"You know, some people would be happy that their client has a conscience and is attracted to non-toxic people."

"I think you're making a lot of assumptions about whether this Jared guy is toxic or not."

Charlie felt a little bit of irritation rising up at that, but he didn't say anything. Sheri was on the brink of giving him a really good telling-off, and he didn't want to make it worse.

"Just trust me that I know what I'm doing," he said. "I won't do anything that would make you ashamed of me."

She frowned, and he knew she didn't believe him.

"That remains to be seen," she said. "But in any case, I'm going to go to bed and try to get at least a bit of sleep. This has been a very exhausting day, and I don't think the rest of the weekend is going to get any better. I strongly suggest that you get some sleep, too. Because the rest of the weekend is going to take a lot out of you, too. Once again, *stay out of trouble.*"

"I give you my word."

She harrumphed at that and left the room.

After she was gone Charlie took off his clothes and got into bed, relishing the feeling of finally being able to relax. Sheri had been right about one thing, at least. This had been a very long day, and he had no idea what the future held for him. He could just about imagine the look on Jared's face when he was informed that he was going to be taking Charlie to meet his family.

Thinking of Jared made Charlie feel all kinds of things. He knew it was more than a little crazy that he was already catching feelings. They'd only barely met, and Jared had been more prickly than welcoming. Even so, there was...something...between the two of them. Charlie wasn't sure that Jared had felt it or, if he did, that he would accept it for what it was. He had the feeling that Jared was the kind of person who would fight back against his feelings until there was no choice but to face them.

*That's okay. I can work with that.*

Exasperated that he wasn't going to be able to sleep, Charlie got out of bed and padded to the window. He threw open the shades and looked out at the city of Huntington spread out below him, with the Ohio River not too far in the distance. Even though he'd never been here before, he still felt like it was home. Maybe it was just being in West Virginia, or maybe there really was something about this little city on the shores of the river that called to him in some way he could barely name.

*Or maybe it's the fact that Jared lives here,* a little voice inside his head remarked. *Maybe you're just so desperate for love that you'll fall for the first guy that crosses your path, and you'll fall in love with the city as a way of getting closer to him.*

Charlie sighed and leaned his head against the window. Somehow life managed to get more complicated despite his best efforts.

He wasn't sure how long he stood there at the window, but finally he started to feel drowsy enough to attempt to sleep again. He wasn't sure that he was going to be able to get any rest at all, but he figured that it was at least worth a try. He got back into bed, and to his relief, was soon asleep.

# CHAPTER 7

*J*ared woke up, and for a blessed few minutes he was able to deceive himself into thinking that everything that had happened the night before was just some weird dream. After all, it just seemed too farfetched that he would have not only managed to meet Charlie Garrett but also had a surprisingly nice time with him in the rose garden, before everything had turned to absolute shit due to the presence of a virulent homophobe and Charlie's unexpectedly violent temper.

Then it slowly dawned on him that all of that had definitely not been a dream and that, in turn, made him realize that he was going to have to deal with all of this now that it was morning of the next day.

Sure enough, as soon as he looked at his phone he saw that every major outlet and minor gossip rag was running a story about how Charlie Garrett, who was trying to make the switch into bigger and better and more prestigious productions, had punched someone in a bar in the middle of nowhere, West Virginia. The snide tone in many of them was impossible to miss.

*How could I have fucked this up so badly?* He kept asking himself.

He guess he shouldn't have been that surprised. Somehow that seemed to be the story of his life. No matter how hard he tried to do the right thing, no matter how close he seemed to get to feeling some sense of happiness and accomplishment, he ended up sabotaging it anyway.

*Makes me think I should just give up.*

That wasn't an option, of course, and so a short time later he got dressed and made his way to the office.

He was painfully aware of many of the angry looks he was getting as he walked through the halls, but he was particularly dreading seeing Rebecca. Indeed, she was in an even worse mood than she'd been in the day before.

"It's about time you showed up," she snapped as he stepped into the main office, and he bit his tongue to keep from telling her that he was actually earlier than normal.

"I, uh, I'm sorry about what happened last night," he said, the words clearly inadequate.

"In my office," she said curtly.

He followed her inside.

As soon as the door was shut Rebecca looked *much* less angry. In fact, she looked more tired than anything as she plopped herself into her desk chair and leaned her head back to look up at the ceiling. Jared took a seat across from her, not yet sure how this whole thing was going to play out. Was she going to reprimand him? Yell at him so that the rest of the office would see that she was doing something proactive? Might she even suspend him or, heaven forbid, fire him?

Not that he would have minded getting fired from this deadend job. Not really, anyway. It's not like he was ever doing much that he enjoyed, with the exception of the Film Festival.

"I hope you know that I'm not really as mad at you as I made it look out there," she said, not taking her eyes off the ceiling. "But one has to put on a certain appearance for prying eyes, y'know? I don't want it getting back to City Council that I'm not being proactive when one of my subordinates messes up."

Rebecca finally turned her attention from whatever she'd been staring at on the ceiling and fixed him in her gaze. Somehow that was even worse than if she'd actually started yelling at him.

"As we talked about last night, this is definitely a very, very bad thing, and we're going to be very, very busy making sure that we get a handle on this." She brandished her phone. "As I'm sure you're abundantly aware, this is all over the news, and it's already threatening to derail all of the hard work we've done for the festival."

"Go on," he said, dreading what was coming next.

"So, after consulting with Sheri, we've decided that Charlie is going to go with you to your parents' house this weekend."

"You're kidding, right?"

Jared had expected many things to come out of this conversation, but he definitely hadn't had "take Charlie to his parents" on his Rebecca's-going-to-punish-Jared Bingo card.

"I'm not, actually," she said, giving him a stern look over the rim of her glasses. "I gave you one thing to do–keep Charlie Garrett out of trouble–and you went and did the exact opposite. Now you're going to have to fix it. And don't even think about yelling at me," Rebecca said, reading his mind in the way that only she could do. "And you might be fooling some people, but you're not fooling me. I can already see that you're getting feelings for Charlie. So maybe this'll give you a chance to work through your complicated feelings about him."

Now that was something he wasn't going to let pass.

"I am not," he said flatly. "I don't know why you would say such a thing."

She didn't need to know that he was quickly–too quickly–starting to find his assumptions about who Charlie really was challenged by the truth he was seeing in front of him. He knew that Rebecca loved him, but he also knew that she could be a bit judgy when it came to his romantic escapades.

"Because I know you better than you know yourself," she said at once. "And I can always tell when you're falling for a guy, particularly when it's one that you know you should be staying a mile away from. I don't think you need me to tell you all of the reasons that getting together with Charlie Garrett would be a monumentally bad thing, but in case you do, here's the big one: he's a star, and he's going to go back to LA when this is all over, and he's going to break your heart when he does so."

"You think I don't already know that?" he said, trying to stay calm. "You think that hasn't already gone through my head a thousand times?" He immediately realized what he'd said and tried to backtrack it. "I mean, I don't know what you're talking about. I don't have feelings for Charlie Garrett."

He was well aware of how weak that sounded, and he was rewarded with one of Rebecca's trademark knowing smirks. Jared hated those, usually because they were the preface to her telling him why she was right about something and he was wrong.

"Mhm," she said.

"And so what if I have a crush on him ?" he asked. "It's not like there's going to be anything that's going to come out of it. Like you said, he lives in LA, I live in West Virginia, and I'm still right about what I said, you know. He does seem to have forgotten the rest of us living back here." He shook his head, though he wasn't sure whether he was trying to convince Rebecca or himself. "Nope. It's not going to happen."

"Do you mean that you're not going to get with him or that you're not going to take him away for a few days?"

"Both."

"Well, if you don't, then the festival is almost certainly going to get canceled, and you're going to have that on your conscience. Is that really what you want?"

Jared really hated it when Rebecca tried to blackmail him, and he hated it even more when it was effective. He knew how important this festival was to her. Hell, he knew how important it was to him, too. They'd worked on it for months, and if spending the rest of the weekend with Charlie was the cost of getting it to work, then wasn't it worth it?

Besides, there were other good reasons to want to spend the weekend with Charlie. Perhaps he could dig a little deeper, find a little bit more about him and the past that he seemed determined to keep hidden...

"Fine, fine, fine," he said, finally giving in. "You probably knew from the beginning that I was going to give in, didn't you?"

She smirked again. "I generally get my own way in the end." She clapped her hands once. "I'm sure that your parents are going to love having Charlie Garrett in their living room. Isn't your mom a big fan of his?"

Jared sighed. "Yes, unfortunately."

"Don't be like that. You're a fan too, even if you don't want to admit it."

Now that he really had to think about it, Jared realized that Rebecca and Sheri had decided on this literally without any input from him at all. Or from his parents, for that matter.

"Wait a minute," he said. "What makes you think that my parents are going to be okay with this? And why their house of all places? And for that matter, what makes you think that *I'll* be okay with just thrusting a very famous stranger on them? What happens if a bunch of reporters find out where we are and show up? My mom's going to be upset enough that I'm dropping someone off on her without giving her a chance to clean up. She's going to have a cow when she finds out who it is."

There. That should put Rebecca in her place.

It didn't.

"How you wrangle your parents is entirely up to you," she said. "If I know them, they're never going to turn away a guest, and they're going to be happy to see you, in any case. As to why your parents' house...well, that was kind of my idea. It just sort of occurred to me, so I ran with it. It's the one place where no one will think to look, since no one knows who you are. They're also far enough away that Charlie should be safe there for a few days—we both know that they're not exactly in the middle of a bustling metropolis, and you've complained enough about how hard it is to get cell service there." She shrugged. "It just seemed like the perfect place, Sheri agreed, and here we are.

"And as for the news hounds, you just leave that to Sheri and me. We'll take care of shielding the two of you. You just make sure that you keep Charlie out of any further trouble. I don't want to hear about any confrontations on TikTok or Twitter, and I most certainly don't want to hear about him getting into any further fistfights. Do I make myself clear?"

Jared nodded his head, because basically that was the only thing he could do.

"How soon do we leave?"

"Right now," she said.

"I guess I'd better get going then," he said, getting to his feet.

"You know, you don't have to look like you're going to your own execution," Rebecca said. "You never know. This might be good for you. You're always saying you need an adventure. And besides," and here her eyes twinkled mischievously, "maybe you'll find out what it's like to sleep with a celebrity. Or at least get some over the pants action."

"You are the absolute worst, do you know that?"

"You just say that because you know that I'm right."

He made a rude noise as he headed to the door.

"Oh, and Jared?"

He turned to look back at her.

"Would you do me a favor and be sure to look like I've just spent the last fifteen minutes tearing you a new one? I want everyone in the office to think that I'm actually doing my job rather than taking it easy on you."

He frowned at her but still nodded his head.

"Yeah, for sure, I guess that's the least I can do."

"You're damn right it is," she said, and then he was back out in the main office.

There was no mistaking the smug look on his office-mates' faces.

*This is going to be a very long weekend,* he thought.


AND SO IT was that Jared found himself, again, parked outside of Charlie Garrett's hotel. This time, though, they'd agreed that he would come out the service entrance, so as to avoid the even larger crowd that was clustered around the front.

Charlie looked a little tired and harried, and Jared even felt a little twinge of pity for him. For the first time, he really thought about what it would be like to be a star, someone whose every slip-up was covered by the news. Even though Charlie wasn't exactly an A-lister–not yet, anyway–he was still someone with his own devoted fans who expected certain things from him. It must be a lot to deal with for a kid from the middle-of-nowhere, West Virginia.

*Careful, Jared, or you're going to end up going soft,* he reminded himself.

It was getting harder and harder to hold onto his resentment, particularly when Charlie flashed him that winning smile and got into the truck, throwing a duffle back into the backseat.

"That's all you're bringing with you?" Jared asked, raising an eyebrow.

"Sure," Charlie said nonchalantly. "We're just going away for a weekend, right? It's not like I have to have a whole wardrobe."

"I just thought someone like you wouldn't dream of going anywhere without a whole bunch of suitcases."

"I mean, isn't the whole point of this exercise for me to go off-radar for a while? I don't think that lugging a whole bunch of suitcases behind me is the best way to accomplish that, do you?"

Jared had to admit that he had a point and, for the umpteenth time in twenty four hours, he had to adjust his ideas of what and who Charlie Garrett was. And, while he would never quite admit it to himself, he was a little resentful of Charlie that he wasn't acting like he was supposed to.

"I guess...I guess we should get going. There's no time like the present and all that."

*What the hell is wrong with me?* He thought. *Why did I just say that?*

"No offense," Charlie said, "but do you know that sometimes you sound just like an old lady?"

Jared laughed despite himself. "You're not the first person to tell me that. I'll try to sound more like a geriatric millennial from now on."

Charlie shook his head. "Don't change on my account. I actually think it's cute."

Jared had nothing to really say to that, and so they started off on this unlikely road trip.

For a while they just drove in silence. It wasn't uncomfortable, though; it was more like a natural lull in the conversation. Each of them had a lot going on, and they didn't feel the need to interrupt one another's thoughts with idle chatter. Without really thinking about it, Jared reached out and turned on the radio.

At once, the plaintive sound of Patsy Cline's "Crazy" came out of the speakers, and Jared felt himself getting a little swoony. Nothing got him square in his feelings like listening to Pasty sing about heartbreak and longing.

To his surprise, Charlie started singing along in a rather lovely, soft baritone.

"*You* like Patsy Cline?" he asked.

Charlie gave him one of those looks that was already becoming very familiar, the type of look that said: "you've got to stop making assumptions about me and the things I like."

Jared shrugged. "Sorry. I just didn't think that you know, you'd like Patsy Cline. It's not like she's the kind of gay icon that everyone loves nowadays. Don't get me wrong. I'm always ready to belt out some tunes with Gaga, Cher, Madonna, and Reba, but for some reason Patsy gets me in a way that no one else does."

If Charlie thought it was weird that Jared was talking about a country music singer that had been dead for several decades in the present tense, he gave no sign of it. In fact, his eyes were dancing with a bit of excitement of his own.

Jared felt something constrict in his chest. It was so rare to find someone his own age that shared his love of Patsy Cline, and that it was Charlie Garrett who was expressing so much interest was...well, it was something. He just didn't know quite what yet. His eyes kept wandering over to where Charlie sat, tracing the way that the sun caught his blonde hair and made it glow, at the way that his jaw was so finely-chiseled that it looked like it could cut glass.

He got so caught up in looking at him while also trying to stay focused on the road that he almost missed what Charlie said next.

"In fact, I've been known to do a deep dive into Cline's discography now and again. I mean sure, everyone knows her signature songs, the ones that come up right away when you search for her on Spotify, and there are quite a few heartbreak songs that she sings, but for my money the best thing she ever did was the song 'Faded Love.' There's just something about that song...it reaches right inside you and tries to pluck your heart out through your chest. I don't think it's possible to listen to that song and not burst into tears."

"Get out of here," Jared said, unable to contain his excitement. "I've always thought the same thing, but whenever I ask other people what their favorite Patsy song is, they inevitably say it's 'Crazy' or 'I Fall to Pieces.' They're definitely sleeping on 'Faded Love,' and they absolutely don't know what they're missing."

He might have been imagining it, but Jared could swear that he felt a tiny little crackle in the air around them, as if something fundamental had changed in their dynamic. They each shared a small little smile.

"I have a feeling I'm going to say this a lot this weekend, but you are definitely not the person that I was expecting when Rebecca told me that we were going to be having Charlie Garrett come to our film festival. To be honest it's kind of rude of you not to be what I expected."

This elicited another laugh. Jared wasn't used to having people actually find his sense of humor amusing.

*Perhaps this weekend isn't going to be so bad after all.*

Then he decided to just give in and start singing along to Cline. Something about her vocals made him forget how nervous and reluctant he usually was to sing in front of anyone, let alone someone he hardly knew.

"You have a really nice voice, you know," Charlie said. "There's a purity to it. Have you ever trained professionally?"

Jared scoffed. "No, I don't think I'm quite that good."

"But how will you ever know until you try?"

"Don't you ever get tired of being the perfect man?" He hadn't meant the words to come out quite that sharply, but there was something just a bit annoying about the fact that Charlie always seemed to know the perfect thing to say. Why couldn't he just be a human being?

"I didn't think that being a kind and supportive person was a character flaw."

Jared rolled his eyes. "Forget I said anything."

"I get the feeling that you say that a lot."

This whole conversation was slipping out of his control again, and Jared reprimanded himself for not being able to just sit and have a pleasant chat without somehow managing to alienate someone.

Strangely enough, however, it was Charlie who came to the rescue.

"Um...so, we're going to your parents' place, yeah? What's it like? And, uh, where do they live?"

Jared laughed at how little they'd actually talked about this weekend before setting out on this journey.

*Thanks Rebecca. Thanks Sheri,* he thought wryly.

"They live up in the northern panhandle in a little house in the country." Aware that Charlie was looking at him with more than a little incredulity, he shrugged his shoulders. "Don't look at me. Rebecca and Sheri cooked this up together, not me. Rebecca said that they'd take care of making sure no one bothered us."

Charlie snorted. "I think you're all underestimating just how difficult it can be to go off the grid."

"We're not all just ignorant rubes you know," Jared snapped.

Charlie sighed. "Jared, you do know that you don't have to take everything I say as a personal attack against you or a veiled criticism of West Virginia in general, right?"

That one hit a little too close to home. Charlie was right; he was probably being a bit too sensitive.

"You're right. I guess if we're going to spend the next couple of days together we're going to have to learn to get along."

"I think it's worth pointing out that that's what I've been trying to do since you picked me up at the airport yesterday."

"Okay fine, you have a point. Again," he said grudgingly. "I'm sorry for being an asshole."

"Not to put too fine a point on it, but yes, you absolutely have. I honestly don't know why, though. We never really got back onto the subject of why you're so dead set against liking me."

Was this really a conversation that Jared wanted to have right now, when they still had a couple of hours left to get to his parents' place? The last thing he wanted was to have some long, drawn-out argument that ultimately ended up nowhere or made them so pissed at each other they didn't have anything else to say. Then again, if they were going to make this whole arrangement work, then they were going to have to establish some sort of peace.

"I guess I do owe you something of an explanation. You did punch a homophobe for my benefit, after all, and while everyone else seems to think that was some sort of horrible sin, I think it was probably better than he deserved."

"You really do have some rough edges, don't you?"

"Yeah, I guess you could say that. It comes from being raised in a state like this one and choosing to stay here rather than running off."

He snuck a look at Charlie to see what expression was on his face, and he wasn't surprised to see a look like a lightbulb had gone off in the actor's head. He decided to just keep going. They hadn't gotten quite this far during their earlier discussion the day before, and he was going to get to the bottom of why Charlie left if it was the last thing he did.

"I know that you're very big on making a big deal about the fact that you're from West Virginia, but I don't see you really acknowledging anything *real*. You seem to just trot it out like it's a nice little garnish, something to make you interesting so people will take you seriously. And, it's more than that. You abandoned your home state, Charlie, and you never really looked back."

Charlie looked like he had several things that he wanted to say, but what he finally said was:

"Was it really such a bad thing for me to want to make a better life for myself and, later, my mom? You know what it's like here. And I really do respect your decision to stay and try to make it better for everyone else. That wasn't the path that I chose, though, and while there are days where I kind of wish I'd stayed, the truth is that I think I made the right decision for me, and I don't have to apologize for that, not to you or to anyone."

Jared was actually impressed with Charlie's willingness to stand up for himself, particularly since he hadn't the first time he'd brought this up. However, he also felt that there was something, or some*things*, that Charlie wasn't telling him.

"You know what? That's fair. You shouldn't have to apologize for your life choices, particularly to someone you don't really know and won't see after this weekend."

That reminder of the essentially ephemeral nature of their encounter cast a pall over their conversation, and they rode in silence for a while.

By this point, they'd managed to talk so much that the trip

was almost over, and as they got closer to Jared's parents' house, it occurred to him that he was going to have to prepare Charlie for what he was about to encounter.

"Listen. There are a few things about my parents that you should know."

"Oh Lord, here it comes. You're going to tell that they're secretly the heads of some secretive and deranged cult, aren't you?"

"Much as my life might have been a bit more interesting growing up if they were and even though this is West Virginia, my parents aren't cult members," Jared said. In fact they're just boring old country Methodists, like almost everyone else around here. When you think of simple country folk, you're probably picturing people like my parents. Picture your average pair of Baby Boomers, and that's them."

"They sound absolutely enchanting."

The strange thing was...Charlie didn't sound sarcastic.

"Are you serious?"

"Why wouldn't I be?"

"I mean, they're my parents, and they're not really very sophisticated." He coughed and cleared his throat, not really sure how to explain what he was talking about. "I guess, well, a lot of my other boyfriends have tended to look down on them when they've visited. It's nothing that they said explicitly, of course, but they had a way of making it clear they thought they were better than my mom and dad."

It took him a second to realize what he'd said.

"Not that I'm saying bringing you home is like bringing back a boyfriend or anything like that, it's just that...," his voice trailed off.

"Jared, calm down. I know you didn't mean anything like that. And I don't know what kinds of guys you've been bringing back to meet your folks, but where I come from you always act polite and interested in whatever your potential in-laws have to say. It's the one way that you can show your significant other that you really care about them and the people who helped them to become the way that they are."

"That's...an amazingly enlightened thing to say. Where have you been all my life?"

"Becoming a bigshot movie star and being too busy and too good to come back to West Virginia, according to some."

"Ouch. Did you have to go below the belt?"

"I don't know. Did you?"

"Would it help if I said I'm sorry again?"

"Yeah, I think it would."

"Fine. I'm sorry for being a jerk. Are you going to continue reminding me of my transgressions for the rest of the weekend?"

Charlie shrugged, somehow managing to make even that gesture look elegant and charismatic. "I might, and then again I might not. I guess it just depends on my mood." And then he flashed that megawatt smile, and Jared suddenly knew that he would be able to forgive him anything if it meant that he was going to get to see it again.

*Easy there, Jared. You're not Julia Roberts in a '90s romantic comedy. There's no need to get all swept off your feet.*

"So," he said, suddenly desperate to change the subject. "Tell me a little something about what it's like to actually be on the set of a movie for the Romance Network."

Even though he couldn't quite see the look on Charlie's face, he thought he could sense the skepticism.

"Are you actually interested, or are you just trying to change the subject?"

"I guess it's probably a little bit of both."

"Well, it's not as exciting as you might think. There's often a lot of standing around and waiting. Then you have to do at least a few takes to get things just right. It all depends on which director you happen to get for a particular project.

Then you have to wait around some more. And then get a few more takes, and then wait around some more."

"You're right. That's not nearly as exciting as I would have expected."

Charlie shrugged. "I told you. That's the secret about the Romance Network, though. They have things set up so that the whole production goes pretty smoothly, and there are times when you feel a bit like you're a cog in some kind of machine. It's not always very glamorous or exciting, but it pays the bills."

Jared had a ton of questions, but some of them would have to wait. After all, they had an entire weekend together, and he didn't want to run out of things to talk about.

They were now passing through Sistersville, one of his favorite places along the route back home. As they passed by the huge mansions on the side of the road, he decided to share a little bit of himself with Charlie.

Or at least try to.

"You see those really nice houses there?" he asked, gesturing toward a trio of opulent mansions on the left side of the road. Charlie nodded.

"Well, they were apparently built back in the days when Sistersville was in the middle of an oil and gas boom. Every time I drive by them, I think about the kinds of mansions that you see in those old movies, somehow both very grand and also a little dilapidated."

"Yeah, I can see what you mean," Charlie said. He gestured at the very last one as they passed. "I think that that one reminds me of Norma Desmond's house in *Sunset Boulevard*. And yes, before you ask, I've seen *Sunset Boulevard*. Several times, in fact. It was actually the movie that made me want to get into acting."

"Did you think that you were going to end up like Norma Desmond someday, holed up in your old mansion and trying to seduce young screenwriters so that you could make your way back to the spotlight?"

"If only I were that lucky," Charlie said with a little laugh. Jared felt some butterflies in his stomach at the sound.

They continued talking about inconsequential things as they finished the last miles of the drive: their favorite books and some of their memories, but then another silence settled down between them. Then Jared's worst nightmare came true: they ran out of things to say.

*Well, that was nice while it lasted,* he thought. *I guess that we just don't have that much to talk about.*

He was saved from having to say or do anything else by their arrival at his parents' house.

"Well," he said, "here we are. Welcome to Chateau Russell. So, just so you know, my parents' names are Joyce and Doug. They don't really like formality, so don't call them Mr. and Mrs. Russell or anything like that."

"You've got it, captain!" Charlie said and gave a mock salute.

"Hmph," Jared said, but Charlie saw the way that he couldn't help but grin a little.

They got out of the truck and started toward the house, and it suddenly occurred to Jared that he'd never gotten around to calling his parents.

*Damn,* he thought. *Well, this should be fun.*

They stepped through the immaculately-manicured lawn–Jared's dad, Doug, did love to keep his yard nice–and stepped up to the front door.

*Here goes nothing,* Jared thought.

# CHAPTER 8

*C*harlie hadn't been sure what to expect when it came to Jared's parents, but he most certainly had not anticipated being bowled over by a couple of very large chocolate labs and one cocker spaniel, nor did he expect the army of cats that suddenly decided to take up residence on his lap as soon as Jared shepherded him to a small couch.

"I, er, hope you don't mind pets," Jared said, as he desperately (and futilely) tried to shoo the cats and dogs away. "As you can see, they've got quite a little menagerie here."

"I love them," he said, and almost thought he saw something like affection flit across Jared's face.

Charlie still hasn't quite forgiven him for the snark about his career at the Romance Network–or for his continued judgment about his choice to leave West Virginia–but he held out hope that Jared would get over his hangups and see him for who he really was rather than what Jared thought he was (or should be).

*It wouldn't kill you to give the guy some grace, even if he's not always willing to give it to you.*

Then it occurred to him to wonder: had Jared even bothered to tell his parents that he was going to be bringing someone along to their house?

"Mom, dad, are you home?" Jared called, wandering away for a moment.

While Jared was trying to find his parents, Charlie took the opportunity to give the house a closer examination. Even though it looked quite small on the outside, it was surprisingly roomy, even though it was also filled with all manner of knick-knacks and trinkets. In fact, it kind of reminded him of the home that he'd grown up in, and he felt a momentary twinge of guilt that he still hadn't had time to call or text his own mom.

"I can't believe you'd invite someone here without telling me!" he heard a female voice exclaim from deeper in the house. "Honestly, Jared, I don't know what gets into you sometimes. I haven't even had a chance to clean the house properly, and you want me to entertain a guest?"

"Mom, the house looks fine," he heard Jared say in a voice that somehow managed to be both strained and patient.

At just that moment Jared returned with the woman that Charlie assumed to be his mother.

She looked nothing like what Charlie had been imagining. She was, he guessed, in her late fifties or early sixties, with blonde hair swept up into a bun. There were a few strands of white here and there, and her deep blue eyes radiated kindness.

*I wish she was my mom*, he thought, and then immediately felt guilty.

As soon as Joyce looked at him, her face seemed to light up like a Christmas tree.

"Oh my goodness," she said breathlessly, "you're Charlie Garrett. You're *the* Charlie Garrett. I just loved you in *A Little Country Romance*. You were wonderful!"

It occurred to him too late that she was exactly the kind of person that he would expect to be one of his fans, and that made him a little wary of this whole encounter. Was she going to badger him with a whole series of questions of what it was like to be on the set of one of his movies? Was she going to ask for his autograph?

"Mom," Jared said, clearly trying to head this off at the pass.

Joyce, however, just waved him off. "Don't worry, dear, I'm not going to drown the poor boy with questions. I'm sure he gets enough of that from all of his other fans."

"I mean, yes, sometimes it does get a bit tiring to get asked all sorts of things by people who don't really have a recognition of privacy, but I think I can make an exception for you. You don't seem like the type to ask me what type of underwear I happen to have on at the moment."

"Clearly you don't know my wife very well," a man that Charlie assumed to be Jared's dad asked as he came into the room. He was about the same height as his wife–both of whom were shorter than either Jared or Charlie–and it was clear that Jared had inherited his looks from his father, because Doug had the same bluffly handsome features and dark hair and piercing blue eyes as his son. They were weathered a bit with age, of course, but he still moved and acted like a much younger man.

"Doug!" Joyce exclaimed, slapping him lightly on the arm. "Behave yourself."

"What?" he said with a shrug. "I'm just telling the truth."

"Sometimes I don't know what I see in you."

"It's my natural debonair charm," Doug said at once. Joyce and Jared both rolled their eyes.

"Anyway, that's enough of that," Joyce said airily. "As I'm sure Jared's told you, I'm Joyce, and this is Doug. None of that Mr. and Mrs. Russell stuff, either."

*Jared was right about that, at least,* Charlie thought.

"We have to figure out where the two of you are going to

sleep," Joyce went on. She wagged a finger at the both of them. "I don't know what type of shenanigans the two of you have been getting up to, but I want you to know that there will be no hanky-panky in this household, at least not until the two of you are married."

Charlie wished he could take a picture of the mortified look on Jared's face. He looked like a fish out of water, with his mouth hanging open and his skin turning several shades of pink.

It made him want to kiss him.

"Mother," Jared finally managed to choke out, "I don't know what idea you have about the two of us, but I can tell you absolutely that the two of us haven't been getting into any 'hanky panky.'" He made a point of using scare quotes to exaggerate how ridiculous he found the situation. All of that just made Charlie want to kiss him even more.

"Don't try to pull the wool over my eyes," Joyce responded. "I may be your mother, but I'm also pretty up-do-date on how things work these days."

"Joyce," Doug said gently, "are you going to go on about this all day or are you going to show the boys where they're going to sleep?"

She huffed.

"Well, I guess we can have Jared stay in the guest room, though the only thing we have in there is the fold-out bed at the moment."

"Don't put yourself out on my account," Charlie rushed to say. "I don't want Jared to not be able to sleep in his own bedroom. I'm totally fine with sleeping on a foldout."

Joyce shook her head. "Absolutely not. You are the guest in this house, and that means that you will have the best accommodations."

Charlie could tell that Jared wasn't particularly happy about this, but he got the feeling that Joyce wasn't the type of person whose wishes could be thwarted, either by her husband or by her son.

"I guess I'll just have to get used to having a backache for the next couple of days," Jared said not-very-graciously.

"There are always sacrifices that we have to make when we have guests," Joyce reminded him.

"In that case we'd better not wait around. Come on, Charlie, and I'll show you *my* room."

"Coming, dear," he said, as they made their way upstairs. The upstairs, like the rest of the Russell house, felt cozy and lived in, with the sort of comfort that could only come from a place that had been home to the same family for years. Even Jared's room still had little reminders of him, including a poster from a '90s movie and a book of the collected poems of D.H. Lawrence.

"So," Charlie said, looking at the room around him, "this is where you grew up, eh? I like to think about all of the hours that a moody and melodramatic young Jared spent listening to Patsy Cline and writing bad poetry."

"What makes you think that my poetry was bad?" Jared asked.

"Because every little gay boy writes bad poetry when they're a teenager."

Jared couldn't help but laugh at that. "I guess you may have a point. Fortunately I threw most of it away, so that no one would have to see the embarrassing things that I was writing about and all of the many crushes that I had as a teen. I did keep most of my journals, though, but mom might have thrown them out. She's not the type of person who likes clutter."

"I heard that!" Joyce shouted from down the hall. "I may like a clean house, but I know when not to throw out something that's actually valuable."

Jared shook his head as his mom was speaking.

"Don't listen to her," he whispered. "I've lost count of the number of things that she's thrown out without even asking me first."

They stood there in a somewhat awkward silence for a few minutes, before Jared finally shrugged and started moving toward the door. "I hope that you're very comfortable in my room, Charlie Garrett," he said.

"You know," Charlie said, hardly believing the words that were coming out of his mouth, "you could always sneak out in the middle of the night and come back into your room. If, you know, you wanted to have a good night's sleep."

He knew that sounded like he was asking Jared to come hook up with him in the middle of the night. In his old bedroom. In his parent's house. It was like the beginning of almost every romantic comedy situation gone wrong. Of course, that was exactly what he was going for, and the thought of Jared crawling into bed with him in the middle of the night made him feel all kinds of ways, and he had to shift position to keep from embarrassing himself.

"As my mom said, we run a clean establishment here," Jared said with a twisted little smile, breaking the tension in a flash. "And for that reason I will be suffering through the ignominy of sleeping on the couch in my own parents' house.

Even so, Charlie couldn't stop thinking about that image of Jared getting into bed with him. The harder he tried to put it out of his mind and think about something else–preferably something far less stimulating–the more insistently it kept intruding on his thoughts.

He was saved from any further thinking by Joyce's voice calling from downstairs.

"Okay, boys, you can come down now. I think you've had quite enough time to get unpacked and get everything in order."

*Keeps a clean establishment indeed.*

"I told you," Jared said, reading his mind. "And one thing you will very quickly learn is that what Joyce Russell wants, she gets. And she most certainly doesn't like to be kept waiting."

They started down the stairs, their arms barely touching one another as they did so. Even though Jared flinched away, Charlie still felt that same little pulse that he'd felt on the few other occasions when the two of them had come this close.

*I just wish that Jared would quit pulling away like he's been shocked,* he thought.

Joyce was waiting for them at the bottom of the stairs, her hands on her hips. She looked like every mother from every sitcom that Charlie had ever seen.

"I hope that the two of you weren't doing anything naughty upstairs," she said. "Like I said. There'll be no hanky panky under my roof."

"Joyce, for heaven's sake, leave them alone. They're adults and they can do whatever they want to," Doug chimed in.

She shook her head. "Don't listen to your father. I make the rules in his house. Now, come back to the living room. I want you to tell me everything."

"Joyce, don't you think they should at least have a chance to catch their breath?" Doug smiled indulgently at his wife as they made their way back to the living room.

"I think we should at least find out what's going on with these two. It's not every day that you have a celebrity in your house, is it?"

"It's okay, Mr. Russell. I don't mind explaining a bit about what happened." He took a deep breath, because he had the feeling that the elder Russells weren't likely to be very approving of his decision to punch another person, regardless of his reasons.

"It's like this," he said, as they sat down in the living room. "Jared and I were at this bar, and there was this guy, and he was being a jerk–on top of saying all sorts of nasty, homophobic things to me earlier in the day–and he shoved Jared and, well, I punched him. Of course there were a lot of people standing around, and they managed to record it all, and, well, here we are."

It all came out in a jumbled rush of words, and for a moment he was afraid that he'd spoken too quickly and that they hadn't really absorbed what had happened.

To his surprise, it was Doug who spoke first.

"Serves him right," he said bluntly.

"Doug," Joyce said. "We don't advocate violence in this house, no matter how awful people behave."

"If someone is going to go chasing after another man and start calling him names right out in public where everyone can see it, and if he's going to push our son, then I don't see why he shouldn't be taught a lesson."

Charlie was starting to see where Jared got his fighting spirit from.

Joyce just sighed and shook her head.

"Go on, Charlie."

And so he told her the rest of what had happened that night and why he was sitting here in her living room.

Just as he finished, however, Joyce leapt to her feet. "I'm so sorry," she said, "but I just noticed how dusty that shelf is!" With that she was off.

"Don't worry," Jared said, leaning in. "She's always like that. All it takes is one speck of dust and she's off like a rocket. She can't stand even the *idea* of anything being out of place, particularly when we have a guest in the house."

"You have no idea how exhausting it gets," Doug said with a rueful shake of his head. "I've lost track of the number of times I've had a cup of coffee whisked away while I was in the middle of drinking it, just because she wanted to get the dish washed and put away."

If Joyce was offended at all of this talk about her cleaning proclivities, she didn't show any sign of it. If anything, all of this commentary just made her clean even more fervently.

"I just can't believe that I have *the* Charlie Garrett sitting in my living room," she gushed as she bustled around making sure that everything was where it needed to be. "I also wish that my son had bothered to tell me that he was bringing home a movie star, or that he was working with him in the first place."

Said son had the good grace to look at least a little bit ashamed.

"I'm sorry, mom," he mumbled under his breath. "I guess time just got away from me." Jared was so cute when he blushed that Charlie wanted to reach out and cup his face and kiss him until he made him turn completely red.

"Well, next time you decide to bring home one of the biggest stars of the Romance Network, why don't you take a moment to call ahead for reservations, hm?"

"Well, since you're both here, you can help me with some of the canning that I was planning on doing this weekend," Doug interjected. "I have a whole bunch of frozen cherries in the freezer, and I want to make sure I get them made into jam as soon as possible."

"You're canning *again?*" Jared asked. "Didn't he just get done doing that a few weeks ago?"

"Well, dear, you know how your father is when it comes to that damn canning machine. He says that you can't have too many jars of jam waiting for you in the cellar."

"I can speak for myself, you know."

"I know you can, dear," Joyce said as she passed behind Doug, patting him (more than a little patronizingly) on the arm. Looking at the two of them, it was pretty clear that Jared had gotten various aspects of his personality from each of his parents. While he had Joyce's fussiness, he also had his father's dogged determination.

What's more, looking at them he found himself wondering what it would be like to be in a long-term relationship with Jared, whether they would bicker like this when they got old.

"Don't get the wrong idea," Jared said, interrupting his thoughts. "My dad isn't some kind of doomsdayer or survivalist or anything. He just doesn't like to be caught unprepared for any eventuality, no matter how unlikely."

"You never know how likely or unlikely something is until it's actually happened," Joyce said.

"There've been a few times when someone in the house lost their job, and it was a bit touch and go there for a while," Jared said.

Charlie could see at once that this was the kind of conversation that made Joyce and Doug uncomfortable, so he decided to smooth things over and keep it moving.

"I always say that you can never be too careful when it comes to money and being prepared. I sometimes think that a lot of people in California should learn that lesson."

Joyce nodded her head approvingly at this, and Charlie congratulated himself on once again being able to get on well with a set of parents.

"You're a very nice young man," Joyce said, reaching up and patting his cheek. "I hope we'll be seeing a lot more of you."

Charlie didn't know what to say to that, so he said nothing.

Doug, not being one to stand on ceremony, announced, "There's no time like the present. Let's get canning!"

He got to his feet and stepped swiftly to the kitchen, leaving Jared and Charlie no choice but to follow him.

As he'd promised, two bags of cherries were already laid

out on the table, along with sugar and jars and everything else that making cherry jam required. It wasn't long before Jared and his dad were elbows-deep in the process and trading light-hearted jokes and jabs while Joyce reminded them to clean up the kitchen when they were done.

There was something almost magical about watching the way Jared interacted with his family. Theirs was clearly a deep bond, and while he had no doubt that they had their fair share of stresses and strains like any family, they'd clearly found a way of working through them and creating something powerful and unique. It was especially refreshing to see Jared be able to let his hair down a little and become a little less guarded. True, he'd begun to open up a bit on the drive here, but Charlie could sense that he was always keeping a little something back. Here, though, he truly looked carefree and joyful, and that made Charlie happy.

Suddenly Jared seemed to remember that he was standing right there and that he had yet to meaningfully contribute to any part of the canning process.

"Charlie, would you mind handing me that bag of sugar?" he asked. "I know this is a bit out of your wheelhouse, but you could at least try to be a little more helpful."

"Jared, be nice to Charlie. He's a guest in our house," Joyce said reprovingly. "Honestly I don't know who raised you to act like that in front of company."

Jared rolled his eyes good-naturedly. As Charlie had still not handed him the sugar, he made to do it himself, and as they both reached for it their hands just barely brushed each other. Jared's face turned that delicate shade of pink again, and even Charlie felt himself feeling a little blush creeping up the back of his neck.

"Sorry," they both said in unison, followed quickly by "jinx."

Charlie's gaze flicked to Doug to see if he'd noticed

anything, but his attention was strictly on the bubbling cherries. He could swear, though, that he saw the ghost of a small on the other man's face.

The rest of the canning process passed in a bit of a blur. As Jared had said, this was very much out of Charlie's realm of experience. However, there was something almost magical about the way that Jared and his dad went through the various steps of the process, from the pouring of the cherries into the little mason jars to setting the jars in the canner. Soon enough the kitchen was filled with numerous *pops* as the jars sealed.

There came a ring at the door just as the last jar went *pop!*.

*Oh crap,* Charlie thought. *Here it comes.*

Even though, as he'd told Jared, he wasn't exactly the type of person to have paparazzi knocking down the door to get to him for a scoop, there would always be those who wanted to get a good story on him. After what had happened at the Stonewall, he had no doubt that there would be at least a few publications who would pay top dollar to figure out where he was, what he was doing, and who he was seeing.

*Sometimes I wish I could just disappear.*

As it turned out, though, the new arrivals weren't some story-hungry reporters from TMZ or some other gossip rag. Instead, they were a cluster of people that Charlie could only assume were members of Jared's family. Or some of them, anyway.

"I cannot believe this," Jared said. "Mother, did you call anyone?"

Joyce put her hands in the air. "I promise that it wasn't me. Besides, when would I have had the chance to call or tell anyone? You've been with me the whole time since you got home."

*I guess this is just some cosmic joke at my expense,* Charlie thought wryly.

Jared shook his head. "Honestly, this family. Doesn't

anyone ever bother to announce when they're going to be dropping by for a visit? And yes, mother, I know how ironic it is that I am the one saying that."

"When you're as right as I am, you don't have to say anything. People just get it."

Jared rolled his eyes at that.

"I guess there's no getting around it. Can we just do the best we can to make sure that everyone keeps this to themselves? In case you missed the memo, the whole reason that we're here is so that Charlie can lie low for a few days and let the chaos of the past day blow over. That's not likely to happen if everyone in the family tells everyone else who isn't here that Charlie Garrett is in your kitchen."

Joyce looked like she was going to have something smart to say, but Doug deftly intervened, which Charlie had a feeling was a fairly regular occurrence in this household.

"Don't worry, son. We'll make sure that everyone knows to keep their lips sealed. You can trust us."

Jared still looked skeptical about that particular claim, but thankfully he didn't push the issue.

Soon enough the Russells' small house was filled to bursting with a surprising number of people. It turned out that both Doug's brother and Joyce's sister had shown up, along with their kids. It was immediately clear to Charlie that this was a family that truly cared about each of its members, as everyone smiled and asked all of the right (and thoughtful) questions.

One of them, a young woman who seemed to be about Charlie's and Jared's age, sauntered up to him.

"So, you're Charlie Garrett," she said nonchalantly.

"I am," he said, trying to keep from blushing. "And you would be?"

"I'm Hannah. And before you ask anything else, I'm Jared's favorite cousin and his protector. If you want to do anything to him or hurt his feelings, you're going to have me to answer to."

"Trust me. The last thing that I would ever want to do is hurt Jared's feelings. He's...," he tapered off, not quite sure just how much he was willing to say to this person he had just met and who was already giving him a very intense look.

She snorted, as if she knew what he was thinking and what he didn't dare say out loud.

"So it's that way already, is it? I can't say that I blame you. Jared is pretty great, even if he has a hard time seeing it sometimes. I meant what I said, though. If you even think about hurting him in any way, I will make it my life's mission to make sure that you never have a moment's peace. Do I make myself clear?"

He gave her what he hoped wasn't too mocking of a salute. "Yes, captain!"

"Oh, knock it off. You might be Mr. Hollywood, but that doesn't mean that you get to be dramatic here. Trust me, there are enough hams in this family without adding you into the mix."

As they settled into a conversation, Charlie felt a warm feeling flowing through him, and it took him a few minutes to figure out just what it was.

It felt like home.

# CHAPTER 9

*S*o far, Charlie meeting his parents (and several other members of the family) hadn't been quite the nightmare that Jared had been expecting. He wasn't sure just how much any of them knew about Charlie's sexuality, but he thought he could see some knowing looks among several of the cousins.

*There goes Jared again,* he could almost hear them saying, *trying to hook up with someone who is so far out of his league as to basically be on another planet.*

He wanted to shout at them that that was definitely not what was happening, that he had no romantic interest whatsoever in Mr. Charlie Garrett, but he decided against it, both because they wouldn't believe him and because he wasn't sure he would have believed it himself. Leaning against the kitchen counter and watching the effortless way that Charlie navigated the family—sharing a story about his own upbringing in the country with his mother, telling his dad some arcane story about the nuts and bolts of filming, or making faces at some of the younger members of the family—Jared couldn't quite believe what he was seeing. As he'd said to Charlie, pretty much every person he'd ever brought home to see his family had looked down on them in one way or another, so his behavior made for a refreshing change.

*I guess that doesn't say much about my own choices regarding significant others.*

"So, cuz, you finally brought home a movie star. I gotta say that I didn't think you had it in you.'

Hannah sidled up to him, smiling sarcastically in the way that she'd perfected. She was always the one who was willing to tell the uncomfortable truths that everyone else was content to just let slip by.

"I wouldn't say that 'I've brought him home'...," he began.

"I know you don't really believe that, Jared."

"And how do you know what I believe?"

"Because I know you better than almost anyone else, either inside this family or outside of it. The two of us have always been more similar than anyone else, which means I can tell when starting to fall for someone and when you don't want to admit it to anyone, including and especially yourself."

"I've only known him for twenty four hours. That's not nearly enough time to really get to know someone, let alone to fall in love."

"Who said anything about falling in love? I implied that you had feelings for him. See the difference? It's like in those movies, where the hero or the heroine starts to realize their feelings for the other person."

"Life isn't a movie," he deflected.

"I know it's not, but there's always a grain of truth in even the most ridiculous rom-com. I'd think that as a writer you'd know that."

"I'm not really a writer, you know."

Hannah gave him the look that said he was being a pedantic idiot and missing the forest for the trees.

"We both know that you love writing. That's why I don't

really understand why you waste so much time in that job with the Huntington City Council. I'm sure it's nice to be involved in the arts in some way, but wouldn't you rather spend your time actually writing something that makes you feel fulfilled?"

As always, Hannah had a way of cutting right to the heart of the matter, but that didn't mean that he liked what she had to say.

"Can we change the subject, please?"

In typical Hannah fashion, however, she shook her head. "I'm not going to let you off that easily. The truth is that the same thing that keeps you from being the writer that you truly want to be is the same thing that's going to get in the way of you making anything lasting with Charlie."

"Hannah," he said, trying to give her a warning about this without being an asshole. "Please."

Hannah shook her head at him. "Fine. Then will you answer me a very simple question?"

"Sure."

"Why are you always so determined to not let yourself just...be happy?"

That question hit him like a ton of bricks, mostly because he'd avoided addressing this question in the privacy of his own thoughts, let alone talked about it with anyone else. And, because he was Jared Russell and hated to feel vulnerable, his first response was anger.

"I find that a bit rich coming from you, considering that you've never liked one of the guys that I've brought home before now."

"Jared, you know that's not true. I've just been honest with you when I thought that you could do better."

"I see. And better according to whom? Has it ever occurred to you that I'm an adult and can make my own decisions about things without constant interference from my family?"

He didn't know why he was acting this way, particularly not with Hannah, one of the few members of his extended family who hadn't ever been an asshole to him.

"Jared, knock it off," she said. "You're just being defensive because you know I'm right, and it's not a good look."

Well, now he just felt sheepish.

"Damn it, Hannah, do you have to know me so well?"

She just smirked. "It's kind of my job, cuz. You've always been the runt, and I've always had to take care of you. That's not going to stop just because you're pushing forty."

"Now you're just being mean and rude."

"Just returning the favor."

This was the kind of banter and repartee that he missed when he wasn't home. Sure, he had a nice bond with Rebecca, and the two of them were able to give each other a hard time, but it was different when it was with someone who'd known you your whole life and who knew you better than you knew yourself and wasn't afraid to be honest about your own short-comings.

"So, uh, what am I going to do about this whole situation?"

"I don't think that you have to *do* anything per se," she said. "Just see where it goes for now. You don't have to make any decisions, unless you want to. I think you might want to remember that you're in charge of your own life, no one else."

Those words were an uncanny echo of what Charlie had said just a bit ago.

"You're wiser than you look, you know."

"That's high praise coming from you."

They continued on bantering like this for a few more minutes, until Charlie ambled over.

"He really is the human equivalent of a golden retriever," Hannah said without missing a beat.

"You'd be surprised how often I get told that," Charlie said, utterly unselfconscious. "In fact, I'm pretty sure that's what got me the job with the Romance Network. They saw the kind of guy I was, the way that my brown eyes are like limpid pools of chocolate, and the rest is history."

"Well listen to this guy," Hannah said. "He's got it all figured out, including his own career."

Even as Charlie was clearly having a good time chatting with Hannah, Jared noticed that he kept looking at his phone, and while he wasn't normally one of those people who was offended when people did that, he thought he could sense that something was wrong.

"Charlie, do you need to take that?"

"Um...no, no I don't," he said, shoving the phone into his pocket. "It's nothing."

Jared tried to give him the kind of look that he was so used to getting from others. "I may not have known you very long, Charlie Garrett, but I can still tell when you're lying. You're not very good at it."

He hadn't thought it was possible, but if anything Charlie got even cuter when he blushed like that.

"I mean, I guess if you want to know the truth, it's my mother. She's been texting a lot, and I haven't had the chance to respond."

"And don't you think that you ought to answer her texts?"

Jared didn't actually think that it was any of his business whether Charlie Garrett texted his mother or not, but he also couldn't help thinking about how his own mother would feel if she was constantly texting her son and not getting a response.

"She might be worried about you, you know. Particularly if she managed to hear about what happened last night."

"Yes," he said, dragging the word out, "I suppose I should." He sighed. "It's just that things with her are always a bit difficult. I know she loves me, but we don't always see eye-to-eye on things."

Before he could think better of it or let his nerves get in the way, Jared was hugging Charlie. At first the other man didn't seem to know what to do, and then he was returning the gesture, sending little jolts of electricity shooting through every nerve in Jared's body.

"It'll be okay, Charlie," he said. "We'll be here for you when you finish the call."

Charlie was the first one to break the hug, but there was still a fond look in his eyes that made Jared's stomach do a backflip.

"I'm just gonna run upstairs and take this," Charlie said, and that quickly he was gone.

"Well," Hannah said, "this should be fun."

# CHAPTER 10

*A*s soon as he stepped away from Jared, Charlie wished he could go back. He knew he wasn't imagining the little spark of connection that had leapt between them, just as he hadn't been imagining it in the kitchen when they were making cherry jam. Jared might like to pretend to the rest of the world that he was ironic and aloof from it all, but in their brief time together Charlie had begun to see a different side of the man, one who was very different from the ice queen that he'd met at the airport just a day ago.

For the moment, though, Charlie had to focus on talking to his mother. As he'd said to Jared, the two of them had never seen eye-to-eye on most things–including, for a very long time, his sexuality–but they'd managed to find a measure of peace. That didn't mean that he stayed in touch with her as much as he should, even if he had moved her out to California.

When he got to Jared's room he closed the door behind him and sat down on the bed, taking another minute to just gaze around at all of the signs of the boy who'd once lived here. He felt a smile pulling at his lips as he thought about what it must have been like for Jared growing up in a house like this one, filled with love and joy and light.

*Okay, enough letting your mind wander. Let's get this over with.*

Even after he'd pulled the phone out of his pocket, however, it took him several minutes to actually type in the number and hit the call button.

As the phone began to ring, Charlie heard laughter coming from downstairs, and he felt the usual pang. Things had never been like that with his family, even when he'd lived at home. His father might have been accepting of his sexuality, but he had never been particularly kind to his wife, who he tended to treat with a sort of casual cruelty.

Why did families have to be so complicated?

It took a few rings, but she finally picked up.

"Charlie, sweetie, I'm so glad you called. I was just thinking about you," his mother's cheery voice said at once. "How are you?" That sweet Appalachian drawl was just as he remembered it, and it made his heart constrict in his chest.

"I'm...I'm good, mom," he said, taking a second to clear his throat. "How are you?"

"I'm good, darlin'. Just trying to get some bakin' done today."

"That sounds great, mom. What's the occasion?"

"Oh, no particular reason. I was just thinkin' about how much I missed the old home place and thought I'd get in touch with my roots by makin' a cobbler."

His mouth started watering as he thought about the taste of her delicious cherry cobbler, but he also braced himself for the guilt trip he knew was coming.

"I saw that you went back to West Virginia yesterday," she said. "I gotta say that my feelings are a little hurt that you didn't ask me if I wanted to come along."

He took a deep breath and pinched his nose. He'd known

this was coming, and he did feel a bit guilty about not inviting her, but he also wished that she would, or could, understand how much of a pain in the ass she could be when she tried this passive aggressive approach to conflict resolution.

"I know, but I just figured that with the whole film premiere and everything that I wouldn't have as much time to be with you as I would have liked, and it doesn't seem like the kind of movie that you would like anyway."

That much was true, anyway. He highly doubted that she would go out of her way to watch some hard-hitting drama about the perils of gay life in the middle of the 20th century.

"But you somehow found time to get into a fight with someone at a bar?"

"Uh, yeah, that probably wasn't my proudest moment," he said, scuffing his foot on the floor, fixating on a knot in the hardwood so that he wouldn't have to really pay attention to what was sure to come from the other end of the line. "That's kind of why I'm holed up for the weekend, so I don't cause any more problems."

There was a heavy sigh on the other end of the line. "Sometimes, Charlie, you're just like your father."

It was a refrain that he'd heard a lot growing up. Any time that he expressed an opinion that his mother didn't like or started to shut down or even came close to losing his temper, she'd tell him that he was being like his father. While he understood where she was coming from, it'd come to a point where he'd decided it was easier to avoid conversation rather than to risk getting in trouble again.

*Typical Charlie Garrett,* he thought. *Face a challenge, run your mouth, and then take the easy way out.*

However, being with Jared and seeing his family had shown him that there might be another way of handling this. Perhaps the pattern of losing his temper and withdrawing wasn't the most helpful way of communicating with her.

"I'm sorry, mom," he said softly. "I know that I'm a bit too much like him sometimes. I...I'll try to do better. You deserve better. We both do."

"Oh, Charlie. You're a good boy. I hope you know that I'll always love you and be here for you. I hope you know that I just want you to be happy. That matters more to me than anything else."

"I really appreciate that," he said, and for the first time in a long time, he really meant it. It suddenly felt as if a great weight was lifted off his chest. It was a small thing, a little thaw, but it suggested that the two of them might be able to work things out, if they took it slow and made meaningful changes. If *he* made slow but meaningful changes.

"So," his mother said, "where are you staying this weekend? I bet Sheri wanted to get you out of Huntington as fast as she could after your little...incident."

"Well, that's the thing. I'm staying with a guy named Jared and his parents. He was kind of recruited into getting me out of town."

He cut himself off before he could blurt out too much.

"I see," she said slowly. "And what are this young man's intentions with my son?"

"Mom, it's not like that," he said.

"But maybe it could be?" she said, making the words half statement and half question.

"I don't think he sees me that way."

"That doesn't answer my question."

*Damn it,* he thought.

"I'm your mother, Charlie. This might come as a surprise to you, but I do know you pretty well, and I know how it goes with the boys that you get with. If you think there's something with this young man, then you should tell him." She paused a minute, as if choosing her next words with care. "Don't be afraid of your feelings, Charlie. And don't be afraid to express them."

*Don't be like your father.* That was what she meant even if she didn't say it.

"Thank you, mom. I'll consider it."

She sighed. "Please do, Charlie. I mean it. I know that you and I don't always agree, but I do want what's best for you. And, well, if this guy Jared ends up being the best, you should let yourself be happy."

*Let yourself be happy.* That was something he hadn't thought about in a while.

"Okay," he said noncommittally.

"So?" she said. "What are you doing just talking to me? Go out there and get him."

"Fine, I'll do it. For you," he said. "I...I love you, mom."

"I love you, too, sweetie," and then the line went dead.

For several minutes Charlie just sat there trying to sort through his feelings about the conversation. It had gone remarkably well. Perhaps *too* well.

He shook his head. What was he thinking? He needed to stop getting in his own way and just enjoy the good things when they came his way. Like...well, like Jared.

*Okay, are you just going to sit here in this room or are you going to go out there and spend some time with the guy you have a crush on?*

That settled it.

He got up slowly and walked toward the door. He had no idea how the rest of this weekend was going to go but, one way or another, he was going to seize his own happiness.

# CHAPTER 11

*W*hen Charlie came out of the bedroom, Jared could tell at once that something serious had happened, though he couldn't quite tell whether it was good or bad.

His mother, however, wasn't one to stand on ceremony. The minute she saw that someone looked like they might be hurting, she swooped in.

"Charlie, dear, is everything okay?" she asked.

"Yes, I'm fine. Or, well, I think I will be, eventually. I just had a rather difficult conversation with my mother." He laughed nervously. "But it went better than I thought. Things haven't always been easy between the two of us."

"Oh sweetie, I'm sorry to hear that," Joyce said, sweeping in for a hug. Jared tried not to feel jealous, reminding himself not to be ridiculous.

"Thank you," Charlie said as Joyce drew away from him, reaching up to flick a stray strand of hair out of his eyes. "I really appreciate that."

"You'll always have a home here," she went on, "and not

just because no one has made Jared smile like you have in a long time."

"Mother," he said warningly, but she just kept talking.

"Sometimes mothers, well, they don't always want to accept that their children are their own people with their own minds and hearts and desires. Give her time. She'll come around."

And there was that folksy country wisdom his mother was so very happy to dish out.

"Thank you for that...Joyce," Charlie said. "I think my mother and I finally understand one another a bit better. Perhaps better than we have in a long time."

As Charlie spoke, it seemed like a weight lifted off his shoulders, and Jared found himself grinning like a fool at seeing it. When Charlie's eyes met his, he started grinning, too, and Jared felt that familiar flush start creeping up his neck.

His mother, instincts sharp as always, sensed the brewing tension between the two of them.

"Now then," she said, "I hope that the two of you aren't going to just loiter around the house all day. Since everyone is here already, I decided to throw a little dinner for the family. Might as well make the most of it, right?"

"Mom, I'm not sure that's a good idea," he began, but Charlie interrupted him.

"That's so sweet of you, Joyce," he said, flashing her his megawatt smile. "Is there anything we can do to help?"

Joyce gave him a mock-stern look. "We don't ask company to help cook here. Jared, why don't you take Charlie around and show him the property while your father and I get dinner ready?"

"If you're sure," Charlie started to say, but this time it was Jared's turn to interrupt him. Grabbing Charlie's hand he pulled him outside, calling out to his mom over his shoulder.

"We'll be back soon!"

They walked for a bit in silence, and it was only when they were several steps away from the house Jared realized that he was still holding Charlie's hand. He dropped it like a hot potato.

*What were you thinking?*

To distract himself from what was almost an intimate moment, he took the time to point out all of the rustic pleasures his parents' place afforded: the small flock of chickens and ducks pecking near their little house ("they call it the Taj McDuck," he told Charlie with a little chagrin), the garden (now faded and filled with corn husks at this time of year), and the numerous Halloween decorations that his father insisted on putting up around the property (including, much to his mother's chagrin, those giant blow-up dolls in the shapes of black cats, pumpkins, and ghosts). As he did so, he found himself feeling a bit reflective about his relationship with his family and with West Virginia as a whole.

" You know," he said into the silence that had settled around them, "I talk a big game about loving it here, but sometimes I'm more than a little ashamed of being from West Virginia. I even broke up with a boyfriend because he called my parents rednecks."

This got a laugh out of Charlie. "Your parents might be simple country people, but they're definitely not rednecks. And neither are you, for that matter."

"I'm glad that you understand the difference. You'd be surprised how many people don't."

"Oh, believe me, I wouldn't."

He was surprised to see sadness on Charlie's face, and he almost reached out and touched his cheek, to see if he could coax a smile out of him. Something still held him back, some fear that doing that would be a step too far.

"They must be pretty awful to you in Hollywood," he said

instead. "I can't imagine them welcoming someone from West Virginia with open arms."

"They all weren't so bad," Charlie said, with a peculiar intensity in his voice. "In fact there were quite a few of them who came from backgrounds similar to mine. And a lot of them were gay, too. They told me that it was better to just go along to get along. That it was better to stay as 'circumspect' as possible.

"I guess you took that advice to heart."

Jared could have kicked himself for saying that outloud but, rather than getting mad about it, Charlie shook his head.

"To you it must look like I left all of this behind, while you've stayed here to fight the good fight."

Jared started to interrupt, to insist that it wasn't like that at all, but Charlie kept talking.

"I should tell you that I don't blame you for feeling resentful. For a long time I *did* give up on West Virginia. I didn't care about the people back here, and I wanted to forget where I came from. It just seemed like it would be easier that way, rather than trying to make peace among the different parts of my life. It took talking to some of my friends back here–who didn't give up on me, even though I'd largely given up on them–to convince me that I might not have as much of the right idea as I thought I did. They convinced me that I was being exactly the kind of person that I'd always said I wouldn't be."

He chuckled sadly and softly. "It also took some long hard looks in the mirror for me to see the truth of things, and I didn't always like what was looking back at me."

*Well, at least some of my suspicions have been confirmed,* Jared thought smugly, but then felt bad about it.

"So, I ended up coming back home for a few weeks at a time in between shoots. I had to do it privately, or at least that's what I thought at the time, because I didn't want to make a big deal about it. I'd done a lot of work to make sure that people didn't know that much about me. In Hollywood it's usually a lot easier to keep parts of your private life private so that everyone else can project what they want onto you."

While Jared was of course quite flattered and honored that Charlie was sharing this part of himself, he was also a little strange having someone who was still basically a stranger be so open about his life and his feelings.

"It wasn't long before I was sending donations and trying to build up some sort of infrastructure for young queer people in the state, Charlie went on. "This would have been...in the mid-2000s, I guess? I was still getting my feet in the business and trying to figure out just what it was that I was going to do with my career. The Romance Network was grooming me to be a part of their regular lineup, and this seemed like a good way to spend all of that money that was coming in."

This time the urge to caress Charlie's face was even stronger, but still he resisted.

*Jared, you're going to have to either pull the trigger on this or let it go,* he thought, followed quickly by, *I'm not imagining this, am I?*

Then Charlie shot him a knowing little look, and he realized that no, he wasn't imagining it. For the moment, though, Charlie was intent on telling the rest of his story, clearly trying to get through it as quickly as possible.

"So, it just kept growing. I was able to do at least some good, but this was in the lead-up to the 2008 election, and that's when things started getting ugly. There were a lot of groups that faced some backlash and pressure. Public libraries started telling me that they didn't want to get in any sort of trouble. And stopped returning my calls. It was the same with a lot of the other nonprofits that I'd been involved in. They just didn't want to have to try to grapple with the vitriol that always came with being publicly seen associating with anything even remotely resembling gayness."

He sighed. "So, I finally just decided that enough was enough. If I wasn't going to make any headway in West Virginia, then I could at least try to make a difference where I was in California. That didn't always work out either, but at least I felt more in control there."

"So...you just gave up on West Virginia?"

"Jared, come on, give me some credit, huh? I didn't just give up, and it didn't happen right away. I tried again a couple of years ago, but things had gotten even uglier in the intervening years. I finally got tired of having doors slammed in my face and gave up. I know that's probably not what you wanted to hear. But then again, maybe it is, because it confirms what you thought you knew about me all along, but I thought you deserved the truth."

Jared took a deep breath, because there were a lot of things that he wanted to say, a lot of pieces of the puzzle that he was still trying to fight together. Charlie was right, at least to an extent. This did confirm what he'd thought, but also it didn't. So much of what he'd thought about Charlie Garrett had been built out of his own assumptions, rather than the truth, and if he was being perfectly honest with himself, it was also about jealousy.

It was time to put all of that away and try something new.

"I can't say that I agree with everything that you did in the past," he said, choosing his words with care, "But I can also see that it was quite a difficult and treacherous path that you had to walk. My real question is: why didn't you just tell me all of this before? Or anyone else, for that matter? I'd think that it would be good for your brand to have everyone know that you were trying to do good things for your home state but that a bunch of religious jackasses were standing in the way."

Charlie shook his head. "It's not like that. I have a very

specific fan base, and they...well, they don't like it when their favorite gay star does anything that's not squeaky clean and nonconfrontational. It's why Sheri has a fulltime job just keeping my name out of the gossip sites, because she knows that if my fans get too much of a whiff of just how much I've been involved in any kind of gay politics, they're not going to be happy. They like their stars to be the good kind of gays, the ones that look pretty on-screen and not much else.

"And as for why I didn't tell you before...well, you can be a bit prickly. And besides, every time I'd get close to getting there you'd change the subject." He shrugged. "I'm glad it's all out in the open. Now you've gotten to see the *real* Charlie Garrett beneath all of the hype."

This was all a lot to absorb, and it didn't help that Charlie looked even sexier and more handsome in the afternoon sunlight, which hit his hair in just such a way as to bring out its darker golden hues. The fact that it also highlighted his biceps didn't hurt.

*Behave yourself.*

"I can see that," he said, because it was the only thing he could think to say at the moment. "It...it must be difficult to always be on and to perform for someone else. It must be even harder to feel like you can never be your authentic self."

"I'm guessing you know something about that too."

Damn Charlie Garrett and his ability to read other people like a book.

"I guess you could say that. It was hard enough to be a gay kid around here without also being the creative type." He snorted. "I think my parents were more concerned about the fact that I wanted to take up such a precarious profession than they were about who I slept with."

"Did they just look at it as a hobby?"

Jared took a moment to consider his words.

"I suppose you could say that. I think it's probably more

114

accurate to say that they just didn't see how that could ever possibly be a way to make money. It turns out they were right."

It hurt to say those words, but there was also something liberating about being able to say them aloud.

"We sometimes have to do what we want despite what our parents have to say about it," Charlie said. "No matter what, though, you should always follow your heart. If there's a book in you that you think needs to be written, if there's a story that you know only you can tell, then you should do it."

Jared almost told him then about his secret plan to write a memoir of what it was like growing up gay in Appalachia. He didn't, though, because he wasn't yet ready to share that particular dream with anyone.

Instead, he settled for just drinking in the beauty that was Charlie Garrett. As he caught glimpses of him out of the corner of his eye, Jared found himself imagining him in one of the movies that he was trying to break into: some brooding hero from a Jane Austen novel, perhaps, or a cold baron with a heart of gold that just needs the right lady, or lord, to melt his heart and open him to a new world of erotic and amorous experiences.

Before he could think about what he was doing, Jared reached out and put his hand on Charlie's, even as that little voice in his mind was screaming at him to stop, demanding to know what he thought he was doing. He steadfastly ignored it, though. Hannah had been right; it was time to seize some of his own happiness, and let the chips fall where they may.

He'd secretly been dreading that Charlie would ask him what he was doing, or that he would be turned off by his presumption. What he didn't expect was for Charlie to turn his smile on him and then, before Jared could say or do anything else, lean over and kiss him.

At first Jared didn't know what to do. It'd been so long

since anyone had kissed him, and also up until a few hours ago he'd resented the guy who was sitting next to him as nothing but a poser and a fake. But also this was *Charlie Garrett* and he was kissing him and, though he would never admit it to anyone else, he suddenly felt light as a feather.

The writerly part of his mind was already trying to fit this whole experience into something that he could write about later, or that he could try to make sense of once he had time to collect himself. The more that the kiss went on, however, the more comfortable he felt just abandoning himself to the pleasure of it, savoring the way that Charlie smelled and the way he tasted, the way that his skin felt brushing against his own.

*Just enjoy this,* he thought. *Don't overthink it.*

So he didn't.

# CHAPTER 12

Charlie hadn't known that he was going to kiss Jared before he did it, but he had most definitely known that he wanted to. There was something about the other man– the way that he was the right combination of sensitive and tough, nerd and country boy, masculine and feminine– that continued to draw him in. He was also unlike anyone else he'd met in either West Virginia or California, which made him that much more appealing, even if he remained something of a tough nut to crack.

He was thus more than a little surprised when Jared actually started kissing him back.

He reached up and put his hand behind Jared's head, running his fingers through his hair, loving the way that the strands passed through his fingers. Jared's breath was coming faster and faster, and Charlie dared to run his other hand up and down his body, savoring the way that his muscles rippled with every move he made. Charlie suddenly wanted to pull off the other man's clothes, but he resisted the urge, mostly because he wasn't sure that Jared was ready to go that far.

Then Jared's hand crept down south and started stroking

Charlie through his jeans, and he knew that this was going to get very intense very quickly if he didn't do something to stop it. The trouble was that he didn't *want* to stop it. In fact, he wanted it to keep going for as long as Jared was willing to let it do so.

Unfortunately, Jared made a little whimpering noise and pulled back, leaving Charlie standing feeling very aroused and a little embarrassed as it dawned on him that they were still within sight of the house.

"Um...," he started fumbling for words, trying to find something to say that would diffuse the awkwardness that was quickly gelling around them. "You're a really good kisser?" He hadn't meant for that last bit to come out like a question.

*Good going, Charlie.*

"You know, when you give someone a compliment like that, you really shouldn't make it sound like you're asking rather than telling."

Charlie chuckled. He should have known that Jared would pick up on that right away.

"You're a very good kisser," he tried again, this time the words coming out declarative.

Jared nodded.

"I don't disagree with your declaration, but I think we're going to need some more experience to make sure that we both know what we're talking about."

Before Charlie could say anything to that Jared's lips were on his again.

This time the kissing was even more intense. It was as if they both wanted to drink the other one up, to erase the boundaries between them, and soon their hands were roaming all over each other. It was intoxicating. It was exciting. It was terrifying.

This time it was Charlie who drew back, though he couldn't have quite said why.

"For the record," Jared said, that elusive little smile flickering on his lips. "You're a pretty good kisser, too. Did they teach you that in Hollywood?"

"They taught me a lot of things in Hollywood," Charlie said.

He wasn't sure just how far things might have gone, because they were interrupted by Jared's mother calling from the house.

"Charlie! Jared!" Joyce's voice came wafting out to them from the house. "Dinner's ready! And don't dally!"

"She does know that she could have just called you, right?" Charlie asked.

"Welcome to my parents' house," he said with a sigh.

They got themselves presentable–or as presentable as they could, anyway–and started walking back. Just before they got to the house, however, Charlie noticed a stray leaf that had somehow found its way onto Jared's shirt. Without saying anything, he reached out and plucked it out, which earned him a startled yelp from Jared.

"What was that for?"

Charlie grinned sheepishly and held it up, as if that was all the explanation necessary. To his relief, Jared just smiled.

He opened his mouth to say something, but just then his mother was at the door to the house, a worried look on her face.

She didn't even wait until they were at the door before she started speaking.

"So, I don't want you to both be mad at me, but I have something to tell you."

Charlie tried not to flinch at that. Jared, however, didn't even try to hide his dismay.

"Who did you call?" he demanded, hands on his hips.

Joyce at least had the good grace to look embarrassed. "I...I might have divulged to your grandmother that Charlie was here and she...well, she might have said she's coming over right away and she might have told a bunch of her friends. I don't *think* they're going to be coming with her, but with your grandmother who can say?"

Jared groaned. "Mom, what part of Charlie's presence here being a secret did you misunderstand? We're trying to keep people from knowing where he is so we don't have to answer all sorts of unpleasant and very troubling questions."

"Now don't take that tone with me," she said. "I didn't really mean for it to get out of hand. It's just that your grandmother was so excited, and she decided to start calling everyone. I hope you're not going to make a big deal out of it when she gets here."

Charlie could tell from the look on Jared's face that he was going to have to intervene before it got any worse. He put a steadying hand on Jared's arm, ignoring the stern look he got in response, and turned on the charm.

"It's okay, Joyce. Really. I'm sure everything's going to be fine. And besides, I'm really looking forward to meeting more of Jared's family and friends." He turned up the wattage on the smile. "I've always thought you can tell a lot about a guy from how he is around his family."

"You always think that, do you?" Jared asked with his eyebrow skeptically raised.

"I do, in fact."

"I really don't know why you two can't just start dating," Joyce said. "It would really make everything so much simpler. Charlie, you're just the kind of man that I've always been looking for for Jared. Are you sure you don't want him?"

This was very uncomfortable territory, not least because Charlie did very much want to put Jared in his back pocket and take him away. Since he knew that wasn't at all what Jared wanted, however, he decided to be as coy as possible, without turning Jared off. He wasn't sure he could pull off that particular juggling act, but damn if he wasn't going to try.

"Well," he began, but Jared interrupted him.

"Mom, Charlie is a guest in our house. Maybe we could save the matchmaking for later?"

Joyce looked like she wanted to keep pressing–and Jared looked like he wanted to melt into the ground–but they were saved from all of that by the arrival of a stately dowager that Charlie could only assume was Jared's grandmother.

"Well, well, well," she said as she approached, "what's this, the welcoming party?"

Marla Grayson–Jared took a moment to properly introduce his grandmother–was one of those formidable dowagers that were a dime a dozen in West Virginia. Though she was probably in her eighties, Charlie thought that she didn't look a day over sixty, with her white hair that had been swept up in a bun at the back of her head, her floral-print blouse, and her polyester slacks. One of her gnarled hands gripped a cane as she came up to the door, but Charlie got the distinct impression she wasn't as feeble as she looked.

"Grandma!" Jared said, stepping forward. "It's so good to see you."

Marla gave him a look, and then her face broke into a smile of undeniable joy and she swept him into her arms. Charlie tried very hard not to be jealous.

"It's good to see you too, sweetie," he said, patting Jared's arm as she pulled away. "And this must be *the* Charlie Garrett. I'm just so happy to meet you!" she exclaimed as they all stepped into the house. "You know, when Joyce said that Jared had managed to bring home someone from the Romance Network, I almost couldn't believe it. It just seemed too good to be true, and yet here you are!"

She looked Charlie up and down for a good few minutes, and he got the distinct impression that she was acting as trial, judge, and jury all at once. He wasn't at all sure that she liked what she saw, but then she nodded her head.

"Well, I gotta say that it's nice that Jared finally brought someone decent around for a change. I never did like a lot of those other fellas that he brought here."

Charlie was familiar enough with the older generation's way of referring to gay relationships to know exactly what he meant, and he felt a little flutter at the idea that people were starting to assume that he was Jared's boyfriend.

*Easy, Charlie. Let's not put the cart before the horse.*

In any case he didn't have much time to really dwell too much on just what he was to Jared, because Joyce swept Marla into the dining room, where the rest of the family had already gathered around the table. There was the usual hustle and bustle and greetings as everyone made Marla welcome and, a short time later, there was an entire spread ready for eating, all laid out with precision on the dining room table.

For the life of him, Charlie couldn't figure out how Joyce had managed to get an entire dinner together in such a short time but, there it was, as pristine and ordered as if she'd been working in the kitchen all day. There was a delicious, succulent roast in pride of place in the center of the table on a gorgeous red serving platter–Fiestaware, of course–while it was surrounded by everything from green beans to baked potatoes, corn on the cob to macaroni and cheese.

It was the sort of home cooked meal that he almost never had when he was in California.

"You'd better take a seat if you don't want to get shut out," Jared said, gently taking his hand and guiding him over to the table, and Charlie thought of the kiss they'd shared such a short time ago. Was that just a fluke, or did it actually mean something? And, just as importantly, was it going to lead to anything else?

They sat down, and just being this close to Jared was more

than a little intoxicating. Charlie flicked his eyes to where Marla sat across from him and saw that she had her eyes on him. He gave her a smile, and she returned it, but he couldn't shake the feeling that she was weighing him in her own private set of scales. She might not know that Jared was gay, but she certainly knew that *something* was up.

For a few minutes Marla was content to let the conversation ebb and flow around her, but it wasn't long until she got right to the heart of the matter. Like grandmothers everywhere, she was old enough to feel entitled to say whatever she wanted, even if it happened to make other people feel a bit uncomfortable.

"I know that everyone else in this family thinks that I'm some simple-minded old lady," she said, "but I do watch the news. And you, young man, were on there." At this she wagged his finger at him.

*Is this really happening?* He thought.

"Now, I know that it's not my place to say this, but I really don't like to see young men fighting, no matter what their reasons are. Violence never gets you anywhere, Charlie Garrett. Remember that."

Charlie wasn't about to disagree with her, particularly since he knew she was right. He almost told her that he'd done it to protect Jared, but decided against it.

*I'm not sure she would approve even if she knew.*

"You know what? You're absolutely right," he said instead. I'm definitely going to be minding my Ps and Qs from now on."

He was vaguely conscious of Jared giving him an incredulous look and mouth and mouthing the letters "Ps" and "Qs" with a very perplexed look on his face.

"See that you do," Marla said, and took a healthy bite of roast and then washed it down with some iced tea. "I don't want to tune into the news and see your name there again, unless it's to hear about you getting some kind of award. I'm sure you're going to be going places, young man, so be sure not to mess it up!"

"Yes, ma'am," he said again. "I'll be extra careful, and when I do get that award, I'll be dedicating it to you."

She scoffed at that. "Don't be ridiculous. There are better people for that. Like my grandson over there. I've lost count of the number of times we've watched one of your movies together."

"I didn't realize that Jared was such a big fan of mine," he said with a smile. Jared at least had the good grace to look embarrassed.

"Oh yes, he talks about you all the time," Marla went on, heedless of the discomfort she was clearly causing Jared.

"I'll definitely keep that in mind," he said. He bumped Jared's knee with his own under the table, smirking as his face turned several shades of pink.

The rest of the dinner passed companionably, and at last Marla made it clear that it was time for her to go.

"This has been a truly fantastic meal, my dear," she said, beaming at Joyce.

Joyce looked so taken aback to be praised by her mother that she didn't say anything.

"Don't look so surprised," Marla said. "I know I don't dish out the compliments as often as I should, but we both know that you're the best cook in the family."

As she made her way out the door, Grandma Marla gestured to Charlie to lean down.

"Don't you dare tell anyone that I said this, but I want you to know two things. One, I think that you did the right thing there in Huntington. That man got what was coming to him. Just don't do it again. Two, you're a good match for my grandson. You *wouldn't* believe the type of people that he's brought up here before. Just don't break his heart like they did, or I will come and find you. I might be old, but I still know how to throw a punch or two myself."

And with that she was gone, sweeping out the door.

Charlie wasn't quite sure how he felt about Marla. He liked her, obviously, but he knew she'd meant what she'd said about defending her grandson. She wasn't going to stand by and let anyone hurt his feelings.

"So, now you've met my grandmother," Jared said as he came back inside. "She's quite the force of nature."

"You could say that. She definitely wasn't quite what I expected, and not at all like my grandparents, or what I remember of them, anyway."

"Did they die when you were young?"

Charlie shifted a bit uncomfortably. "Neither of my parents were very close to their parents, and so they didn't really want me to be, either. I think I might have met them a handful of times before they died."

He hadn't been aware until he said it just how much he'd missed out on that sort of relationship, and once again he found himself being a little envious of the life that Jared led.

"Are you absolutely sure that she doesn't know you're gay?" he asked.

He thought that she must, given what she'd said to him.

Jared made a very complicated face. "Well, it's a little messy, actually. I think the best way to put it is that she 'knows' but she doesn't really 'know,' if you know what I mean."

Charlie laughed at that. "Yeah, I think I have a good idea of what you're talking about. It's one of those things that older people do that allows them to keep pretending that you're the same person that you were when you were growing up. I guess that we all have some sort of fiction that we use to keep ourselves sane."

"What are you two boys whispering about?" asked Joyce,

who'd managed to sneak up on them without either of them being able to hear her. "I hope that you haven't been saying anything mean about your grandmother. You know that she thinks the world of you."

"Of course not, mom. We were just talking about how funny older people can be."

"Don't make fun of your grandmother," she said sternly. "That's not nice."

"We weren't making fun of her, mother," Jared said. "We were just commenting on how she can still pretend like my... guy friends are nothing more than just roommates. She still talks about Paul that way, even though we were together for five years and lived in a house with just one master bedroom."

"She's from a different generation," she said.

Charlie wanted to point out that neither Charlie nor Jared were exactly "young" anymore, but he figured that in this case discretion was the better part of valor.

"I know that, mom," Jared said. "But don't you think that sometimes it would be nice if gay people like me were able to just be themselves openly and without fear of judgment from the members of their own family?"

This was quickly becoming something more than just a spirited disagreement about the nature of the closet, and Charlie knew that he had to do something before it got really out of control. It was clear that Joyce and Jared could really get into it when they both had their feelings hurt.

"Look, I think we can all admit that sometimes older people would be better off just admitting the truth rather than hiding from it, but sometimes we also have to take people where they are rather than continuing to demand something that they're not able to give...right?"

Surprisingly enough, his interjection worked. Joyce and Jared suddenly backed off of one another, though there was still that bit of crackling tension in the air. Charlie found himself silently begging Jared to just let this one go and to let his mother work through this in her own time.

Jared nodded a tad reluctantly. "I guess you're right, Charlie."

Joyce gave him a smile and a little pat on the cheek.

"Now see, Jared, this is the kind of boy we've been waiting for you to bring home, someone with a good head on his shoulders. He's a keeper."

Now that that little bit of unpleasantness was over, they retired to the family room, where the rest of the family was still gathered. Somehow Charlie found himself seated next to Doug, who leaned over to whisper confidentially in his ear.

"I have to give you credit, Charlie. You're able to defuse tense situations pretty well," he said. "Usually when these two start going at one another I find somewhere else to be and hunker down until the whole thing has blown over."

Joyce, sitting nearby, blew out a very theatrical sigh. "Really, Doug, do you have to be so dramatic about it? It's not like we've ever thrown anything at one another. I mean, except for that one time."

"I just hope you know that just because you've won this round doesn't mean that I'm not going to go at it again," said Jared, and Charlie almost rolled his eyes at his obvious need to have the last word.

Joyce looked like she was going to give her son a good smack for that bit of impertinence, but then seemed to decide against it. "What I wouldn't give for a son who is nice and obedient."

"Ah, but then you wouldn't have me, would you? And think how boring your life would be if we didn't have these little sparring matches. Besides, it keeps you sharp."

And just like that, the tension that had been building up like a bad thunderstorm was gone.

*What I wouldn't give to have a family like this one,* Charlie thought, and then immediately felt guilty.

"Charlie," Jared said abruptly. "Would you like to go for a walk, maybe somewhere a bit further away this time. I'm dying for some fresh air and, well, to get away from these yahoos for a bit."

Every eye was suddenly on them, and Charlie had no idea what he was supposed to say. If he said yes, then might make the rest of the family feel like he wanted to get away from them. If he said no, then he would probably hurt Jared's feelings.

"I think that's a very good idea," Joyce said. "You two could use a little bit of alone time, and I promise I won't interrupt this time." She gave them both a very knowing look, and this time it was Charlie's turn to blush.

"Thanks for that, mom," Jared said, his own face also starting to flush. "Well, Charlie? What about it?"

This was the chance he'd been waiting for, and Charlie would be a fool not to take it.

He flashed his most camera-ready grin. "I'd love to."

# CHAPTER 13

*J*ared hadn't really been sure he was going to ask Charlie to go for a longer walk until the words were out of his mouth. Once they were, though, he was...actually kind of glad that he'd asked. Watching him with his family had been a bit of a revelation, but more than that, he was really amazed at how skilled he was at defusing the argument between Jared and his mother. That was something that Jared himself could never get the hang of, no matter how much it sometimes threatened to derail his relationship with her.

*Sometimes, I think I like being right more than I like the people in my life.*

Charlie, on the other hand, was about as far from that as possible. The easy way that he'd interacted with Jared's grandmother had been more evidence that he had that knack of being a people person, someone who was able to get along with pretty much anyone that he came into contact with, a skill Jared had never mastered

Now they were walking outside again, and he wanted, very

badly, to kiss Charlie like he had before, to feel his lips against his own, but he was afraid to initiate it.

He looked nervously over at Charlie, but he was just taking in the beauty of the surrounding hills.

*Damn, he really does look beautiful here. But then, I guess he'd probably look beautiful anywhere,* Jared thought.

"So, where shall we go?" Charlie asked suddenly, turning to look at him with those startlingly blue eyes. He gestured at the surrounding farm. "I'm sure there's all sorts of nooks and crannies that you had time to explore when you were young, right?"

Jared wanted to believe that there was a hint of something else in those words, but he was afraid to let himself get his hopes up.

*Just take it easy, Jared,* he said. *He's probably just being curious. Don't try to force anything, and whatever you do, don't mention that damn kiss.*

"Um...," he said, mind suddenly devoid of all rational thought.

*Say something, idiot!*

"Yes, I know where we can go," he said, gesturing vaguely to one of the larger hills that surrounded his parents' house. "Do you feel up to climbing to the top of that hill? It's a bit of a trek, but I promise you that the views from it all are simply breathtaking."

Once again he was rewarded with that smile.

"If you're game, then so am I. I have to make sure that all of those physical trainer lessons are worth something out in the real world."

*Great,* Jared thought. *He's probably going to make it to the top of the hill long before I do.*

They set off up the hill, and it became clear very quickly that, indeed, Charlie was in much better shape than Jared. While Jared started huffing and puffing after about only ten minutes of climbing, Charlie didn't seem like he was even breathing hard or breaking a sweat. Jared shot him what he knew was a rather venomous look but Charlie, in typical Charlie fashion, just flashed him a smile.

"Sorry," he said with a shrug. "I told you that I pay good money for a personal trainer. I'd be rather annoyed if I couldn't even make it to the top of a hill without getting winded, you know?"

By the time they finally reached the top Jared was very thoroughly winded and very, very sweaty, but to give Charlie his due he hadn't left him behind. Now that he was completely worn out, Jared threw himself on the ground and just stretched out, enjoying the feel of the grass beneath him and the cleanness of the country air.

"I think I'm going to regret this tomorrow," he said. "I haven't walked like that in a very long time. Probably too long."

Charlie gave him a mock stern look. "You really should try to stay active, you know. Neither of us are spring chickens."

"Ugh. I know. You're right. I'll be sure to walk to the top of this hill every time I come home." He didn't bother mentioning that that was exactly what he used to do before he got so caught up with other stuff and didn't come home as much as he used to.

"So," Charlie said, flopping down beside him, "was there a particular reason why you wanted to come up here?"

*Because I thought that it was one of the few places where you and I could make out without anyone knowing what we were doing.*

"Because...well, I guess because this has always been one of the most peaceful places that I've ever known," he said aloud. "It was only up here, under the sky and in the field, that I could ever really feel like I was just by myself."

Charlie gave him a wistful smile. "I like the sound of that," he said. "We never really had anything like that where I grew up. The coal mines had already stripped most of the hills away, and they hadn't really done much to reclaim the land. We couldn't even go into the creek most of the time because it was just so polluted."

Jared sighed. "Yeah, there are a lot of places in West Virginia like that. It's not so bad up here, or at least it wasn't until all of the natural gas drilling started. Now you can't even go two or three hills over without running into some place that's been totally stripped of its trees. It's really awful."

A bit of an awkward silence settled over the two of them as they each thought about what it meant for the natural beauty of their state to be stripped away. While Jared knew it was a very important subject—and it was one that was near and dear to his heart, considering he lived here—he wanted to talk about something else, something more romantic, or at least not as depressing.

"I'll be honest, though. There was also something about being able to look out over the land nearby that made me almost feel like a prince in a castle, like this was all mine." He laughed at that. "Of course, my parents only really own this little sliver of land." He gestured at the other houses scattered on the other hills. "Those are all different parcels of property. It all used to belong to our family at one time or another, but over the years people have moved away to other states and other folks have moved in. There are still enough of us left that people associate this land with us, but it's not like it used to be."

"You really love it here, don't you?" Charlie asked.

Jared paused a minute before answering. "I do. I think it's one of those things that it took me a very long time to accept, but I really do love it. It's like nowhere else in the world."

"Have you ever thought about moving back here?"

Leave it to Charlie to ask the one question that Jared himself had managed to avoid over the past several years. Of course, the truth was that he *had* thought about moving back to live on one of the hills around his parents' house. He'd toyed with the idea for a long time–after all, it wasn't like he had much of a life in Huntington, much as he hated to admit it–but something always held him back. He didn't want to be one of those people who moved back to be with his family when there were so many other things that he could be doing, so many other places to explore and see and do. If he moved back here, it would be like admitting that he'd failed at all grand ambitions that he'd had as a young person.

"Jared, are you okay?"

He brought himself back to the present and decided to give Charlie the most honest answer that he could.

"Yeah, I've considered it a bit here and there over the years. But...I don't know. I just don't think I'm ready to admit that I've let myself down. If I move back here, it'll be like I haven't been able to make it, as a writer or as anything else. You know what I mean?"

Charlie paused for a moment, and then he nodded his head. Or maybe shook it. It was honestly kind of hard to tell, because it seemed to be a bit of both.

"I think you might be looking at this the wrong way. It's not always a bad thing to come back home. Sometimes it's the only place where you can really discover who you are and what you want out of life. And besides, you have a good relationship with your family, and if you really want to be a writer, that's something that you can do anywhere, right? It's not like you have to live somewhere fancy to become a success.

"You know," he went on with a bit of a rakish smile and a glint in his eye, "I've heard there's this thing called the internet that lets you get in touch with people all over the world."

Jared plucked a few strands of grass and threw at Charlie, but he deftly dodged them. Somehow, not a single one of them managed to land.

"Oh come *on*," he said.

Charlie laughed and then, much to Jared's surprise, he actually tackled him, bearing him to the ground and pinning his arms above his head.

"Do you want to try throwing some grass at me while your arms are pinned down?" he said, a grin that was mischievous and...something else...on his face.

This had all caught Jared by surprise, but there was one part of his body that was responding accordingly. He tried to get free, but that physical training had made Charlie quite strong in his upper body, which in turn meant that he was able to keep Jared pinned without much trouble.

For a few minutes more Jared tried to look anywhere but at Charlie, knowing that if he dared to look up that he would almost certainly lose himself in Charlie's eyes. That, he knew, was the last thing he wanted. Or was it the thing that he wanted more than anything else?

"Jared," Charlie said gently. "Look at me."

There was a quiet power in Charlie's voice that Jared found impossible to resist. He looked up, and what he saw in Charlie's eyes was a strange mix of tenderness, affection, humor, and desire. Jared felt as if the entire world had fallen out from underneath him.

Then Charlie leaned down and kissed him again, and he found himself in a paradox. On the one hand everything about this moment was crystal clear—the way that he could hear the birds trilling off in the distance, the slight breeze that moved through the brown grass, the rustle of the autumn leaves. On the other hand, it felt like he was totally out of his body, as if he'd been transported to some other place beyond this time and place, somewhere where there was just him and Charlie.

Before he could second-guess himself he reached his hands up and wrapped them around Charlie's neck, drawing him ever closer. Suddenly he couldn't get enough of Charlie–the way he smelled, the way his own hardness was brushing against Jared's, the way his lips felt pressed against his own lips–and he moaned before he could help himself.

Charlie chuckled softly, and Jared pulled away.

"Did you just laugh at me?" he asked. He wasn't even sure whether he was offended or not.

Charlie didn't even have the grace to look sheepish or ashamed. He just shrugged those broad shoulders and flashed that dazzling smile. "I wouldn't say that I laughed *at* you. I would just say that I was a little surprised, but pleasantly, about how much you got into kissing me."

Jared was tempted to throw another bit of grass at him, but considering how that last bit had worked out, he decided not to.

"Is that so?"

"It is. In fact," Charlie said, smirking, "I think that you want me to keep kissing you."

Jared did, in fact, want that very much, but he wasn't going to give Charlie the advantage by admitting that aloud.

"I think you're very full of yourself, Charlie Garrett," he said.

"And I think I'm a very good judge of character."

Jared felt a laughter bubbling up from inside of him, as well as a lightness to his soul that he hadn't felt in a very long time.

Oh, fuck it.

"Okay fine. I want you to kiss me again," he said. "And I want to kiss you back, and lots of other things." Just what those other things might be he left unspecified. There'd be time enough to figure that out later.

"Well, that's good, because I very much want to keep kissing you."

And with that he leaned in and pressed his lips to Jared's again. This time, the electric sparks flying between them were even more intense. Their bodies just seemed to fit together, in some way that went beyond the physical. As Jared let his hands explore Charlie's body, he was amazed at how lean and muscular it was, and he found himself thinking that his body was as close to perfect as he'd ever encountered.

He wrapped his hands around Charlie's butt and gave it a squeeze.

*God, even his ass is perfect,* he thought.

Charlie laughed deep in his throat and, before Jared could do anything, he pulled his lips away and started making his way down his throat, planting gentle kisses. Even that was enough to make Jared moan and start writhing.

*How did he know that was my sensitive spot?* He thought distractedly.

It quickly became clear that Charlie definitely knew his way around a man's body, and he knew when he'd done something to bring his partner pleasure. He started to kiss Jared's neck with more intensity, even daring to suck on the skin for a few minutes. Each time he did so a bolt of electric pleasure shot through Jared's body, causing him to moan and writhe, losing whatever shreds of his dignity he had left.

"Something tells me that you like having your neck kissed," he murmured, continuing to do just that while Jared felt his body thrumming like a finely-tuned violin.

"Charlie," he managed to gasp, "if you keep doing that...I don't think I'm going to be able to hold back."

Charlie looked up at him impishly. "Oh, now we wouldn't want that to happen, would we? I would hate to go back to your parents' house with you having made a mess."

Rather than responding to that, Jared just pulled him back up, resuming their kissing. Kissing was safe. Kissing didn't require other things, the kind of vulnerability that he was very reluctant to share with any other man, no matter how handsome they were. There was a part of him–and an increasingly urgent and prominent part of him–that wanted to throw all of his caution to the wind, to just let Charlie Garrett do whatever he wanted to him.

*Relax,* he thought to himself. *If you want to have sex, wouldn't it be okay to do it with someone like Charlie? He looks like he knows what he's doing, and he's not an asshole. Even if this doesn't go anywhere—and let's be real, it's not going to go anywhere–at least you can say that you actually slept with* the *Charlie Garrett.*

But didn't Charlie deserve more than that?

Charlie immediately sensed that something was wrong. Rather than reacting with impatience or anger, he instead took Jared's face gently in his hands and pressed a firm but loving kiss on his forehead, then looked into his eyes.

"Are you okay, Jared?"

Oh, how to answer that question? How to tell Charlie–sweet, adorable, compassionate and empathetic Charlie–about all of the things that were ricocheting inside of his mind? Why couldn't he just let himself relax and enjoy this little erotic encounter without all of the other familiar emotional baggage coming up to bother him?

"I'm fine," he said, not entirely convincingly, and made to start kissing Charlie again.

Charlie, to his credit, didn't reciprocate, though he didn't reject his overture outright. Instead, he gently deflected.

"Jared," he said, voice serious, "I don't ever want you to think that you have to do anything you don't want to do. We'll only go as far as you want to go and no further. I promise that

I won't try to pressure you, and I certainly won't think less of you in any way."

Jared wanted to roll his eyes at this display of sensitivity on Charlie's part, but the truth was that he was actually quite touched by it. Every new thing he learned about Charlie Garrett made him see him in a better and more positive light, and while that brought some complications with it, he was also glad that he was being made to re-evaluate his feelings.

"I'm really fine," he said, this time more sure that he actually believed what he was saying. "It's just, you're one of the first guys that I've been with or had any kind of sexy times with in a long time, so it takes me a bit to, you know, kind of figure out how it goes. You know what I mean?"

Charlie smiled.

"Of course. It's been a while for me, too." He paused, and then he bit his lip in a very sexy way. "Do you want to keep going? Or would you rather stop?"

In answer, Jared reached up and pulled Charlie down again. He had no idea how this thing was going to end up or how far they would end up going and, for once in his life, Jared didn't care.

They continued to explore one another's bodies for several more moments. Jared quickly found out that Charlie *really* liked it when someone nibbled on his earlobes, while Charlie continued to torture him by making love to his neck, until he was fairly certain that he was going to have several hickies that were going to take some explaining.

"Charlie! Jared!" his mother's voice, once again interrupting at the worst possible time, floated up from down the hill. "Sorry to interrupt, but everyone's leaving!"

"Your mother really does have the worst sense of timing, doesn't she?" Charlie asked ruefully. "I thought she said she wasn't going to bother you this time?"

Jared sighed. "Yeah, well, she's a mom. That's what they do: they walk in on you when you're trying to be intimate."

"You have a very skilled way of talking about sex without actually talking about sex. Or, for that matter, masturbation," Charlie said. "I can see why you're a writer."

Jared scoffed at that as they got to their feet, smoothing out their clothes so that they at least wouldn't look like they'd been having a literal roll in the hay. "I'm not a writer," he said. "I wouldn't even say that I'm an aspiring writer. That's a part of my life that I put away."

That hurt to admit out loud, but it was also freeing, in a way.

"I think that if you love writing and you do it for any length of time, then you're a writer. Like, even if I gave up acting I would still feel like I'm an actor. It's just a part of who I am, and nothing I'm ever going to do is going to change that."

Jared didn't want to get into this particular argument with Charlie. Besides which, maybe Charlie was right. Maybe the only thing standing in the way of his success was himself.

That, in turn, made him wonder if the same might be true of Charlie. He didn't want to admit it–not yet, anyway–but there was something taking shape between the two of them. He couldn't yet see what that shape was, and he most certainly didn't know if there was anything even resembling a future between the two of them but, for a split second as they stood there on the hill that had been one of his sanctuaries as a gay teen, he allowed himself to think of what it might be like to actually *do* all of the things that he thought about doing, rather than just letting them sit in his mind as ideas.

As they made their way back down the hill, Jared's hand kept itching to reach out and take Charlie's, and though he might have imagined it he thought Charlie wanted to do the same.

*Just hold his hand, Jared.*

But he didn't, and he was saved from having to think any more about it by their arrival back at the house, where his mother was already standing there waiting for them.

"Welcome back to the madhouse," Jared said with a wry smile.

# CHAPTER 14

*E*ven though Charlie enjoyed being made to feel that he was genuinely a part of Jared's family, he wished he could have had at least a few more private minutes to share with him. He'd been on the brink of a breakthrough with him–physical, emotional, hell maybe even spiritual–but then Joyce had called out to them and interrupted the whole thing.

Of course he wasn't going to show how annoyed he was to anyone, least of all Joyce, who genuinely seemed to enjoy having him in the house. The last thing he wanted to do was annoy or upset the parents of the man that he was trying to court.

*Is that really what I'm doing?* He thought. *Am I courting Jared? Also, who the hell says "court?"*

He looked at Jared, but the openness that Charlie had seen in his face just a few minutes before had been replaced by his usual rather ironic expression.

*Jared, I'm going to figure you out if it's the last thing I do,* he thought.

He didn't get to think about it much more, however, because as soon as they were back to the house they were enveloped once more in the casual warmth of the Russell family. As Joyce had said, however, everyone was getting to leave but, as Charlie knew quite well, a West Virginia goodbye could take a *very* long time.

Finally, there was just Hannah left and, as she pulled Charlie into a hug, she whispered in his ear.

"I'm really glad you're here, Charlie," she said. "Jared's a special guy, but I think you'll be good for each other. Just be warned. There's probably going to be a time when he's going to try to push you away. That's just what he does. It doesn't mean that he doesn't care about you. It just means that he's afraid of getting hurt and is willing to do whatever he needs to do to make sure that doesn't happen. Don't let it discourage you."

Before he could say anything she went on. "Also, Remember what I told you. If you break his heart, I'll end you." Then she was gone, giving her farewells to Jared and his parents.

Just as she left, Doug was suddenly there, giving him his friendliest dad smile.

*Something's up,* he thought.

"Charlie, would you come into my study for a minute?" he asked.

Suddenly his happiness evaporated. He couldn't imagine what *this* was going to be, but he couldn't very well say no, though, could he?

Doug led him down the hall and, after casting a look back at Jared sending a silent plea for help–a look that Jared somehow managed to ignore–he accompanied Doug inside.

It looked exactly like he'd expected. There were book-shelves on each wall, though only a couple of them held books, with the others occupied by model ships. There was a large polished desk in the middle of the room, with a chair both behind and in front of it. Doug took the one behind and, with a gesture, indicated that Charlie should take the other one.

Charlie couldn't shake the feeling that this was a meeting with the high school principal.

"I suppose you're wondering why I've asked you in here." He held the solemn look on his face for a split second more, and then he burst into a laugh.

"You should see the look on your face," he said. "You almost look like you're facing the electric chair."

Charlie smiled sheepishly.

"In my defense, it's not every day that the father of the man that you're interested in calls you into his study."

As soon as the words were out of his mouth he knew that he'd said more than he intended to.

*Oh no*, he thought. *Oh no no no no no.*

Doug, however, looked completely unphased by this. In fact, he looked like this was exactly what he'd been waiting to hear.

"I was wondering when one of you would actually say it out loud," he said. "I know people your generation seem to think that Baby Boomers live on another planet and another time, but we dated, too, and I remember having that same look on my face when I was interested in Joyce."

At this exact moment Charlie was the one who felt like he was on a different planet.

"Um...I guess that's a good thing, right?" he asked. "Better to be open and honest about this rather than hiding it?"

*What is wrong with me?* He thought. *Why am I blurting all of this out to Jared's dad of all people?*

"I've always thought that, too," Doug said. He folded his hands in front of him on the desk and leaned forward.

"Which is why I'm going to level with you. I know that Jared has feelings for you. And, if you want the absolute truth, I think you're just the kind of guy that he needs. You help to

143

bring him out of his shell. I haven't seen him be this happy in a long, long time. I don't suppose I need to tell you but Jared, well, he struggles with some things, and I've always felt kind of lost when it comes to trying to help him. You, though, you help him just by being there."

Charlie's heart was singing at the thought that he might actually be good for Jared. He wanted so badly to get under that prickly mask that he kept putting up around him, and to know that he had Doug's approval meant a lot.

"I guess what I'm saying is that I'm giving you my blessing to pursue Jared, but," and here Doug held up a warning finger, "I don't want you to hurt him. I'm his dad, after all, and I've gotta look after his best interests. If you hurt my boy, Charlie Garrett, I wouldn't want to be you for all the tea in China."

Charlie knew that Doug might seem nice, but he knew better than to try to cross him.

"You have my word that I won't hurt him. In fact, I intend to make sure that no one ever hurts him again. I think he's been through enough of that."

Doug snorted. "You can say that again. Jared's a good boy, and a smart one, but he sometimes doesn't make the best choices when it comes to men. Don't get too far ahead of yourself, though. You know how prickly he is. It's going to take a lot of doing on your part to get him to open up to you, but I think you'll discover that it really is worth it."

*You don't need to tell* me *that,* Charlie thought. *I know that well enough already.*

"Now, I'm going to tell you something that's probably going to make you feel a bit awkward, but I don't want it to."

Charlie cringed inwardly. He had a feeling that he knew exactly where this was going.

"Now, I know you're going to be embarrassed because you're in your thirties, but I'm going to be frank with you about sex. If it were up to Joyce she'd say that the two of you shouldn't get into anything while you're in her house, but what she doesn't know doesn't hurt her. All I ask is if the two of you are going to be intimate under this roof, that you at least make sure that you're protected and take all the necessary precautions. Do I make myself clear?"

By this point Charlie's face had turned about ten shades of red. It was one thing for Jared's dad to tell him that he gave him his permission to pursue his son; it was quite another for him to speak so cavalierly of gay sex. What was even going on right now?

Doug, however, was clearly waiting for Charlie to say something, and so he just blurted out the first thing that came into his head.

"Of course, sir," he said. "I take that sort of thing very seriously, and I know that Jared does, too." He of course did not know anything of the sort, but it felt like the best thing to say.

Doug nodded.

"Good. I was hoping that this conversation would be easy. You seem like a nice and easy going guy. Like I said. I think you'll be good for Jared. What do you say we get back out there and rejoin the rest of the family? I'm sure they're starting to wonder where we are."

Charlie's head was spinning by how quickly this whole situation had unfolded. That conversation had been very unusual, but he had to admit that there was also something a little touching about the fact that Doug was so open-minded about, well, about his son having sex in his own house.

When they got back to the living room Jared gave them both an inquisitive look, but since he didn't ask, Charlie didn't tell.

By now it was night, and Doug and Joyce began to get ready for bed. Charlie was relieved; it could get very exhausting having to be on for everyone all the time. Soon enough they were all in their separate rooms, and he finally had a chance to think.

As he laid down Jared's old bed, he found himself wondering what it would have been like to know him when he was that age. It was the same kind of thing that he thought about every time he got interested in someone new. He always felt a bit sad at realizing there would always be a part of that person's life that he couldn't fully share, but there was also something exciting about learning about their past.

Once he started thinking about Jared's past, then he started thinking about the present, and that was even more complicated. No matter what Doug might say, he had his doubts that Jared would ever really open up to him. Their conversation after the meeting in the study had been stilted and impersonal, and Jared had barely had two words for him before he went to bed.

*It's time to stop thinking about this and try to get some sleep,* he thought. *You're not going to solve all of your problems right now. Maybe tomorrow will be a bit easier.*

Charlie had just closed his eyes and was finally feeling sleep beginning to steal over him when he heard the door to the room crack open, the light from the hallway casting a slender glow. He didn't move at first, thinking that maybe it was Joyce coming by to check on him. However, when he opened his eyes a little, he could tell that the person standing there was not Joyce, but Jared, and his heart started beating so hard he thought it would come out of his chest.

"Charlie," Jared whispered, voice hardly audible. "Are you still awake?"

"Yes," he said, even though his throat felt like it was trying to close up. "I'm still awake."

"Can...can I come in?"

"Of course," he said right away. "It's your bedroom isn't it?"

There was a chuckle from Jared at this, and then he was slipping into the room, padding through a beam of moonlight that came in through the window.

A heavy feeling permeated the air, making Charlie feel a complicated mix of emotions. He was aroused, obviously, but it was more than that. Maybe it was his conversation with Doug earlier, or maybe it was the moonlight, or maybe it was those things and a whole host of others, but something made him feel like whatever was about to happen was going to irrevocably change things between them.

Jared sat down gently on the edge of the bed, almost as if he was asking permission to be there.

"So," he said, running his hand in intricate patterns over the bedspread. "Do I even want to know what you and my dad were talking about in his study?"

Charlie cleared his throat nervously. He should have known that Jared was going to ask him about this sooner or later, but now that the moment was here he once again found that he didn't quite know what to say. *Well, he told me that we were good for one another and that if we had sex that we should make sure that we were safe,* didn't seem like quite the right thing to say.

However, that was pretty much exactly what came out of his mouth.

For a few minutes Jared didn't say anything, and Charlie was worried that he'd overstepped some hidden boundary. Finally, though, Jared just laughed softly.

"You would never guess that it was my dad who would be the one to talk to you about gay sex, would you?"

"I have to admit that that wasn't exactly what I'd been expecting," Charlie said. "It's not every day that the father of the guy you're interested in starts telling you that he thinks you should make sure to be practicing safer sex. Particularly not when you're in your thirties. I almost felt like a teenager talking to his boyfriend's dad."

Once again, Charlie's mouth got too far ahead of his brain. He half expected Jared to go bolting from the room the minute that he said he was interested in him but, to his surprise, he reached out and rested his hand on Charlie's leg. A bolt of electric desire jolted through him at just that slight touch.

"So you're interested in me?" Jared said. The uncertainty and longing in his voice was enough to break Charlie's heart.

He fought down the temptation to laugh–he knew that that would be the worst thing he could do–and instead reached out a hand and placed it over Jared's. "I'm *very* interested in you," he said.

Even though it was dark somehow they found their way toward one another, and once again their lips touched. Just like when they were up on the hill, Charlie lost himself in everything about Jared, his senses overwhelmed with his simple proximity.

Neither of them had to say anything else. Instead, they let their bodies do their talking for them. Their clothes were soon on an untidy pile on the floor, and their lips were back together, their hands roaming freely over one another's bodies.

Even though they both knew they had to be quiet, every so often one of them would utter a moan, and then the other would shush them.

Finally, though, Charlie had Jared right where he wanted him, sprawled out on the bed below him.

Charlie was simply in awe of Jared's body, of the way that he seemed to open up like a flower as he ran his fingers down his chest and swirled his fingers around his nipples. Jared wasn't ripped like so many of the LA guys that Charlie had been with, but he had a lean build that made him feel even more protective of him.

It was when Jared looked up at him, though, that he thought his heart might burst.

"You're so beautiful," he whispered. He knew the words were inadequate, that they didn't even come close to describing what he felt for the man below him, the way that he'd felt from the moment they met, actually. But how did you say something like that to someone? How did you really get them to understand how much they meant to you?

Pushing those thoughts aside he leaned down and pressed his lips to Jared's, once again relishing the taste of him, the sweetness of his breath. He reached up and ran his hands through Jared's thick hair, then let his hand cup his cheek as the two of them continued to kiss, their passion becoming more intense and all-consuming with every moment. There was nothing else in the world right now—there was no film festival, no family worries, no anxieties of any kind. There were just the two of them.

It was Jared who drew back for a moment, his breath coming in short gasps.

"Um...," he said rather nervously, "do you...do you want to take this further?"

*God yes.*

Aloud he said, "I mean, I do, but only if you do. I don't want you to do anything that you're not comfortable with."

There was no mistaking Jared's chuckle, somehow both affectionate and exasperated.

"I don't think you need to worry about me wanting to take things further." He thrust his hips up ever so slightly. Charlie swallowed, his own hardness becoming so intense he thought he might go crazy with it. He had to resist the urge to just have his way with him right there.

Jared reached up and cupped his face. "Are *you* okay? If you don't want to go any further,. I'm happy just being with you."

Charlie was somewhat surprised to find out that he believed him.

"I really do," he said, finally finding his voice. "Want to take things to the next level, that is."

Once again that laugh. "There's condoms and lube in the nightstand right there."

"Do you have sex in your old bedroom a lot?" he asked.

There was a moment of quiet. "Well, my exes and I certainly weren't celibate when we were visiting my folks."

There was one more nagging question, but Jared answered it before he could ask it.

"I'm a bottom, in case you didn't know that already."

Charlie had had a feeling, but he didn't want to say that aloud.

"I know you were probably thinking that already, but I just thought I'd make it easy for you. Now, are you going to get the condom and the lube, or do I have to do it for you?"

That settled it. Charlie reached over and got them out of the night stand, and even though this was very much what he wanted, he could still feel his hands shaking.

*Easy, Charlie. It's not like this is your first time.*

That might be true, but he didn't want to hurt Jared, either physically or emotionally. He knew that he was probably making too much out of this, but he also knew that Jared tended to be a lot more vulnerable than he was willing to let on.

He got the condom and lube out and, while he got the package open and began to put it on Jared prepared himself. Charlie took the bottle of lube and did his part, and then it was time.

"Are you ready?" he asked Jared, his voice thick with desire.

"Oh my God, yes," Jared said. "I'm not a wilted little flower."

"Okay then," Charlie said with a little growl.

Their bodies melded together perfectly. In fact, Charlie didn't think that he'd had this kind of immediate physical connection with anyone that he'd ever been with. It was as if their bodies were two halves of the same whole, that each of them had just been waiting for the chance to finally be with the other. As soon as they came together they fell into a steady rhythm, each of them knowing just how to bring the other the most pleasure.

Usually whenever Charlie had sex with someone his mind always stayed active. No matter how hard he tried, he just couldn't shut off his intrusive thoughts. This time, though, all of that disappeared, as he lost himself to the physical experience of being with Jared. He kissed him up and down his throat, he whispered sweet and dirty nothings into his ear, he ran his hands through his hair. He wanted to be as close to Jared as he could possibly get, he wanted Jared to know in this moment that he was protected and safe and that Charlie would do everything he could to bring him as much pleasure as he could.

They tried to stay as quiet as possible, but neither of them could stay entirely silent. Truth be told, Charlie enjoyed the sounds of pleasure that Jared was making, and he loved the fact that he was the one making him make them.

When they both found release it was like Charlie had been taken to a different planet. The pleasure filled his entire head and his body and his soul, and he clamped his lips to Jared's so that their moans blended together. Wave after wave of pleasure crashed through him.

As the tide of his orgasm began to recede, he started to pull out but Jared reached behind him and pulled him deeper again.

"Please," he whispered, "I just want to feel you for a few more minutes."

Charlie was happy to oblige, but eventually nature took its course. Even then, though, he didn't move away from Jared. They lay there, each of them catching their breath.

When Charlie thought about the sated feeling that people always described as afterglow, this was what he'd thought of. He'd never actually experienced it before–most of the guys he'd been with couldn't wait to get done and leave. He wasn't sure what he'd done to deserve this piece of good luck, but he wasn't about to mess it up by saying or doing anything that would disturb it.

Suddenly a small bedside light came on, and Jared turned to look at him.

"You always look like you're thinking about something deep and profound," Jared said. "And that always makes me wonder about just what's going to come out of your mouth."

Charlie couldn't help but smile at that. "I think that's funny coming from you of all people, considering how often you say things that aren't always tactful. I've never met someone who is so good at being unintentionally mean."

Rather than being offended, Jared smiled and snuggled closer to him, pulling the blankets up as he did so.

"You might not believe me, but I usually don't mean even half the things I say. I usually just say something snarky or mean as a defense mechanism." He huffed. "I can't believe I've just told you that deep dark secret about myself. Now that means I have to kill you."

"Do you really think that you're that successful when it comes to convincing the world that you're some sarcastic ice queen? You're not Bette Davis you know."

"I've always thought of myself as more of a Joan Craw-ford, actually," Jared said.

"Well, that's it,"Charlie said mock-seriously. "I'm afraid I can't possibly date a man who's a Joan Crawford fan."

It was a mistake to mention the word "date." That much

was clear at once. Though Jared didn't pull away, there was a slight but very noticeable change to his posture, a stiffening that suggested he was very uncomfortable with the direction that this conversation was starting to take.

*Way to go, Charlie. Can't you have one conversation with this guy without it turning into something weird?*

It only took a couple of seconds for the awkwardness to pass.

"Let's just enjoy the moment," Jared said at last. "Let the future take care of itself."

Charlie held his breath for a moment, but since there was nothing more forthcoming, he decided to just let it go at that. He planted a gentle kiss on top of Jared's head and felt a flush of warmth when Jared once again snuggled up to him, as if he was seeking comfort. He put his arm around him and pulled him close.

*This is good enough,* he thought. *Like he said, deal with the future when it gets here.*

With that comforting thought in his mind, he finally let himself relax and slip into sleep.

# CHAPTER 15

*a*s Charlie's breathing grew slower and slower with sleep, Jared tried to get his body to do the same. No matter how hard he tried, though, it refused to cooperate. He simply couldn't unwind enough–and his thoughts wouldn't slow down enough–for him to get to sleep.

*Figures,* he thought. *I finally get some of the best sex that I've had in...well, probably ever...and then I can't sleep.*

The reason wasn't really that complicated. The sex with Charlie might have been mind-blowing, but his mentioning of dating had forced Jared to really think about what it was that they were doing. Were they, in fact, dating? What would that even look like, considering their different circumstances? This wasn't a fairy tale or a rom-com, after all. There were very real consequences and material conditions that had to be taken into account. They couldn't just coast along on vibes and good wishes and hope that everything would work out okay in the end. That just wasn't how real life worked.

Was it?

He fought down the urge to toss and turn like he usually would. He really did enjoy the closeness to Charlie. There was a way that their bodies meshed together that he didn't think he'd ever experienced with another person. At the same time as it made him feel complete and whole, however, it also frightened him. When you got close to someone like that, it was only a matter of time before they found a way to hurt you.

Jared's breaths were starting to come faster and faster, and his thoughts were starting to race so much he knew he was going to have a full-on anxiety attack if he didn't calm down.

*Take deep breaths, Jared. Deep breaths.*

He finally managed to get himself back under control, and he could think clearly again.

It was better to just enjoy what they had and let it go at that. After this weekend they would each go their separate ways, back to their regular lives. They could remember this as a particularly nice interlude in both of their lives, a rare opportunity to really connect with someone out of their social circles.

*See? That wasn't so hard, was it?*

It hurt a little to admit that all of this was just going to be temporary, but Jared had always tried to live life as it was rather than what he wanted it to be, and he took a perverse sort of comfort from hurting his own feelings like this.

And with that, he finally let himself drift off to sleep.

JARED WOKE up just before dawn. Looking over at Charlie he could see that he was still fast asleep, his chest rising and falling with his even breathing. He felt his heart swelling with...well, he didn't want to say it was love because they'd only known each other for a few days...but even so, it was something more than just affection.

He reached out and picked up his phone to see what time it was. He knew that his parents were still early-risers and, while his dad had basically given Charlie permission to seduce him in his old bedroom–and that was *still* weird–he thought there might be a difference between his parents approving of such a thing in the abstract and actually seeing their son in bed with another man.

Moving quickly and quietly, he managed to get out of bed and slip into his clothes. He was tempted to plant a parting kiss on Charlie's forehead but decided against it. Instead he tiptoed out of the bedroom and made his way back to the guest room and slipped inside. He had no way of knowing whether his mother had decided to look in on him during the night (as she had a tendency of doing whenever he was home), but he really hoped she hadn't. He didn't want to have to feel embarrassed at the breakfast table.

Jared got into bed, but it was quickly clear that he wasn't going to get any more sleep, so he just lay there staring at the ceiling, trying not to think of anything in particular.

Not long after, he heard the rustle and clatter as the dogs woke up first, followed by his parents. He closed his eyes and just let himself enjoy the homely sound of them moving through the house, his mother uttering a few choice words for the dogs (the morning was really the only time she was ever really grumpy). It all took him back to his childhood, and there was a comfort and a pleasure in that.

Soon enough, he heard his mother's footsteps outside the guest bedroom, and then she was knocking gently.

"Jared, sweetie, are you awake?" she asked.

He debated pretending to still be asleep, but then he figured that, since he wasn't going to get any more sleep anyway, he might as well just admit to being awake and get the day started.

"Yeah, I'm awake," he said. "I'll be right down."

"Okay," she said. "I'll start making breakfast. "How do waffles sound?"

"They sound great, mom!" he said.

There was another pause on the other side of the door.

"Would you mind telling Charlie that breakfast will be served in a little while? I don't mind making another batch, but I thought he might like to have breakfast with the rest of us."

Jared stifled a sigh. His mother was the master of making nagging sound like she was only thinking about you.

*Be nice, Jared,* he reminded himself. *She's been nothing but kind and welcoming to you and Charlie since you got here. The least you can do is not be snarky.*

Summoning up all of his politeness, he said, "Of course, mom. I'll see if he's up."

"Thank you!" she chirped, and then she was gone.

In his experience sex–particularly good sex–always changed things, and not always for the better. The longer he put off waking up Charlie, the longer he could put off avoiding what that change would look like.

*Okay, that's enough. Get off your ass and go wake up Charlie.*

The few feet between the guest bedroom and his old room felt like a mile and, once there, he just stood, uncertain what to do. Even when he pushed the door open and stepped inside he couldn't bring himself to wake Charlie up, choosing instead to look at his face, still peaceful in sleep.

"Are you going to just stand there and look at me all morning or are you going to invite me to breakfast?"

Jared almost jumped out of his skin.

"I wasn't staring at you."

Charlie leaned up in bed and gave him a look. "I think we both know that's not true. Don't worry, though. I thought it was kind of cute. But also kind of creepy."

Once again Charlie gave him that feeling that his whole world was spinning out of control, and if there was one thing that Jared did *not* like, it was chaos and a lack of control.

*Pull yourself together, damn it.*

"Well, anyway, mom wanted me to tell you that breakfast was going to be ready in a little while. I hope you like waffles."

Charlie's eyes lit up at that. "I actually love waffles, but I don't get to eat them very often." He looked rather sheepish at that. "Carbs."

Jared rolled his eyes. "Okay, Mr. Hollywood. Always obsessing about carbs or something rather than just trying to enjoy life's pleasures. I'll never understand it." He stood there for another minute, but when Charlie didn't move he started tapping his foot. "I'm not leaving until I see that you're out of bed."

Charlie actually blushed a little.

"Uh, I'm not actually dressed right now."

Jared smirked at him. "I don't think we need to worry about seeing each other naked, do you? Besides, you're...," he gestured at Charlie, "you're Charlie Garrett, the guy who works out all the time and has an actual physical trainer."

Charlie rolled his eyes. "You're really not going to move or close your eyes, are you?"

"Not when the view is this good, I'm not," Jared said.

"Fine."

Jared wasn't lying. Charlie was as beautiful naked as he was with his clothes on, of that there was absolutely no doubt. It wasn't just that he was muscular and toned; he was perfectly proportioned. It might have been cliche, but Jared was reminded of the statues that the ancient Greeks had sculpted of young male beauty. In fact, it occurred to him that Charlie Garrett would have made a very good Alexander the Great.

Now that he had an audience, Charlie moved very deliberately. Whatever his initial hesitation, he clearly liked showing off for Jared, and Jared enjoyed the show just as much.

Finally, though, he managed to get dressed, though Jared was more than a little disappointed to see his beautiful body disappear beneath his clothes. Charlie gave him a smirk in return.

"Don't look so sad," he said. "I'm sure you'll get to see it again, soon."

Jared once again felt that little prickle of unease at the thought of continuing whatever this was with Charlie, at least beyond this weekend, but he pushed it away.

"Boys!" Joyce's voice came from downstairs. "Are you about ready? Breakfast is on the table!"

"I guess I should have warned you that my mother can be a bit of a nag sometimes."

"Don't be so hard on her. She's just trying to be a good host. Like mother, like son."

Jared gave him a scathing look, but Charlie just laughed.

A few minutes later the four of them—Charlie, Jared, and Jared's parents—were seated around the table tucking in to a very delicious helping of waffles. His mother, of course, had made sure to put bowls of strawberries and bananas on the table, too, as well as a very large bottle of syrup that she proudly told them she had bought on their most recent trip to New England.

Jared had to admit that it was very good syrup. In fact the entire meal was delicious, and it brought back some very warm and pleasant memories of his childhood. He kept looking at Charlie, to see what he was making of all of this, but he was so invested in his waffles that he didn't even look up.

"So," Joyce said at last, as they were all planning on doing today?"

To be quite honest Jared hadn't really thought that far ahead, but now he realized that he should show Charlie something other than just his parents' property.

"Uh, I guess I could show Charlie Annamoriah? I mean, I'm not sure he'd want to see my old stomping grounds, but at least it would get us out of the house a bit."

To his surprise, Charlie greeted this idea with enthusiasm.

"I think that's a great idea," he said. "I'd love to see where you spent part of your childhood."

"Don't get too excited," Jared said. "There really isn't that much there that's worth writing home about."

"It wouldn't hurt you to show some pride in where you come from, son," Doug said.

"I'll do my best, dad," Jared said.

The rest of breakfast passed in mostly companionable small talk, as Jared and his parents reminisced about their shared past and the many happy memories they had in this house. This was a regular part of his visits home, since it was often easier to find shared understanding and joy in the past rather than the thorny present. Any time they got close to one of the subjects that Jared preferred not to talk about—particularly anything to do with his love life—he neatly parried and moved them to more comfortable territory.

Finally breakfast was done and it was time to start getting ready to leave for Annamoriah, since that was clearly what they were going to spend the day doing. Considering the fact that it took about ten minutes to get from one side of town to the other, he wasn't sure just what he was going to show Charlie.

*Don't be so negative,* he thought, his echoes echoing his father's words. *If you want Charlie to understand who you are, the least you can do is show him where you grew up and the places that shaped you. And who knows? You might even learn something about yourself.*

That was a bit of a strange thought, but he decided to go about this with the spirit of openness that it deserved.

Both he and Charlie took showers, and the whole time Charlie was in there Jared kept wondering what it would be like to be in there with him, their bodies touching each other as the hot water streamed over them. Sex was great, but so was the kind of intimacy that could only come from taking a shower with another man...

"Jared," his mother said, breaking into his thoughts. He turned to where she stood in the doorway to the guest bedroom. She had that serious look on her face that said she had something very important to tell him but didn't quite know how to start. "Do you have a minute?"

He gestured vaguely toward where Charlie was still showering down the hall. "Sure, mom. What's up?"

She came in and sat down on the bed next to him. He suddenly had a flashback of when they'd had "the talk."

"Don't get that look," she said. "I'm not here to lecture you."

"Well, that's a relief," he said.

"I just wanted to say that I love the way that you've been the past day or so," she said. "I'll admit that I was a bit surprised when you brought Charlie here without telling me, but I'm glad that you did. You seem so carefree when he's around, almost as if that weight you're always carrying is finally starting to lift a little bit." She leaned in then and gave him a quick peck on the cheek. "I know you don't need a mother's advice, but if you ask me you might want to give this one a chance."

Before he could say anything to that–before he could even thank her for offering her advice–she was up and gone.

A minute later Charlie came into the room, wearing a very tight-fitting pair of jeans and a plain white T-shirt. He looked so much like a teen idol that Jared almost wanted to scream.

"You look...really nice," he managed to choke out.

"If you could see your face right now," Charlie said. Before Jared could respond to that Charlie had thrown himself onto the bed beside him and took him into a rough embrace.

"What are you doing?" Jared said, the scent of Charlie's

cologne and that smell that was just *him* making him feel very aroused.

"Just giving my favorite guy a hug. You looked like you could use it."

*I could always use a hug from you,* he thought but didn't say.

"So, when do we head off to your hometown? I meant what I said. I'm genuinely looking forward to getting to know the place that you grew up and spent your formative years. One of these days I'll return the favor, I promise."

There was something enticing about that promise of the future, of a time when the two of them would be able to get to know more about one another. He smiled at the thought.

"We're leaving right now."

IT TOOK ABOUT twenty minutes to get from Jareds' parents' place to Annamoriah, and the road was, like so many others in West Virginia, full of twists and turns. Charlie, of course, was used to this type of thing, as he reassured Jared when he started to apologize for the road.

"Believe me, they're even worse down south below Morgantown," he said. "Not only do they curve and switch every which way. There are also pot holes that could easily swallow a car."

They both had a good laugh at that.

The real joy of the drive, though, was just how beautiful it was. The road curved along the ridge, which meant that you could look out on the hills and valleys on either side. Small farms were scattered along the hilltops, and the trees were also in their most beautiful state. It had been just the right amount of wet and dry this year, which meant that the splendor was even more vibrant than usual.

Even though he would never have admitted it aloud, Jared actually felt like he was home.

Finally they came within the last few miles of Annamoriah.

"Are you ready to see the sprawling metropolis that I spent my formative years in?" he asked.

"I told you before that I was looking forward to getting to see the place that you grew up," Charlie said, "and I meant it. I do wonder, though, why you're so intent on being so down on it. Was it really that bad?"

Jared was honestly not sure how to answer that. He hadn't had the worst time of it in high school. A select few people had known he was gay, and for the most part people didn't make a big deal out of it, but there was still a pervasive feeling of homophobia. It was there in the way that people would look at him while he walked down the hallway, and the way that they would sometimes lean over to whisper to one another.

He tried to explain some of this to Charlie, but he finally got frustrated with his inability to convey exactly what he meant and went silent.

"I guess a lot of it might have been in my head," he admitted.

Charlie shook his head. "I don't think you were necessarily imagining all of it," he said. "Things were different when we were growing up, and it's true that West Virginia, particularly small-town West Virginia, can be very reluctant to change its ways and come into the 21st century. But still, don't you have any fond memories of high school and your hometown that you like to think about sometimes?"

Jared rather wondered why Charlie was being so insistent about this, but he decided to humor him and try to think about some of the things about his home that he actually liked. It ended up being surprisingly easy.

"Well," he said, drawing the word out, "I like the way that

my school was small enough that you knew everyone from the time that you were in kindergarten until you graduated from high school. By the time it was over you felt like you really understood everyone else, that you'd been through it and survived. I like the way that we'd all get together to go to the two restaurants in town, gathering every Friday night after the football game. I love the ice cream shop that used to make sundaes that were even better than Dairy Queen's."

His face fell. "Unfortunately most of those places aren't in business anymore." He barked a bitter laugh. "I'm afraid that the 21st century hasn't been as kind to Annamoriah as it has been to some other places in West Virginia." He sighed. "I wish that it was different, but that's just the way it is sometimes."

For the first time, Jared really took a minute to think about what it meant that Annamoriah wasn't the same town that it had been when he was growing up. He still felt a lot of fondness for it, but it was a shadow of its former self, and this impression only got more intense as they came within the limits of the town itself. There were far more empty storefronts than there had been when he was in school. The saddest were those that still had a few objects left in their front windows, a reminder of what they used to be.

"It's not much to look at, is it?" Jared asked as they drove down Main Street.

*At least the library is still open,* he thought glumly.

"I wouldn't say that," Charlie said, as always trying to look on the bright side. "There's something cute about it. Looking around at it, you can see what it used to be, and you can also see what it might be if someone cared enough to pour some money and energy into it."

Jared tried to hide his skepticism about that particular idea. It wasn't that he didn't think Annamoriah and its residents didn't deserve another chance to flourish; it was just that he didn't think there was likely to be any sort of movement on that front, not anytime soon, anyway. Still, he wasn't going to pour water on Charlie's idea.

"You know," Charlie went on, "I can actually see a way in which this town could reinvent itself as a little artist colony, like a lot of the small towns in the southern part of the state have been doing. There could be little galleries and shops. Local artisans could offer classes and stuff. Surely there are enough people here with the artsy spirit to make it work, right?"

"I honestly don't know," he said. "I haven't been that plugged into things here for a very long time."

"You should think about asking your parents about it. They might even want to get in on the act."

Jared didn't think that much was likely. Neither of his parents were particularly artistic in temperament, but maybe it was worth a try.

For a while he just sort of drove around the town aimlessly, showing Charlie all of the places that meant something to him: the public library (obviously), but also his old high school (which had been converted into a community center once the whole county consolidated), and the small town market which doubled as a pizza shop (and which, like the library, was still miraculously open). Charlie kept asking questions, as if he really did want to know about both the place and Jared's relationship to it.

*This guy is really too good to be true,* he thought.

There was, finally, just one last place that he wanted to take Charlie to, the one place that he'd always been able to find peace and welcome, even when the rest of his life felt like shit.

He was going to take him to Streeter Park.

There was something more than a little miraculous about this little bit of green space that sat on the edge of town. It had been in Annamoriah since its founding in the 1800s and, despite all of the ups and downs it had faced over the years, it had somehow managed to stay largely the same. It was as it always had been: a little island of green beauty in the midst of a town that had seen better days.

Even though it was fall, there hadn't yet been a hard frost, so the roses were still blooming in their beds. Once upon a time Jared had actually been pretty good friends with the gardener, but he'd passed away while he was in undergrad. Jared didn't know who was in charge of them now, but whoever they were, they were doing a very good job at making sure that they were kept pruned and fertilized. Their heady scent filled the air, while the nearby creek chattered away in its bank.

"Other than the hill near my parents' place, this was the one place where I could always go and feel at peace with the world." He ducked his head shyly, still a bit uncomfortable at sharing this little piece of himself with Charlie, still afraid that he might turn his nose up at it.

"Well, what are we waiting for?" Charlie asked. "Let's get out and explore it a bit!"

Jared was a bit nervous to get out of the car–there was no point in keeping Charlie out of the spotlight if they managed to get spotted by someone, after all–but Charlie waved that concern away, gesturing toward the empty park.

"I don't see anyone out there, do you?"

Jared had to admit that he did not but, as he reminded Charlie, this was also a small town and all it would take was one person and then they would have everyone here gawking at them.

"You worry too much," Charlie said and then leaned over and kissed him. While Jared was still wrapping his head around that–and trying not to be paranoid about being seen by someone–Charlie got out of the car and bounded off across the park. Once again, Jared was reminded very much of a golden retriever, and he felt his heart do a little backflip.

He got slowly out of the car, still always keeping an eye out in case anyone was watching. As Charlie had rightly pointed out, however, there wasn't a single person nearby, nor did it look like there was going to be anytime soon.

They leisurely strolled around the park, their hands coming very close to touching but never quite making it. The truth was that he was still nervous about showing such explicit attention to another guy in the middle of his old hometown.

*Old habits die hard, I guess,* he thought. *Particularly the bad ones.*

Suddenly Charlie grabbed hold of his hand and led him over to one of the benches that were scattered throughout the park. Jared wasn't sure whether to feel nervous or excited or some combination of the two.

As soon as they were seated Charlie took his hand in his and planted a gentle kiss on it.

"Jared, I want you to know how much I've enjoyed the last couple of days with you. I know that we got off on a bit of the wrong foot, but I like to think that I've shown you that I'm not the person that you think I am, or at least not entirely that."

Jared's heart was beating faster and faster. For some strange reason he felt like this was the moment in a rom-com where the hero would ask the heroine to marry him.

*He's not going to ask me to marry him,* is he?

But no, it was something far simpler that Charlie was going to ask, even if it was no less momentous for Jared.

"I know that there's a lot standing in the way of a relationship, but, well, I guess I was wondering if you might like to try dating me?" Charlie laughed self-deprecatingly, showing off those dimples that were so irresistible. "I know it's going to be long-distance, but I think we can find some ways to work it out. It's just...you make me feel like an actual person, and I flatter myself into thinking that you have some feelings of some sort for me, too. Or am I wrong?"

This was the moment that Jared would usually tell someone that was interested in him that, while he was very flattered by the attention, he just wasn't in the market for a relationship. Those exact words almost slipped out of his mouth, but instead he surprised himself.

"I feel the same way about you," he said. There was a part of his mind that was screaming at him to cut and run while he still could, that this was a one-way ticket to heartbreak, but he kept forging on, some brave, romantic part of himself that he'd almost forgotten existed managing to take over. "I'll admit that when I first picked you up I thought you were the arrogant golden boy that everyone that I'd always thought you were, but now I see there's something special about you."

He paused to gather his thoughts and his courage. "So, yeah, I think I would like to date you. I mean, I have no idea how this is all going to work but, somehow, I think the two of us can figure it out. I'm starting to think there's nothing we can't do together."

Before he could second guess himself he leaned in and gave Charlie a very passionate kiss. When he pulled away, he could feel his own face flushing, and Charlie's was, too.

"That was unbearably sappy of me, wasn't it?" he said.

Charlie laughed. "Probably, but I liked it. And besides, you know you don't have to add a sarcastic remark to every heartfelt thing you say, right?"

"Oh, just shut up and kiss me again," Jared said.

"With pleasure," Charlie said.

# CHAPTER 16

*a*s he kissed Jared, Charlie's heart felt like it was doing somersaults. He hadn't felt this happy about something in a long time, and the fact that Jared seemed willing to at least entertain the possibility that they might try to build something together was more than he'd dared to hope for.

*You should learn to have more faith,* he reminded himself.

"I don't have words to tell me how happy you've just made me," he blurted out as he pulled away. "I know that it's not always easy for you to open yourself to other people, and it means the world that you've done that with me. I hope I can reward your trust."

He noted the way that Jared forced himself not to roll his eyes, and he smiled. Some things, it seemed, never changed when it came to Jared.

"You know," he said. "It would probably help if you didn't roll your eyes every time someone tries to be a little vulnerable with you. It's okay to just feel, you know."

Jared gave a little laugh. "And that, my dear, is where you're wrong," he said. "The best defense against the cold world that we live in is to simply pretend that you don't care. That way, no one can ever really have the power to hurt you."

Even though it was said in jest, Charlie still thought there was a great deal of honesty there. It made him sad, to think that Jared had been hurt so often that he thought that he had to erect all of these barriers to keep people out. If it was the last thing he did, he was going to convince Jared that he was worthy of being loved and cared about, that there was nothing wrong with him.

As they sat there in the peace and tranquility of the park, however, it also occurred to him that there were going to be some high logistical hurdles when it came to their relationship. They still lived on opposite sides of the country, for one thing, and he doubted that Jared was going to make it easy on him in that regard.

Strangely, though, that was exactly what drew Charlie to him in the first place. He wanted to just lean in and take care of Jared in all of the ways that no one–except possibly his parents–had ever really done.

On an impulse, he reached over and took Jared's hand in his. For a split second he thought that he would pull away, but instead his grip tightened.

"I've really enjoyed these past couple of days," he said. "You're nothing like the Charlie that I thought I knew via the internet. You're sweet and kind, and not fake at all." He laughed softly. "I didn't think that people in Hollywood were capable of being so authentic."

"Just because we pretend to be someone else for a living doesn't mean that we aren't also people with souls," Charlie said. He was learning to be patient when it came to Jared's assumptions about what people in the entertainment industry were like. In fact Jared's assumptions weren't that far off about some of the people that he'd met while he was out there. Being plastic and fake and concerned about appearance was in fact the norm for far too many people, but it had never felt right for him.

*I just have to make Jared aware of that.*

He suddenly had an idea. "Would you mind walking around town a bit?" he said. He'd meant what he said to Jared when he'd proposed that they think about investing in Annamoriah. There was a lot of potential here; he could just feel it. He wanted to get a better idea of what the town actually looked like to a pedestrian, though.

"I would love that, actually," Jared said.

Soon enough they were walking down Main Street, and Charlie was critically examining all of the buildings. A lot of these had been here for quite a long while—since 1837, at least according to the sign that proclaimed the downtown was officially part of the National Registry of Historic Places—and though a few were probably dilapidated beyond repair, there were some that he could see being renovated spaces for artists and other creatives. One building in particular stood out to him.

"What's this place called?" he said as they came to a stop in front of it. It was one of those buildings that had been very popular during the 19th and early 20th centuries, all pillars and elegant brickwork. Even though it had clearly seen better days it was still a beautiful building, particularly with its stained glass windows.

Jared laughed a little. "It's actually called the Hope Building, though it's been a while since this town had any of that."

"You know," Charlie said, tapping his chin thoughtfully, "that would actually make a great gallery space. Everyone is really getting into the local art stuff. We'll have to ask around and see if there is anyone who might be interested in setting up shop there. We could use it as sort of the anchor to help reinvigorate all of downtown."

He flicked his gaze at Jared to see how he was reacting to

all of this, suddenly conscious that he might be stepping on his toes, which was the very last thing that he wanted to do. Jared, however, actually looked like he was getting invested in this idea, too.

"You know, I hate to admit it, but you might just be onto something. I honestly have no idea whether any of this will work, but I guess it's worth a shot?"

"You never know until you try," Charlie said and, before Jared could say anything, he slipped his hand back into his. "Don't worry," he rushed to reassure him, "I won't hold it forever. I just wanted to touch you again."

To his immense satisfaction, he saw a grin spread across Jared's face.

They spent a bit more time walking around the town, and with every bit of it that they saw Charlie felt like he understood Jared a little better. However much he might have become a "big city boy" (if one could consider Huntington with its population of less than 50,000 a big city), there was still a part of him that seemed to thrive in a small town setting like this one.

That, however, raised a whole new series of questions. If they decided to start a future together, where would they live? Charlie might get irritated with the shallowness of California, but the truth was that he'd also grown used to many of the things there. Did he really think that he'd be able to get used to the rhythms of small town life again?

*There's time enough to answer those questions in the future,* he thought. *Let's just enjoy the present. And who knows? You might find out that you like the simple life of a small town more than you thought.*

There was definitely food for thought there.

Even though Annamoriah was an incredibly small town, Charlie still felt like he could have spent all day there and never batted an eye. However, he was also conscious of the fact that every moment they spent there risked someone seeing them. He'd almost managed to forget that they were trying to be inconspicuous, and even a small town like this one was likely to have someone with an iPhone who would only be too happy to announce that they'd seen *the* Charlie Garrett.

Jared seemed to be thinking along the same lines, because he suddenly sighed.

"I hate to be a party pooper, but I think it's probably about time that we start getting back to my parents' place. I'm really glad that you came here with me, though. You really gave me a chance to appreciate my hometown in a way that I hadn't before."

Charlie smiled in return. "It was my pleasure. It's always hard to see the beauty of where we come from, at least until someone points it out to us."

"You probably have a point there, even though I hate to admit it."

Charlie took his hand out of Jared's and draped a companionable arm over his shoulder.

"I think you'll find that I'm right much more than I'm wrong."

For a split second it seemed like Jared might take his arm off of his shoulder, but then he actually snuggled closer together as they made their way back to his car.

"We'll see about that."

*Oh that we will,* Charlie thought. *That we will.*

# CHAPTER 17

$\mathcal{T}$hey were both quiet on the drive back to his parents' house, the kind of quiet that only two people who are absolutely comfortable with one another can share. At one point Jared reached out and took his hand again, and they stayed like that for the rest of the drive.

The whole drive there, though, Jared kept playing their conversation over and over in his head. He still couldn't believe that he'd actually agreed that he wanted to pursue something long-term with Charlie. Now that he had a little time to think about it, he realized this was truly what he wanted. If he was willing to take a really hard look at his innermost thoughts, he would acknowledge that this had been the case for a very long time, ever since he saw Charlie on the cover of *People* magazine ten years ago.

*I guess Rebecca was right,* he thought. *She's been saying for years that I have a crush on him and, well, I guess I always did.*

And it wasn't just that he was physically attracted to Charlie, though the sex *had* been very good, and Charlie *was* very handsome. It was more that Charlie had the almost supernatural ability to bring out the best in him. Something about his mere presence made Jared want to try harder and to be better. It also made him want to do something more with his life and to do his part to help Annamoriah become a better and more vital version of itself.

All of his life he'd been running away from his home. Thanks to Charlie, though, he'd come to realize that most of his fear and anxiety was a product of his imagination more than anything that in the real world. It wasn't that things were perfect, either with his parents or Annamoriah, but neither were they as bad as he'd always convinced himself they were.

*I don't even know who I am anymore,* he thought, and for some reason that thought didn't scare him. In fact, it excited him.

Just as they pulled in the driveway, however, he felt his phone buzz, and even before he looked at it, something–either his sixth sense for doom or his generally pessimistic nature–told him that this wasn't going to be good.

Sure enough, he could see that it was Rebecca texting, and that sick feeling just got worse.

"Jared, what's wrong?" Charlie asked, genuine concern in his voice.

"It's Rebecca," he said. "I didn't really see what the text said, but I have a feeling that it's not going to be good. Why don't you go into the house, and I'll be in in a few minutes?"

Jared could tell that Charlie wanted to argue with him, but he did as he asked. When he looked down at his phone his heart fell.

*I need you to call me. NOW.*

The words glared at him, and he felt like they were trying to sear into his brain. Whatever this was about, he knew that it must be serious if Rebecca was taking that tone with him.

For a split second he thought about just lying to her and saying that he hadn't received the text. He quickly decided against that, though, not just because it would be a betrayal of his friendship with Rebecca but also because he knew quite well that she would never believe him.

So, he nervously hit the button and put the phone to his ear. Unfortunately Rebecca picked up right away, which was yet another piece of evidence that whatever this was, it wasn't good.

"Hi," he said when she greeted him. "You told me to call you so, uh, that's what I'm doing."

"I'm glad you did," Rebecca said. "She took a deep breath, and Jared knew this was going to be even worse than he thought.

"See," she said without preamble, "it's like this. The Council was very much not happy about what happened with Charlie and the guy at the bar. Even though he didn't press charges, there were some members of the Council who wanted some heads to roll for the embarrassment."

"By 'some members' I assume you mean Councilman Rhodes," he said. He was actually surprised at how calm he sounded, considering that there was a slight roaring in his ears and a feeling that his whole life was falling apart right in front of him.

"Actually, it might surprise you to learn that there are other members of the City Council other than Councilman Rhodes, and they weren't particularly happy about the big star of the film festival clocking someone in the city's only gay bar. For that matter, the owners of the bar weren't pleased about the negative publicity either, even if they privately agreed that the guy really did have it coming."

Jared felt the same flare of impotent rage that he'd felt before, the same sense that he was being punished not for Charlie punching someone but for the mere fact that they were both gay in a city that, until recently, had not been partic-ularly friendly toward its queer residents.

"I'm aware that we fucked up," he said. "But we're doing

the best that we can to repair things. I've kept a very good eye on him this weekend."

"There's worse, I'm afraid," she said. "I wanted to be the one to tell you this," she said, "but I want you to know that it's not easy, and that I did everything I could to keep this from happening..." Her voice trailed off.

Jared sighed. "Rebecca. Just tell me what you've got to say and get it over with."

"The Council has decided that they're going to officially terminate your employment. Starting immediately."

At first Jared couldn't believe that he'd heard correctly. This couldn't be happening. She couldn't have just told him that he was about to lose his job. That couldn't be right, not after all of the hoops that he'd jumped through to get it in the first place, and certainly not after what he'd done for the film festival. There was no way that that was going to happen, and there was surely no way that Rebecca would just stand there and let it happen.

"Jared, are you there?"

"Yes, I'm here," he said, his voice sounding like it was coming from a thousand miles away. "I'm just trying to figure out what all of this means."

"I'm sorry. I did everything I could. Really."

He knew it was irrational, but something about the way that she said that suddenly made him wonder if she was telling the truth, or if this was another of those cases where she was trying to deflect blame because it was easier than admitting the truth of her own complicity. He hated himself for thinking it, but he had a feeling it was the former. And *that* thought shook him out of his shock and made him genuinely angry.

"You threw me under the bus, didn't you?" His voice was no longer distant but was instead hard and brittle and ugly. He truly hated this part of himself, but he couldn't seem to help himself. It was out there and there was nothing he could do about it.

"I...I...I...," she stammered, and he knew it was right. He pressed on, each word feeling like a knife in his hand.

"You were afraid it was going to come down between you keeping your job or me keeping mine, and so you decided I was expendable." He snorted. "I should have known."

"It's not like that," she said. "They told me if someone's head didn't roll that they were going to pull the plug on the festival, and I just couldn't let that happen."

"So what you're saying is that you chose the festival over me, your supposed best friend."

There was no mistaking the sigh on the other end of the line, and he knew that he was pushing her to say something he knew both of them would regret. Jared was too far gone by this point, though, as he knew all too well. His tongue was like an avalanche: nothing was going to stand between it and absolute destruction.

"You know, I guess I shouldn't be surprised by this. You were always the kind of person who put yourself above anyone else. I'm just shocked it took this long. You've always looked down on me and not taken me seriously, so of course it wouldn't even have occurred to you to defend me when the chips were down. Did you even really try, Rebecca, or did you just roll over the first chance you got? Did you just go ahead and offer me up without them even asking?" He snorted. "Some queer advocate you are."

Rebecca greeted that with an ominous silence, and there was a perverse part of Jared that looked forward to what was coming next.

"You know, you're such an asshole sometimes. You think that you're the only one who stands up for queer people, you think that you're some sort of moral purist who gets to stand on the high road and look down on everyone else. You do it with me, you did it with your parents when you first came out, and you're doing it with Charlie. You didn't even give him a chance before you were already judging him for what you saw as his faults. However, that's ultimately a *you* problem, Jared, and you're going to have to address it sooner rather than later."

"Do you have anything else you'd like to say to me?" he grated out. "Or have you finished pointing out what you see as my glaring personal failings? I wouldn't want you to leave anything on the table so you can throw it in my face the next time we have a big fight like this one."

"I don't think there'll be another fight like this one," she said. He almost thought that he could hear some sadness in her voice. "I don't think I want to see you for a while."

*Say something, you idiot,* that voice in the back of his head was screaming. *Don't torpedo your friendship like this. You deserve better and so does she!*

But, like so many other members of his family–and so many Appalachians in general–he was stubborn to a fault. He'd committed to this course of action, and he wasn't going to back away.

"If that's the way you want it, then I'm happy to oblige." He waited a moment. "Is there anything else that you'd like to say, or are we finished with this conversation?"

"We're done. Goodbye, Jared."

"Bye."

The line went dead.

For several minutes he just sat there in his truck, not sure how to feel about what had just happened. On the one hand, he was genuinely angry that Rebecca had betrayed him. On the other, he understood that she'd done the best she could with nothing but bad options, and he regretted losing his temper like that.

Even more distressing was the fact that she had a point

about his moral sanctimony. He didn't like to admit it about himself, but he knew that he tended to look down on people that he didn't agree with. He knew there were reasons for why he looked at the world that way—both good and bad ones—but he wasn't really in the mood to look at them with any detail at the moment. At this point, he just wanted to go inside, throw himself in Charlie's arms, and forget about everything.

He got out of the truck and wandered toward the house, feeling like a zombie. Getting fired by the City Council wasn't the absolute worst thing that could happen, not financially, anyway. He had some savings, so he wasn't going to be on the street anytime soon, but he honestly had no idea what he was going to do or what kind of job he was going to pursue.

As soon as he stepped inside Charlie was right there, and he couldn't help but wonder if all of this would have been happening if he'd never met Charlie Garrett and managed to get sucked into his drama.

"Jared, what's wrong?" he asked, even his compassion managing to get on Jared's nerves.

*Just once, couldn't he just be thoughtless like so many other men?* Jared thought sourly.

"Well," he said, determined not to lose his temper, "I got fired. And Rebecca was the absolute worst about it. We had a pretty ugly fight. So, yeah, that's about it."

He knew he sounded surly and unpleasant, but he was past caring.

Someone else might have taken a few minutes to figure out just what Jared needed or wanted to hear. A different kind of person, knowing Jared's peculiar and mercurial temper, would have tried to comfort him or offer him some sort of empty words of comfort, and he might even have welcomed it. Charlie Garrett, however, wasn't that type of person.

"I mean, maybe there's a bright side," Charlie said tentatively, as if he was afraid that Jared was going to yell at him. "I mean, you didn't seem very happy in that job, anyway. Maybe you can really turn your attention to writing like you've always wanted." He paused. "And maybe you could even think about moving out to California. I know that it's too early to talk about us living together or anything, but I could help you get on your feet, maybe connect you with the right kind of people."

Rationally, Jared knew that Charlie was just trying to be helpful, that his offer came from a place of love and affection rather than pity and condescension. However, that was literally the opposite of what Jared needed or wanted right then and so, as he'd done with Rebecca, he lashed out.

"Charlie, I hate to break it to you, but you can't just drop in whenever you think it's convenient and solve a problem. In fact, that's exactly what got us into this mess in the first place. You always rush in to try to solve a problem, but you just make things worse. If you hadn't punched that asshole in the bar none of this would be happening. I'd still have my job with the City Council, I wouldn't have had to drag you here to meet my parents, and we could have all been a lot happier."

He was conscious as he was saying it that his voice was getting higher and higher and louder and louder, and that his parents could no doubt hear every word. He suddenly didn't care, however. He just wanted to get Charlie as far away from him as possible. He wanted to hurt him so that he would see the kind of person that Jared really was.

"And while we're on the subject, I *still* think it's pretty rich that you think you can just helicopter into your home state whenever you want to and then just leave. You have no idea what it's like to live here these days, because if you did you might actually put in a bit of effort to make sure that it's the best place that it can be for all of the queer teens who still live here. Instead you're always off in Hollywood getting to hobnob with all of the other rich and shallow people, who I'm sure fawn all over you and tell you how absolutely wonderful and noble it is that you still care about all of the people living back home."

He snorted, just in case his contempt wasn't absolutely clear by now. "Well, I don't think there's any point in sitting around here. We should get you back to Huntington. To be honest, I don't really want to have any more to do with the film festival than I have to."

*Or with you.* Those were the hurtful words that were on the very tip of his tongue, but somehow he managed to keep from saying them.

It was at this moment that Jared's parents decided to put in an appearance. He couldn't decide whether that was a good or a bad thing.

"Jared, Charlie, let's all just take a breath," his mother said, as always rushing in to try to smooth things over before they got out of hand. "I'm sure that this is a tough time for you, dear, but there's no need to lash out at Charlie like that. Charlie, would you give us just a few minutes?"

This was quickly becoming one of those moments where Jared basically saw red. Once again the rational part of his mind knew that his mother was just trying to help, but talking to Charlie as if he, Jared, wasn't there and, moreover, acting as if he was some kind of dangerous animal that needed to be tamed, well, it was just too much (even if it was also somewhat true).

"Mother, don't take this the wrong way, but butt out," he said, which was about the nicest thing he could think of. It was bad enough to be having this very unpleasant conversation with Charlie without either of his parents trying to make things better.

Unfortunately, that was the exact wrong thing he could have said, but the reprimand came not from his mother but instead from his father, who almost never raised his voice or spoke a word in anger.

"Jared, that's *enough*. You will not speak to your mother like that, not while you're under this roof."

Jared was so surprised that his father actually raised his voice that he couldn't think of what to say. He just stood there with his mouth hanging open.

Suddenly the only thing he wanted was to be out of there and going back to Huntington. Jared didn't know how all of this weekend, which had so far been so filled with joy and self-discovery and happiness, had come crumbling down, but he wanted it all over with as quickly as possible. In fact, he really wanted to bolt right to his car, get in, and start driving.

Then Charlie once again stepped into the breach.

"Why don't we all just take a few minutes to cool off, huh?"

Jared took a deep breath. He was working on one hell of a headache—it was already starting behind his eyes, and he knew that it wouldn't be long before it took over—but even through the pain and his anger and his hurt feelings, he knew that Charlie was right. And, of course, he resented him for that, too. How did he know how to make things better between Jared and his parents when Jared himself could never entirely figure out how to do that, even after all these years?

"Fine," he said, and stormed upstairs.

As soon as he was back in his room all of the complicated and ugly feelings came roaring back to the surface again, and he thought for a minute that he was going to actually go crazy.

*I've gotta get out of here,* he thought. *I don't care what happens or where I go, but I gotta get out of here.*

Which is how, fifteen minutes later, he was sneaking out the door of the house, heading toward his truck, his suitcase beside him. In the far reaches of his mind a little voice was screaming at him that he couldn't just leave Charlie here—he had to get back to Huntington, after all—but the louder voice became the more determined he became to leave. Charlie was a star, after all, not a child. If he was so good at figuring things out with Jared's parents, then he could figure this out, too.

Jared got in his truck, turned the key in the ignition and, before he could think any more about what he was about to do, he was gone, his parents, and Charlie, already in the rearview mirror.

# CHAPTER 18

*A*fter Jared stormed out of the room and went up to the guest room, Charlie just sort of stood there with Joyce and Doug, none of them quite able to believe what had just happened. Somehow, between one minute and the next, the romance that had slowly been taking shape between Charlie and Jared seemed to have been burned entirely to the ground.

"Would you like to sit in the living room?" Joyce asked, finally recovering some measure of her equanimity. "I'm really sorry that you had to see whatever that was. Sometimes, I don't know what gets into that boy's head. Lord knows I love him, but I'd like to shake some sense into him."

Charlie had a feeling that that was about as aggressive as Joyce ever got, and it surprised him. Jared must have shaken her up a bit with his little outburst.

They all retired to the living room, where they sat around in a semi-awkward silence, none of them quite sure what to say. They all seemed to have reached an unspoken agreement that the best thing to do was wait for Jared to cool down on his own, however long that might end up taking. It wasn't until they heard his truck's engine starting that they thought things might have gone off the rails a bit more than they thought, but even then none of them thought there was any reason to panic.

"I'm sure he's just blowing off some steam," Charlie said, and both Joyce and Doug nodded in agreement. It was clear from the looks on their faces, though, that they weren't entirely sure.

When an hour passed and Jared still hadn't returned, Charlie started to wonder, too.

Finally, it was clear what had happened. Jared had ditched them all.

"Well," Doug said, slapping his knees, "I guess Jared has pulled a Jared."

Charlie did a double-take at that, even though he was pretty sure he knew exactly what Doug meant, unfortunately.

"Doug," Joyce said, a note of caution in her voice, "don't."

"No, Joyce. This is unacceptable," he said, gesturing at Charlie. "He's hared off again, and now Charlie is left here to fend for himself. It's unacceptable and inexcusable. He should know better. He's an adult."

"Look, it's no big deal," Charlie said, deciding to head all of this off at the pass. "I'm sure I can find some way to get back to Huntington. Jared was nice enough to drive me here. I didn't really expect him to have to drive me back too. I can just rent a car." He chuckled, trying to set them both at their ease. "I think I can afford it."

"You'll do no such thing," Doug said. "*I'll* drive you back to Huntington, and once I get there I'm going to give my son a piece of my mind."

Charlie looked outside. It was already starting to get dark. Suddenly it all came crashing down on him, all of the things that he still had to do, all of the aspects of the film festival that still had to go on, no matter how much his life had changed.

There was a part of him that just wanted to get on the nearest plane and get back to California, forgetting that all of this had never happened.

*I'm not proud of that, but that's the truth,* he thought.

"You don't have to do that, really," he said.

"Yes, I do," Doug said, and it was clear that he wasn't going to take no for an answer. "How soon do you think you can be ready?"

This whole situation was spinning out of control much faster than Charlie would ever have expected, but he supposed it could have been worse. He did like Doug and, if nothing else, a four-hour car drive would give him more of an opportunity to get to know the other man.

It wasn't long before Charlie and Doug were in the latter's old Buick, headed back to Huntington and whatever waited there.

Charlie had to admit that this wasn't exactly the way that he had envisioned this weekend coming to a close, but he supposed it was what he'd deserved. Much as he hated to admit it, Jared was right. None of this would have happened if he hadn't let his temper get the better of him. For that matter, none of this would have happened if he'd stayed in California where he belonged rather than trying to be a white knight bullshit hero.

"I know that you probably don't want to hear this right now," Doug said, "but I want you to know that I think Jared really has feelings for you. It's just that he sometimes has a hard time figuring out what to do with those feelings. As you know, he's had a rough time of it with some of his exes, and none of them have really treated him like they deserve."

Charlie knew that much was true, and he said as much.

"Now, I know that doesn't excuse his actions today," Doug went on. "In fact, I'm going to give him a good earful when I see him again. However, if the chance presents itself, I hope you can find it in your heart to forgive him. I think you'll be glad you did."

*I'm not at all sure that's true,* he thought but didn't say.

"I'll do my best," he said instead.

After that conversation most of the trip passed in a bit of silence. It wasn't awkward, at least not entirely. Instead, it was more or less a peaceful interlude between two people who were comfortable enough to not have to fill the air with chatter, despite the fact that they barely knew each other. Charlie thought with a pang about the future he'd dared to begin to imagine with Jared and his family. He doubted that Doug and Joyce would want to have anything to do with him after what had happened this weekend.

They finally reached the outskirts of Huntington, and Charlie breathed an internal sigh of relief. He just wanted to get back to his hotel room, maybe have a drink at the bar, and try to get as much sleep as possible before tomorrow.

*Fuck,* he thought. *I still have to write my speech for the festival. Assuming that Sheri hasn't done it already.*

Thinking of Sheri reminded him of all of the things that he was going to have to deal with now that he was back in town. The idyll with Jared had ended before he had come up with any satisfactory solutions to any of his myriad problems, and he didn't think they were going to get any better.

"Where would you like me to drop you off?" Doug asked.

"Um...I guess at the Huntington Grande?" Charlie said, somehow making it seem more like a question. "I guess I should try to get my life together before tomorrow."

"I know it doesn't seem like it right now, but I have a feeling you'll get it all figured out. You strike me as the type of guy who always lands on his feet. You must be pretty special if Jared found something about you that he liked so much."

The mention of Jared's name seemed to cast a cloud over their conversation again, and they didn't say anything more as

Doug made his way through the streets of Huntington. Being back here brought Charlie back to the moments when he'd first gotten to know Jared–had that just been a few days ago?-- and how much everything had changed.

*Maybe I should have just stayed here and weathered the news storm,* he thought.

Then they were in front of the hotel, and before he quite realized what he was doing he was standing outside and waving to Doug as he pulled away, disappearing down the street.

*Well, that's one thing taken care of,* he thought.

Charlie wasn't sure whether to be relieved or offended that there was no one outside the hotel waiting to attack him with cameras and shouted questions. In any case, he made his way up to his room without being seen but, as he swiped the key in the lock, he felt another pang, thinking about what Jared was doing and how he must be feeling about all of this.

*Jared,* he thought. *I hope you know that you're worth love, even if you can't see it right now.*

Just as he stepped inside, however, he heard someone behind him clear their throat, and he froze.

"And just what are you doing back here?" Sheri asked him in that no-nonsense voice that he'd learned a long time ago to fear. "I thought you were supposed to be out of town with your boyfriend and staying out of trouble?"

He turned around. Sheri was standing there in her usual pantsuit, arms crossed, one stilettoed foot tapping up and down while her fingers.

"Well?" she asked when he didn't say anything at once.

"Let's just say that things didn't work out quite as well as I'd hoped," he said.

There was a flicker of something that might have been sympathy on her face, but then it hardened again, no doubt as she thought about all of the complications that his being here was likely to cause.

"Please," he said, holding up a hand, "I really don't need any 'I told you so's' right now."

"Actually," she said, "I was going to say that if you don't want to do the talk before the film festival you don't have to. In fact, it might be better if you didn't. Perhaps we should just get back to California and forget that all of this ever happened."

Charlie couldn't deny that there was a part of him that was desperate to do just that, to get away from all of the mess and madness that had characterized his time coming home. In particular, he wanted to get away from all of the memories of Jared that being here would continue to conjure.

*Jared, how did this all go so wrong?* He wanted, desperately, to believe that this had all been a blip, that he hadn't meant all of what he'd said. The more he thought about it, however, the more convinced he became that the ugly side of Jared that he'd revealed back at his parents' house had, in fact, been the real person. Oh, he was sure there was something else there, that there was a core to him that was really beautiful and as sensitive as Charlie had thought at the beginning, but it was so buried beneath all of the other baggage that Charlie didn't think he'd ever be able to dig his way out of it.

*As he's made clear, that's someone else's problem,* he thought sourly. It was time to get this whole festival over with and put in the rearview mirror so that he could resume his life back in California.

"No," he said. "I'm done with running away. We're going to see this through to the end."

Something about just saying those words aloud made him feel confident about his choices in a way that he hadn't been in a long time. Whatever else happened during this trip—and he had a feeling that there was a lot more to come—he could at least take comfort from the fact that he'd seen it through to the end.

"Now that you're back," Sheri said, breaking into his thoughts. "I have something important to give you." She walked over to his desk and grabbed a folder, which she then handed to him without even the slightest bit of ceremony.

"Do I want to know what this is?" he asked with a raised eyebrow.

"Since I figured you'd decide to go through with the speech no matter what I said, I took the liberty of writing a draft. Trust me, it's already made it through all of the revisions that it needs. This is the type of speech that will impress everyone and not piss anyone off, let alone the members of the Huntington City Council, who have been on the warpath ever since you left. If you just read this, I think we can smooth this whole thing over and take control of the narrative."

Charlie reluctantly opened the folder and skimmed the speech. He could tell right away that this was exactly the opposite of what he would have liked to say even if, as Sheri had said, it was exactly the type of anodyne speech one might expect from such a gathering. It was full of expressions of gratitude to Huntingotn and to speaking in general terms about how much had been gained but how much there was still left to do.

*Yeah, I'm not reading that,* he decided right away. He didn't say that to Sheri, of course, because she wouldn't understand. In fact, he knew that she would reprimand him for being foolish enough to do what he was thinking about doing.

But if being here in West Virginia this past weekend had taught him anything, it was that it wasn't worth bending yourself out of shape for someone else. You had to be honest about what you were doing, and let the chips fall where they may. What he was about to do might cost him his career, it might cost him everything that he'd already built, but he was going to go through with it.

There was no going back.

After getting rid of Sheri, Charlie spent the next several hours writing a new version of his speech. He decided to write by hand, because that always made him feel more connected to his thoughts and, as the hours passed and he kept writing, he found that it was a lot easier, and also a lot harder, than he had expected. There was a lot he needed to cram into a relatively short speech but, by the time that three hours had gone by, he felt like he'd written something he could be proud of.

He also realized he was incredibly hungry, so he ordered some room service, had a light dinner, and then went to bed. It was going to be a very busy day tomorrow.

As he drifted off, his thoughts kept returning to Jared, wondering where he was and what he was doing. Charlie tried to resist the effort, but he even checked his phone several times, just to see if somehow he'd missed a message. He hadn't and, after about the dozenth check, he decided that it was time to go to sleep. Tomorrow he'd face the world.

The next day passed in something of a haze. Sheri informed him over a light breakfast that she'd already made plans for the jet to take them back to California after his speech was done that night. She'd already booked him a meeting with several producers of a new project, and she thought it was in his best interests to capitalize on at least a bit of the goodwill from the festival in order to get some things set in stone.

*If only you knew what was coming,* he thought but didn't say.

Still, he packed all of his bags and got things ready for his departure. He resolutely kept Jared out of his thoughts, because he knew if he started to give in to thinking about him—and about the fact that he hadn't even tried to reach out—then he was going to lose his focus, and he needed all of his resources to be able to focus today.

*You can do this,* he kept reminding himself.

At last all of his belongings were packed away, and he was left staring at yet another empty hotel room. For the briefest of moments his mind flashed back to that first night, and the way that Jared had brought him here after the incident at the Stonewall. A small smile flickered across his lips at the memory.

*If only things could have stayed like that,* he thought.

Then Sheri was knocking on the door, and it was time to go.

WHEN THEY GOT to the theater it was clear at once that there was an even bigger crowd than they'd expected. Part of Charlie was excited and happy—and even a little proud—to see that so many people had come out to see him. Or, at least, he assumed they'd turned out to see him and his new movie, rather than the controversy of a few days earlier. As they started clapping and waving, though, he smiled, knowing that they really were there for all of the right reasons, so he plastered on the usual smile and waved in return.

The Keith Albee was one of the oldest theaters in Huntington, and even though its best days had seemed to be behind it, it had experienced a bit of a renaissance thanks to some wise investment. Being inside of the building, Charlie could see why it was a true local landmark, and he almost felt like he was walking through one of the old theaters from the early days of Hollywood, with its pillars and its carpeted floors and its magnificent painted ceiling.

There was, of course, quite a lot of hustle and bustle as everyone was still getting ready for his big screening. He was whisked into a backroom–there would be enough time to give interviews after the screening, assuming that Sheri still wanted that to happen after his speech–where he was given another once-over to make sure that he was ready for the cameras.

"You've got your speech and everything?" Sheri asked as she walked in. She was dressed in a pantsuit, as usual, and her heels made their usual menacing click on the tiled floor. "Did you make any changes?"

Charlie almost told her the truth. It didn't seem fair to go through with this without at least giving her some kind of warning of what was to come. However, just when he started to confess, his tongue just seemed to stick to the roof of his mouth. Instead, he just said, "Yes, I've got the speech and no, I didn't make any changes."

For a second he thought that she might press him on it, but instead she just nodded her head.

"Good. Once you're done with your speech we'll start the movie, and then after that you can take a few questions, give a couple of interviews, and then we'll get to the airport and go home." She took a deep breath. "I don't know about you, but I'll be glad when this whole thing is over."

"Yes," he said simply.

"You sure are quiet," she said. "Is everything okay?"

He wanted to tell her that of course everything wasn't okay, but he knew Sheri well enough to realize she wouldn't be particularly sympathetic to matters of the heart. That just didn't compute with her when they were in the middle of business.

"I'm fine," he said tersely.

She shrugged as if that was good enough and then went off to attend to some last minute details.

Time seemed to pass both very quickly and very slowly, and as it did Charlie looked around, seeing if perhaps Rebecca was going to try to touch base with him before he went on. He badly wanted to know whether she'd made any kind of peace with Jared or whether the two of them were still fighting. However, when it came time for him to deliver his speech she hadn't shown up, so he had to step up in front of those gathered to hear him.

As soon as he stepped out on stage the enormity of what he was about to do came crashing down on him. If he went through with this, nothing was going to be the same, and he had to be okay with that.

*You can do this,* he reminded himself. *Besides, you only have one copy of the speech with you, and it's the one that* you *wrote.* The one that Sheri had written for him—with its platitudes and stale compromise—had been left in the trash can when he left the room.

Taking a deep breath, he walked to the podium, conscious of all of the claps and approving smiles beaming up at him. Somehow, the fact that everyone there seemed to be in his corner made him feel better about all of this, giving him the strength to go through with it.

Finally the crowd quieted down enough so that he could start.

"When I first came back to West Virginia for this festival," he began, "I thought that this was going to be one of those lovely speeches that people coming back to their home states from Hollywood always give, thanking everyone for helping to make them who they are, and you'll get some of that tonight. What you'll *also* get, though, is some tough talk, because the truth is that those who are in charge of governing various places in the Mountain State haven't done as good of a job as they should have when it comes to protecting the most vulnerable."

He rattled off a series of statistics that he'd quickly researched while revamping this speech. Some of them had been truly gut-wrenching, but he needed those people out there in the audience—particularly the straight ones who believed they were allies—to see just how bad the situation was. In fact, he'd been surprised by some of what he'd read, and he liked to think that he was on top of LGBTQ+ issues in his home state.

When he was finished delivering those stats, he could see there were a few people in the audience who looked uncomfortable, as if they hadn't been expecting him to be this real in front of them. That was good, though. He wanted them to realize that they were all complicit in what was going on, in one way or another.

"Now, I don't want to pin this blame on anyone in particular, but the truth is that there are some people right here in this town who are willing to either turn a blind eye to homophobia or to practice it themselves. I know for a fact that there is at least one member of City Council who likes to say homophobic things and thinks that he can get away with it. The ugly reality is that he *has* gotten away with it, because people are often too willing to cause a fuss. They're more afraid of making things awkward than they are of the very real damage that's being caused by letting homophobia go unchallenged."

He could tell at once who Councilman Rhodes was in the audience, because there was only one man there whose face had turned about ten different shades of red as Charlie had continued speaking.

*Well, that's good*, Charlie thought, *because he needs to realize and come to grips with the fact that his time of terrorizing the people of Huntington is coming to a close.*

More importantly, though, Charlie was struck by the

hopeful smiles on the faces of so many of the young people out there in the audience. The thought that he was doing something good for them was enough to give him the strength to continue.

"The film you're about to watch today is one that's very near and dear to my heart. It's one of those movies that reminds you that queer people of all sorts have always been around, even if their stories have either been papered over or pushed into the margins. This is a story about a love that is forbidden not just because it transgresses social classes but also because it's between two queer men. It's a crucial story, and I'm very proud to have been a part of it."

He was conscious of Sheri behind him, and he could just imagine the look on her face as he set his entire career on fire right in front of her.

*I don't care anymore,* he thought. *The only thing that matters is being honest to and with myself. I have to speak my truth, and these people are going to listen to it, no matter how uncomfortable it might make some of them.*

"It's also a story about power, particularly the power of being true to yourself, of not letting the social expectations of others dictate your every behavior. That's a lesson that hits home with me the older I get. I hope that everyone sitting in this theater, and everyone out there in the world tonight who might see this speech on YouTube or TikTok or somewhere else, realizes how much power there is in speaking up and speaking your truth. I'm happy to have been able to do so tonight. Going forward, I'm going to continue speaking out and doing everything I can to make life better for all of the queer folks who still call Appalachia home. They're as much a part of this region as their straight counterparts, and it's time that they're seen that way.

"Thank you all so much for this chance to speak to you all

tonight. I hope you enjoy the film, and I hope you've enjoyed the festival."

And then he was done. The speech was over. There was a moment of pregnant, heavy silence throughout the auditorium, and then a few scattered people started clapping. As Charlie watched, they got to their feet, followed by several others. His stomach clenched as he thought of the rest of the crowd leaving the room. He needn't have worried, though. While a few did storm out–most notably Councilman Rhodes–far more stayed there, and as they did the clapping grew louder and more enthusiastic, until practically everyone in the auditorium was on their feet giving him a standing ovation.

*Looks like I made the right call, after all,* he thought, heart swelling with joy and euphoria.

Then he turned around, and the look on Sheri's face told him that he had definitely crossed a boundary and that she was very, *very* pissed about it.

"Sheri...," he started to say, but she held up her hand. He closed his mouth with a snap.

"Save it," she said. "We're leaving."

# CHAPTER 19

When he got back to Huntington, Jared went straight to his apartment, determined to never come out of it again. He knew that he'd acted like an absolute asshole to Charlie and that he should have told him that he was sorry. For that matter, he should have offered to drive him back to the festival, regardless of what his parents might have had to say about the matter.

If he was being honest with himself, he was also a little hurt that neither his parents or Charlie had called to check in on him.

*You could make this better in a heartbeat if you'd just call them—your parents, Charlie, Rebecca—and tell them you're sorry.*

But, with that typical West Virginia stubbornness, he just couldn't bring himself to do it, and it was only when his phone started buzzing that he even looked at it. Rebecca's name blinking on the screen, because *of course* it would have to be her.

*I just can't with her right now,* he thought. He put the phone back down, hoping to ignore her as much as possible, but when she kept calling he knew that he was going to have to pick up eventually.

"What?" he snapped.

"Don't you *dare* take that tone with me," she said at once. "I'm not the one who has been acting like an absolute dunce about this whole Charlie thing."

He rolled his eyes and tried to calm himself, taking several deep breaths. He knew that this was just her way, that she was trying to give him the tough love that she thought he needed. He wasn't in the mood for it, of course, but he knew her well enough by now to know that she was going to bulldoze him if he didn't at least try to stand up for himself.

"Rebecca, I'm really not in the mood for this right now," he began, but she immediately cut him off.

"I don't really care what you're in the mood for, Jared Russell. Can you imagine my surprise when Charlie Garrett showed up at the hotel *without you*? I'm just going to assume that it was your parents who brought him. Either that or he had to rent a car to get back to Huntington, and God help you if that was the case. The last thing we need is for our star attraction to have had to drive himself all the way back here from your parents' house."

"Rebecca, listen," he said and took a deep breath to calm himself and give himself the strength to go on. "I'm sorry about all of this. I was being stupid, and I have no idea how to fix any of this, not Charlie, not the stuff with the film festival, or my parents, or the City Council. Or you, for that matter." He barked out a bitter laugh at that last part. There was a time when he would never have imagined feeling so lost or desperate, certainly not where Rebecca was concerned. The two of them had always seemed to understand one another at a deep, instinctual level.

"I know you didn't ask for my advice, but given the way that you've been acting, I'm going to give you some tough love. It's going to take you a while to dig yourself out of the hole you've put yourself in, and the more honest you are with yourself about that, the better off you're going to be. Take a bit to figure yourself out, and then start making amends."

Now it was her turn to take a deep breath.

"For what it's worth, I forgive you. You've been a really good friend to me when I needed it, and sometimes even though I made it really difficult to love and be loyal to me. Even a fight like the one we just had isn't going to demolish that, even if you did act like an asshole.

"And I know that it might be easy to contemplate, but I also think that you need to say sorry to Charlie. He might not accept your apology, but it's the least that he deserves. I mean, I don't know exactly what went down between the two of you, but if I know you, you were probably the one who started it."

*Damn it. I hate when she's right,* he thought.

"You're right," he said, "even though I hate to admit it. But...thank you for being willing to forgive me. I know that I can sometimes be a bit of a pill as a friend. And you really do mean the world to me."

"Get therapy," she said.

"I will," he promised.

"Okay. Well, I have to get off of here. I know you might have forgotten, but I have a film festival to put on." She paused. "Are you sure you wouldn't like to come?"

Jared shook his head even though he knew that she couldn't see it.

"I think I'm going to have to pass on this one," he said. "I really want to come, but I think it's best that I stay away. I don't want to distract Charlie from his big day."

"Fair enough. Well, goodbye, Jared."

"Bye."

After hanging up with Rebecca, Jared wasn't quite sure where to go or what to do. He felt even more aimless than he usually did and, considering the fact that he usually felt pretty aimless with his life, that was really saying something.

Suddenly it hit him. There was one place where he could go where he would at least find a measure of peace. It was one of the few places in Huntington that gave him the same feeling of serenity that he was able to find on the hill back home and at Streeter Park. Leaving his apartment yet again, he made his way to the campus of Marshall University.

Even though he'd lived in Huntington ever since finishing his undergrad, he'd rarely been back to Marshall's campus. Perhaps it was because he still hadn't achieved all of the ambitions that he'd had as a college student, or perhaps he was just lazy and didn't have much reason to come to this end of town. Either way, he'd avoided it, and now that he was here he found himself in a very strange mental and emotional space.

Walking through Marshall's campus, Jared reflected on the person that he had been twenty years earlier. Back then he'd been a nervous young gay just trying to make sense of himself, his place in the world, and his feelings. He'd grown up a lot since then, even if he hadn't achieved all of his goals and dreams.

*There's still time for that, you know,* he reminded himself. It was a familiar refrain, something that he'd been telling himself for years now, so that he wouldn't get so depressed that he quit functioning altogether. It was becoming less and less convincing with the passing years, though.

He sat down on one of the stone tables that sat outside of the library, and for a split second he almost felt like he was the same student that he'd been all those years ago, when the whole world had seemed so ripe and full of promise. He wasn't sure whether he felt sad or happy or perhaps some combination of the two.

However, Jared soon found that he was restless and that he didn't want to stay in one place for very long, and so he moved on, until he was standing in front of the Memorial Fountain, that strange but oddly beautiful piece of sculpture that had been built in memory of the football team who'd died in a plane crash in 1970.

Even though he hadn't even been born yet –not even a twinkle in his parents' eyes–when the plane crash had happened, he'd always found himself moved by the fountain in all of its austere and strange beauty. The waters weren't running now, of course, because it was too late in the year, but standing there he found himself thinking about Charlie, about how much the two of them had managed to share in just a weekend.

*You would have fallen over yourself trying to get with a guy like that when you were younger,* he thought. *You would have sold a kidney to get his attention, and when you finally had it... what did you do? You threw it away like it was nothing.*

He thought about the way that it had felt to be with Charlie, the way that he'd seemed to see him as a person. And, of course, he thought about the sex which had, in fact, been good. Very, very good.

"You could just go to him and tell him how you feel, you know." He hadn't even heard his dad approach, but when he heard his voice he turned around to face him.

Doug would have been well within his rights to be truly furious with his son, but instead Jared saw on his face what he always had: unconditional love and acceptance. He thought of all of the times that he'd tried to talk to his dad and always chickened out, believing that he wouldn't understand what he was feeling. No matter how much Doug tried to reach out to him, he'd always recoiled. He'd built up an image of what his father was like, and no matter how much reality was different, that was the one that stuck with him.

He sighed. "I'm really sorry, dad," he said. "You deserved better than me throwing a temper tantrum while we had a guest at your house, particularly after you'd gone out of your way to make Charlie feel so welcome." He barked a bitter little laugh. "I guess I can be a bit of a jackass sometimes."

"Yes, you can," his father said at once, "but you also have the biggest and most loving heart of anyone I've ever met. You just don't like anyone to see it."

"I guess that runs in the family," he said.

"It does," his dad said. "Your mother makes a good show about being friendly and loving, but she sometimes has a hard time letting people in to see the real her."

Jared sighed. He hadn't really counted on having a heart-to-heart with his dad at just this moment but, now that the cat was out of the bag, he supposed there was no point in giving this conversation short-shrift.

"I'm really sorry about that," he said. "And now I've not only managed to damage my relationship with you and mom; I've also done the same with Charlie." He could feel his throat trying to close up, and he knew it was going to be a struggle to get through this whole bit without crying. "Like, he was one of the few guys that I've ever known who treated me like a person with real feelings rather than just someone that they could take advantage of, and the first thing I did was try to push him away." He gestured vaguely in the direction of the theater. "And now I know he's not that far away, but he might as well be on the other side of the world for all the more good it does me. If I was him I wouldn't even give me the time of day."

Doug didn't say anything for a moment, but Jared could see the wheels of his mind grinding as he worked through that. One thing that he'd always admired about his dad was his deliberate approach to things. He wasn't the type of person to just rush in and say the first thing that came to mind. He wanted to make absolutely sure of what he meant before he opened his mouth.

*I wish I'd inherited that particular character trait.*

"If you want my fatherly advice, I would say that if you really like him, that you should go and apologize. I know that it's not easy to let anyone in, and I know it's even harder to admit that you've done something wrong." Jared made to say something, but Doug held up a hand to stop him. "I also know that apologies are very hard for anyone, because you're leaving yourself open to the possibility that someone might not be able or willing to forgive you. If you really like this guy, Jared, you shouldn't give up on him just because you did something stupid."

Now it was Jared's turn to work through all of this.

"I really do like him, and I think in time I could even come to love him," he said slowly. "But how can I go back and tell him all of this, when I've already acted like such an asshole?"

Doug actually laughed a little. "Do you have any idea how many times I've acted like a total asshole to your mother? Do you know what a jerk I could be when we were young and had first started dating? I don't think a month went by that I wasn't putting my foot in it in one way or another. Somehow, though, we found a way to get through it all. We realized that we truly loved each other, and that it was worth making our way through the complicated things that come up when you're in a relationship with someone.

"Look, there are always going to be difficulties, and only you know your own mind. However, if you want my advice, and it's going to sound very cliche, you should go to him. At the very least you can tell him how you feel. If you want to know something else that I've learned through the years, it's that you should never not do something because you're afraid. That's just going to make you regret not having taken the chance. And regret is something that you do not want to have to live with."

"You know, dad, you're actually pretty wise," he said. "I

guess if I have a regret it's that I didn't listen to you more often growing up. I probably would have been a lot happier."

"Well, when you're a parent you get very used to your kids not paying attention to anything that you have to say. As a rule they only decide to go along with something when they've decided that it's their own idea."

A comfortable silence settled down for a moment, and then Jared made a decision.

"I'm gonna go to the theater right now," he said. "Do you want to come?"

He knew his dad was going to say no, but he still felt like he should ask. Indeed, Doug shook his head.

"Nah, son. I gotta get back to your mother. And besides, I think this moment is for you and Charlie, not me."

They gave each other a hug, then Doug was walking away and Jared was left to make his way back to the theater.

Jared could have driven back to the Keith Albee, but since it wasn't that far at all he decided to just walk. He needed that last little bit of time with his own thoughts in order to figure out just what it was he was going to say. He knew in the broad strokes how he wanted this to go, but he had no idea whether it was going to end up ending how he wanted or whether, as he feared and suspected, it would blow up in his face, with Charlie telling him that he wanted nothing more to do with him.

When he got there, he looked at the theater across the street, and he thought of all of the things that Charlie might then be doing. Was he giving his talk? Was he wondering why Jared wasn't in the audience, or was he just glad that he didn't have to put up with another potential outburst?

It took him longer than it should have to work up the nerve to actually go in there, and by the time he started to cross the street the doors were already opening and a cluster of people were coming out. When Jared saw one of the faces in that knot of people, his heart fell.

It was Councilman Rhodes.

"You really have a lot of nerve showing up here," he said, face turning an alarming shade of red when his eyes fell on Jared. "After what your boyfriend said in there, I should have you run out of town on a rail!"

"I don't think that will be necessary," said Councilwoman Tate, who'd clearly exited with him. She'd always been one of Jared's favorite members of the City Council. Not only had she launched an investigation of Councilman Rhodes; she'd been one of the first to give her unapologetic support for the film festival. "In fact, I think that we'll be taking a vote very soon to see whether or not you are really the one best positioned to represent your constituents on the Council."

Rhodes' face turned an even more alarming shade of red. "I was duly elected, and you can't remove me without a full hearing."

"Oh, believe me, I know the rules as well as you do," she said crisply. "You may rest assured that it will all be done according to the book. I think that once we start digging into your finances we're going to find some very suspicious dealings. You've gotten away with things too long, Rhodes, and it's time to clean up City Council."

Rhodes looked like he wanted to keep arguing the matter, but he was also smart enough to realize that he wasn't likely to win this fight. He knew, probably better than most, that *no one* won an argument with Councilwoman Tate whenever she had decided that something was going to happen. With a growl and a huff he stormed off.

This was almost too good to be true, and Jared tried not to let himself look or feel too smug. However, there was no denying that it would be a bit of poetic justice if Rhodes was brought down by his own rampant corruption.

*It's just a shame that he wasn't removed for being a raging homophobe,* he thought.

Now that Rhodes was gone, Tate turned her attention to him, and he wasn't entirely sure that he was going to like what she had to say. Indeed, she put her hands on her hips and looked him up and down.

"You sure have caused quite a lot of trouble, young man," she said. "I honestly don't know who I'm madder at, you, Rhodes, or that movie star that you brought here. Do you have any idea how much trouble he's caused with that little speech of his?"

Jared wasn't sure whether or not he wanted to ask what speech she was talking about, but his curiosity got the better of him.

"Um...I'm not sure I know exactly what you're talking about," he said cautiously. "What speech?"

Tate gave him a look, as if she wasn't quite sure that she believed that he had no idea what she was talking about. However, she just shook her head.

"Your *friend* in there gave quite a rousing speech accusing certain members of the Huntington City Council of not being supportive enough of the gay community. It was a good speech, I'll give him that, but it's not what I expected. I respect him, though. For a guy who's always been taught to keep an eye on his reputation, he sure does know when to cause a fuss at the worst times."

Jared almost couldn't believe what he was hearing. Charlie Garrett had actually gone out of his way to challenge the status quo? His heart swelled with pride and, he had to admit it, with love, to think that Charlie would actually do that, when the stakes were so high and he had so much to lose.

*The studio isn't going to like this,* he thought.

"If you're going to go after him, you'd better do it soon,"

she said. "Because from the look on his publicist's face I don't think they're going to stay there very long."

"Thank you, Councilor. I'm going to do just that!"

Jared made his way into the theater. Even though most of the people were still inside watching the movie, there were quite a few people milling about the lobby, and it was clear that they, too, had heard about Charlie's speech. In fact, it was all anyone could talk about. Jared had a feeling that this was going to be the topic of conversation in every piece of media that came out of the festival.

He honestly wasn't sure how he felt about that. It might have been the thing that he was pushing Charlie to do since they'd met, but it was also one of those things that could have far-reaching consequences for his career. Jared doubted that he was going to be able to make any forward momentum with this kind of baggage weighing him down.

For the moment, though, Jared had more important things on his mind. He had to find Charlie before he left. Nothing else mattered. He'd been stupid to let the other man slip through his fingers in the first place, and he wasn't about to let that happen again.

Fortunately, he knew his way around this theater better than most, and it wasn't long before he was in the modified green room that they'd managed to rig up. To his dismay, though, Charlie wasn't there. He looked around, desperate to find someone who might be able to tell him where he'd gone, but there was no one.

*No*, he thought. *This can't be happening. I can't be this close just for everything to have everything fall apart. That...that just wouldn't be fair.*

He knew even as he thought those things that he was being both tedious and childish. The universe didn't owe him anything, and he certainly didn't deserve anything from Charlie after the way that he'd acted.

Jared knew that his only chance now was for him to get to the back parking lot before Charlie managed to get away. Something told him, though, that he wasn't going to make it, that he was going to be too late and all of this was going to fall apart.

Sure enough, he got to the back lot just in time to see what he knew to be Charlie's limo driving off. After all, who else but Charlie would have a limo at the premiere? He could have almost sworn that he saw Sheri's face in the window looking back at him, but he couldn't have sworn to it. He supposed that he wasn't surprised that she'd rushed him out of there as soon as he'd finished with his speech. Whatever else she might be, she was a good publicist. She'd want to make sure that she was protecting Charlie's legacy as much as possible.

*Well,* he thought, *that's that. I guess maybe it's for the best after all. Maybe this is the universe's way of telling me that this wasn't meant to be and that I should just accept that.*

He stood there for several more minutes, not quite sure he knew what he was hoping for. He knew that he could have gone back to his apartments, gotten into his truck, and gone racing after Charlie. For that matter, he could have called him up on the phone and told him how he felt. Somehow, though, Jared couldn't shake the feeling that if this–if *they*–had been meant to be that the universe would have made sure that he'd made it here in time. Since he hadn't, it was best to just make peace with that and start putting his life together. Without Charlie.

*Goodbye, Charlie Garrett. It was nice while it lasted.*

# CHAPTER 20

*A*fter they left the theater Sheri didn't say anything, her face an expressionless mask. Even though Charlie tried to convince himself that it wasn't that bad, he could tell that she was well and truly furious with him, more than she'd ever been in all of their years of working together. The fact that she'd swept them out of the theater before the movie had even started–thus denying him the chance to explain himself to the waiting reporters–made it even clearer. He'd fucked up, and she was surely going to let him know about it.

There was a car waiting for them, of course, because Sheri wasn't the type of person to ever leave anything to chance. She'd probably figured that he was going to pull some stunt like this and had made sure that she had the means to get him out of there as quickly as possible. He paused for a split second and looked back–was he hoping to see Jared come running out of the theater, or was he just trying to get a last look back at the place where his next great venture just went down in flames? He honestly couldn't say–but there was no one there waiting for him, no one running out to say anything.

*I guess I left them in shock,* he thought a little bitterly.

Then they were in the car and racing toward the airport, and he didn't really have time or energy to think about much of anything.

The trip there took a remarkably short amount of time, and he was pretty sure the driver ran more than a few red lights. Clearly Sheri had told him that getting back to California as quickly as possible was of the paramount importance, and what Sheri wanted, Sheri got. She didn't say a word to him, of course, but she seemed to radiate anger and frustration, and he didn't feel brave enough to try to start a conversation: not when they drove up the hill toward the airport, not when they got out of the car, and not even when they started to get on the plane.

As he got on-board the jet, Charlie cast one look back in the direction of Huntington. He'd only been here a short time, but for some reason it had already cast a spell on him. He knew well enough why that was—it was the place that Jared called home—but he also knew that there was nothing more for him there. Jared had already made quite clear how he felt, and Charlie had to live with that.

He settled into a seat and buckled up, Sheri seated across from him. As the plane taxied and began to take off, he couldn't help but wonder what Jared was doing at that exact moment, and there was a tiny part of him that wished that he would see Jared come racing up that hill, desperate to get to Charlie before he took off.

But, of course, that didn't happen.

"You're not going to believe this, but your socials are blowing up right now, and the news is actually *good.*"

It took him a few seconds to realize that Sheri had started speaking to him and that she'd actually given him a piece of good news. When it finally sunk in, he couldn't help thinking that it paled in comparison to the disappointment of Jared not showing up, either to the screening or afterward.

*Just accept it,* he thought. *He told you how he felt, and that's all there is to it.*

But had he? Yes, he'd been cruel and hurtful, but Charlie thought he'd seen something else beneath all of that bravado; he suspected there was a sensitive boy there that was still trying to figure things out and to decide how he felt about...well, everything.

"Is that so?" he asked.

"Don't be like that, Charlie," Sheri said. "This is good news for you. You could have really shredded everything with that speech. For once in your life, can you just take the win and make both our lives easier?"

He knew that he should just tell Sheri what she so clearly wanted to hear and at the very least make this plane trip more enjoyable. However, something about giving that speech had opened up all kinds of opportunities for him, and he was going to start standing up for himself, even if that meant going against what Sheri wanted.

"Yes, it's great," he said, measuring his words with care, "but I'm sorry that I didn't start saying what I thought sooner."

Sheri gave him one of her level looks that suggested he was being unnecessarily dense.

"Really, Charlie? You're really going to start in on that again? How many times do I have to tell you that sometimes you have to just do what's expected of you so that you can make bigger gains later? You might have notched a win this time, but let's not get ahead of ourselves."

He opened his mouth to say something, but then he decided against it.

"Okay," was all he said.

They settled down into a quasi-comfortable silence after that.

· · ·

WHEN HE GOT BACK to California, Charlie tried to get back into his old routine. As Sheri had predicted, he was fending off offers left and right, and while some of them were projects that really did appeal to him, he still couldn't quite get the motivation that he needed in order to take on any of them. There was still a part of him that was back in West Virginia, and he was starting to think that there always would be.

Finally, when he couldn't take it anymore, he decided that he was just going to have to talk to Sheri about it. She might not completely understand where he was coming from, but she would at least be able to give him some advice that he badly needed.

As soon as he got to her office, he could tell from the look on her face that she knew why he was there.

"You're thinking about Jared, aren't you?" she asked as soon as he took a seat. She sighed and shook her head. "I knew this was going to happen. I'm starting to think that I should have just told you that he was waiting for you outside the theater that day."

"Wait, what do you mean Jared was there outside the venue?" he asked. For a minute it felt as if the room was tilting around him, but he forced himself to remain calm.

If Sheri was aware that she'd just dropped a bomb on him, she gave no sign of it. In fact, she looked utterly unperturbed. They could have been talking about the weather for all the more emotion she showed.

"You already told me how much of an asshole he'd been to you," she went on. "I didn't, and don't, think you need any more of that kind of energy in your life. You have a career, Charlie, and I hate to be the bearer of bad news or to be the adult in the room, but that has to be the thing that you work on the most right now. You don't have time to get into some long distance relationship. They don't last, anyway. Trust me."

Charlie wasn't sure whether to be bitterly amused or infuriated by this turn of events.

In the end, he opted for the former, and he actually found himself laughing.

"What's so funny?" Sheri asked.

"It's just...it's all like a rom-com, isn't it? I didn't know that he was standing right outside the whole time, or that he was trying to get to me, and I've been eating my heart out for nothing."

This seemed to get to Sheri in a way that nothing else he'd said had.

"You really do love this guy, don't you?"

Charlie knew the answer to that question, but he still felt a little shy about admitting it. How could you fall in love with someone that you'd only known for a couple of days? For that matter, how could you love someone who had already made it abundantly clear that they weren't really that interested in you?

"Yes," he finally said, because he was tired of lying about it to both himself and to Sheri and to everyone else.

Of course, Sheri rolled her eyes, because that was the type of thing that Sheri would do when confronted with someone else's feelings that she considered to be misguided. Which was to say...most of them.

She huffed and blew a stray bit of hair out of her eyes. "Well, there's really only one thing to do, as you should know, having starred in quite a few rom-coms of your own. You're going to have to go back and find him and tell him how you feel."

He was so surprised at this unexpected generosity that it took him a moment to think of something to say. Since she was clearly in a giving and sympathetic mood, he decided to go ahead and ask her for her advice. After all, what harm could it do?

"But he hasn't reached out to me. What gives me the right to go back to him when he already made it clear that he doesn't want to be with me and, in fact, wants nothing more to do with me? I mean, even if he *did* come to the theater, he said some hurtful things, and I'm just...I'm just not sure that he wants to be in a relationship."

Charlie wasn't sure why he was throwing up all of these roadblocks, but he thought it might be because he wanted to see what Sheri would say. Perhaps she'd be able to show him something he was missing.

She did not disappoint.

"Do I have to spell it out for you, Charlie? People say and do all sorts of things that they don't really believe, particularly when they're afraid of their own feelings. And from everything you've told me about this guy, he is most *definitely* afraid of his own feelings. Now, if that's the kind of guy that you really want to be with, that's your business, but you at least have to be a little bit aware of what that entails. If you're going to be with someone who's afraid of commitment, then you have to be okay with being the one to make the first move."

Charlie knew she was right, even as his mind tried to come up with a whole bunch of other reasons that he could back out of this before he got his feelings hurt again. However, he knew that he wasn't going to be able to find any kind of peace unless he found out Jared's feelings for him one way or another.

"Well?" she demanded. "What are you going to do?"

He scuffed his foot on the rug.

"Why are you being so insistent about this, Sheri? I thought you wanted me to get ahead with my career and ignore all of that other stuff."

"I guess because when it comes down to it I know you're not going to be able to do anything or focus on anything related to your career as long as he's out there and as long as this situation isn't resolved. If I'm going to get you to the next level as an actor I need to make sure you're not being burdened with distractions."

Before he could say anything to that rather cold-hearted and cynical approach to his love life, she went on.

"However, you have to recognize that that boy is a mess. I know you're smitten with him, and I'm sure that you're going to be very happy together, but I want to make sure that you do the right thing, the thing that's going to make you the happiest and that's not going to make you miserable. I know I give you a hard time, and I'm sure you think I'm a real hardass. The truth is, though, that I really do care about you. I want you to be happy. The question is: is Jared the person to make you happy?"

Charlie knew the answer to that. He supposed he'd known it from the moment that Jared pulled up to the airport in that old truck of his, that smirk on his face. Jared was the person that he wanted to try to make it work with, and he could already envision the kind of future that they could build in West Virginia.

"Yes," he said at last, his voice more assured than he thought it would be. "He's the one."

This time, rather than a hard look, Sheri actually smiled at him.

*This can't be the same Sheri that I've known all these years, can it?*

"I don't want to get all sappy and stuff, and don't get used to this, but it seems to me that there's really only one thing you can do at this point. You're going to have to go after him."

This was what he'd wanted all along, of course, and it certainly seemed as if the universe was sending him every sign it could to tell him that this was what he *should* do, but

Charlie still couldn't quite bring himself to believe that he was thinking about doing this.

"But what about all of the offers, and all of the studio calls?" he asked.

"Oh for heaven's sake, Charlie, are you really going to sit here and debate with me about whether you should go and get that silly boy? I've already told you that I think it's what you should do. I don't know what else I can do. Paint it across the sky, maybe? And as far as the studio offers and all of that?" She waved her hand. "I'll take care of it. We'll find some way to iron out all of the details after you make sure that you get your happily ever after. You're a hot commodity right now, and that means that you have a lot more leverage than you did before." She snorted. "I guess being a bit of a social justice warrior does give you some cultural cache when you need it."

"I guess there's just one thing to do, then," he said, getting to his feet. "I'm going to go get Jared."

THIS TIME, Charlie opted not to take his private jet back to West Virginia. He wasn't sure why he decided to drive, other than that he just needed the chance to clear his head. He wasn't sure whether spending several days in a car was going to be just what the doctor ordered in that regard, but he figured that he might as well give it a try and see what happened.

Surprisingly enough, it worked. Something about being out on the open road allowed him to think more clearly than he had in years. With each passing mile, he became more and more convinced that he was, in fact, doing the right thing. With nothing but the road in front of him, he allowed himself to really see why going back for Jared was the best choice that he could make.

He just hoped that it wouldn't be a waste of time.

Charlie had decided that he would go to Jared's parents'

place first. He didn't know this for sure, but something told him that this would be where Jared would be. Call it artistic intuition, or just a lucky guess, but he had a feeling that when he got there he'd find Jared, probably holed up in his old bedroom, trying to work through some bit of writer's block.

He tried not to let himself think too much about what might happen when he actually got there, but he wasn't blind to the possibility that Jared might not want him now, or perhaps his parents would tell him to get off their property. There were a million different possibilities, but Charlie tried to focus on the positive ones, with somewhat limited results.

Perhaps the best thing about the whole road trip, though, was how easily he was able to avoid detection by other people. By choosing little out-of-the-way motels and truckstops, he was able to keep other people from seeing him as Charlie Garrett and instead as just another guy who was on the road.

When, at last, he got off of the exit that would take him to Jared's parents' house, he felt absolutely confident in his decision to come. Whether Jared rejected him or not, he would at least know one way or another, and he wouldn't have to torment himself with endless "what ifs?"

Then he was pulling into Jared's parents' driveway, and he felt his confidence begin to flag. Was he really going to do this? Was he really going to act like one of the heroes in his own movies? Now that he was in the real world and not just in the in-between world of the open road, it all seemed much more complicated.

*You've come this far,* he reminded himself. *You're not going to turn back now.*

Jared's parents met him out in the yard before he'd even made it halfway to the house. His heart sank as he thought about what they might say, the disappointment that would be in their voices when they told him that he should probably just leave, because Jared just didn't want to see him.

To his pleasant surprise, however, they both met him with smiles on their faces. Even though he knew they'd had no way of knowing he was coming, the way that they were looking at him told him that they'd anticipated his coming and had actually been looking forward to it.

"We're so glad you're here," Joyce said, taking his hands in her own and then giving him a big hug.

"Good to see you back here, young man," Doug said, giving him a firm handshake and then pulling him in for a hug. "I was beginning to think that Jared might be the one who'd come to his senses first, and we both know that wasn't likely to happen."

They all shared a smile and a slight laugh at that, the shared amusement of a group of people who loved someone dearly but weren't blind to their foibles.

"Is he here?" he asked at last.

They both nodded their heads.

"He's in his bedroom," Joyce said. "Do you want to come inside and talk to him?"

At first Charlie almost said yes. Then he had a better idea. There was one place that would serve as the perfect setting for the reunion that he'd imagined with Jared. He had no way of knowing whether Jared would approve or not but, since he'd come this far and taken this many risks, he figured it was worth seeing through to the end.

"Do you think...do you think it would be okay if I went up to the top of the hill? And do you think you might send him up there in about, say, fifteen minutes?" He gestured at the hill behind them.

Once again they both smiled, as if this was exactly what they'd hoped–or expected–to happen.

"Of course, dear," Joyce said, reaching out and patting him on the cheek. "We'll give you a few minutes to get settled and then, if Jared hasn't noticed that you're there, we'll send him up."

Charlie was so overcome by their kind welcome that he had to swallow a few times to get his voice to come out clear.

"I really appreciate that," he said at last. "This and...well, just everything."

"That's okay, son," Doug said. "No thanks necessary. We're the ones who should be thanking you. You're the best thing that's ever happened to Jared, and I think even he's come to accept that. Now, you head up on the hill. You don't want to spoil your Hollywood ending, do you?"

Charlie smiled and gave them both another hug, and then he was traipsing up the hill.

As he reached the top of it, the view took his breath away. Part of that was because he was reminded of the time that he'd spent up here with Jared, but it was also because, as Jared himself had pointed out, this was like nowhere else in the world. Everything that they both loved about West Virginia–its beauty, its antiquity, its closeness to nature–was here, on this hilltop.

He turned to look back at the house, uncertain just how long he was going to have to wait up here. No sooner had he done so, however, than it opened, and Jared stood there.

*Well,* he thought, *here goes nothing.*

He waved and, to his everlasting delight and surprise, Jared waved back and, his face beaming with a smile that was visible even at this distance, he began to walk up the hill.

# CHAPTER 21

*A*fter missing Charlie at the theater, Jared decided that he couldn't stay in Huntington any more. He'd made peace with the fact that things there were never going to be the same, not now that he'd learned what it was like to know love. He would need to take some time to really get his life back on track, and he knew that he'd gotten as much out of Huntington as he was likely to. Even though he hated to admit it, his best bet was to spend some at his parents' place. They'd welcome him back–they were always telling him that it was a shame that he didn't live closer so they could spend more time with him–and while he was there he could finally get to work on his book and hopefully actually finish it.

Of course, he also knew that it was going to be a bit rich for him to go back home when he'd left his parents in the lurch when it came to Charlie, but if his dad was willing to forgive him, he knew his mother would be, too. She was just that type of person.

The drive back to his parents' place was a lot longer and lonelier than it had been just a couple of days earlier. The whole time, Jared kept mentally kicking himself that he'd let a guy like Charlie slip through his fingers.

*Well, there's no use complaining about it any more,* he thought. *You made your choice. Now you have to live with it.*

When he pulled into his parents' driveway, he didn't get out right away. He was still embarrassed by how much he knew he'd hurt his mother with his little scene and his leaving without saying goodbye.

But being with Charlie had shown him that there were better and healthier ways of being with his family and that he couldn't, and shouldn't, just keep on acting as if his emotions and feelings were the only ones that mattered. Because that was what he'd been doing for a lot longer than he realized. While it was more than a little painful to have to look himself in the mirror and see himself for what he really was, being with Charlie for just a weekend had shown him that it wasn't all bad.

Finally he felt like he was ready to face his mother again. His feet felt heavy as he walked across the yard, and that feeling only got worse when he saw his dad standing at the door.

"She's in the living room waiting for you," he said, opening up the door and giving Jared a hug. "Don't worry," he whispered, "it's fine."

Jared was incredibly relieved to hear that but, at the same time, he wouldn't quite be able to believe it was true until he actually talked to her himself.

When he got to the living room he found his mother sitting in her favorite chair, a bundle of knitting in her lap. She looked like the quintessential mom, as her fingers moved deftly with the needles and yarn.

"Well?" she said without looking up, "are you just going to stand there all day or are you actually going to come in and sit down?" She nodded with her head toward the chair opposite her. Jared, knowing that this was his cue, did as she said.

"So, uh, I guess I need to apologize to you," he started, his tongue already stumbling over the words. "The way I acted wasn't okay at all, and I know that. I also know that I apologized to dad, but I didn't to you, and I want to apologize for that, too. It was really immature of me, and you definitely deserve better."

For a few minutes his mom didn't say anything, and he thought for sure that she really was mad this time. Then, slowly, she put her knitting down and looked him right in the eye.

"You don't have to go through all of that song and dance," she said, voice rough with tears. "Just promise me that you won't do that again. I was scared that you were going to do something to yourself or get into an accident." She wagged a motherly finger at him. "I know how you drive when you get mad. That's what upset me more than anything else. Well, that and throwing away a perfectly good guy like Charlie." She snorted. "But I guess that didn't surprise me, either. You never did know what was best for yourself."

He could have pretended to be outraged, but the truth was that he was actually touched that, as always, she just wanted what was best for him, even after he'd been an asshole.

Even so, he cringed a little at the mention of Charlie. "Yeah, I'm not exactly thrilled about the way that I handled the whole Charlie thing, either, to be honest. I don't know what was going on in my head, but I guess I just let my own insecurities get in the way of happiness."

She nodded her head as he was speaking.

"So what are you going to do now?" she asked. He could always count on his mother to get right to the heart of the issue, particularly if she thought she already knew the answer.

"Of course you can stay here for as long as you want," she said. "In fact, I'm going to have to insist on it. I want you to start working on that book you keep talking about, and I want you to take some time to really get yourself into the headspace that you need to be in."

"Headspace?" he asked. "Since when are you the type of person to use the phrase 'headspace?'"

"Since my son began acting like an even bigger silly goose than usual," she said at once. "You know that I try to keep my nose out of your business, but I just couldn't keep it to myself. Charlie was good for you, Jared, whether you want to accept that or not. I saw the way he looked at you and, more to the point, I saw the way that *you* looked at *him*. I've never seen you look at another man like that."

"Well, to be fair, you've only known me as a gay man for the last decade and a half or so," he said. "So technically you..."

His mother immediately gave him that look that said very eloquently that he was being deliberately obtuse and she wasn't going to have any of it.

"You know that's not what I meant," she said. "He's a good man, and he's rich, and he seems to be head over heels for you. So why don't you give him a call and try to patch things up?"

That was something that Jared had given a bit of thought to, but he knew that he couldn't take that step. He was trying to look forward and not back and, much as he had grown to love Charlie–he could admit that to himself if not to anyone else–he knew that he couldn't embrace that part of his past.

"I just can't, mom. I know that you want us to be together, but that's just not going to happen, for a whole host of reasons. Trust me when I say that I've given this a great deal of thought, and I'm very okay with my decision."

"Jared, the most important thing to me is that you're happy. If that means you're happy without Charlie, then I'm not going to try to tell you otherwise. Ultimately you're the only one who can decide who and what makes you the happiest. That's not something that I can tell you, and it's not something that your father can tell you. It's not even something that Charlie could tell you. It has to come from inside of you."

Coming from anyone else those words would feel more than a little cheesy and trite. Somehow, though, his mother had the ability to say those kinds of things and make them sound and feel like they were absolutely sincere.

"Thanks, mom," he said and meant it.

She gave him one of her smiles. "Of course, dear. I'll always be here for you."

THE NEXT COUPLE of weeks were some of the most peaceful that Jared had ever experienced. Cut free from his dead-end job with the City Council, he was finally able to turn his attention back to the writing that he'd been ignoring for far too long. Almost as soon as he put pen to paper–he was one of those old-fashioned people who really did enjoy writing by hand rather than computer all the time–he could feel the words flowing out of him. He hadn't had this sensation in so long that he'd almost forgotten what it was like, and it didn't take long for him to figure out why he was suddenly so inspired.

It was Charlie, of course.

He knew that he shouldn't bind all of his creativity to one person, but there was no doubt in his mind that it was Charlie Garrett who'd made him feel as if he could really do this, as if his own voice was worth exploring. Of course, he had no idea whether anyone, let alone a publisher, would be interested. However, there was something exciting and exhilarating, maybe even life-giving, about the act of creation.

*This is what I've been missing out on for years,* he thought. *It's a shame I wasted so much time at that stupid City Council job, when I could have been doing this.*

He'd finally decided on writing a sort of quasi-fictional

memoir. He'd always been a fan of Truman Capote's *In Cold Blood* and other types of creative nonfiction, and the form continued to recommend itself to him as the way that he might be able to come to terms with some of his own past.

Of course, he didn't spend all of his time just bent over his pen and paper. He also made sure to spend time outside enjoying the nice weather, and he helped his dad care for the chickens and the garden. It felt good to be getting in touch with his roots again, in a way that he'd never been able to do before. It was exciting and yet also calming at the same time, and he was glad for the chance to get closer to his parents.

Jared was happy, but it still felt like he was missing something. He tried, he really did, to put Charlie out of his mind and to just focus on the present and the future. Every time he turned on the TV, though, there was a reminder of Charlie, and the same went for his computer, his phone, and even his watch. Everyone was speculating about who Charlie Garrett might be in a relationship with and whether he'd had his heart broken in West Virginia, but either Sheri was even better at managing the press than she'd let on or else they really had been lucky to escape being found out.

Either way, Jared pretended that it didn't hurt him to think about Charlie being with anyone else, but he couldn't hide the truth from his mother.

"You could just call him, you know," she said one day, and then immediately put her hands up in a sign of surrender. "I'm not trying to tell you what to do or manage your life. I'm just saying that I've seen you moping around the house, and I know what that usually means."

It was at just that moment that he looked at the TV and there was Charlie. He was giving an interview to one of the talk shows, and Jared felt like he'd been kicked. All of the breath left his body, and he actually had to sit down.

*Ugh. Of course he looks better than ever,* Jared thought resentfully. *Would it hurt him to look at least a bit lovelorn?*

The truth was, though, that Charlie looked positively radiant. That smile of his still had the power to light up an entire room, and he laughed and joked with the interviewer with the sort of effortless charm that he'd exerted from the moment that Jared had met him.

"I can turn it off if you want," his mother said, interrupting his thoughts.

"No, it's fine. Go ahead and watch him. I'm gonna head back up to my room and get some writing done."

His mom gave him that concerned look, but he pretended he didn't see it as he went back upstairs and, true to his word, started writing.

SEEING Charlie on the TV seemed to unleash yet another wave of creativity, and over the next couple of days the words just seemed to pour onto the page of their own volition. In all of his years of composing Jared had never felt the muse strike like this before, and it made him feel incredibly alive.

It was a few days after seeing Charlie on the TV, and Jared had just finished a remarkably productive day of writing, plumbing some depths of his own psyche that he hadn't known existed. He'd just set his pen down when he heard a car door outside. He assumed it was someone who'd come to see his parents–he'd learned very quickly that there was an almost constant stream of family and friends coming in and out of their house on a daily basis–and even when the front door didn't open he didn't think anything about it.

It wasn't until he looked out his window–which looked out on the hill behind the house–that he saw a figure walking up it.

*It can't be,* he thought. *It just can't be.* He wasn't sure if he was trying to convince himself that it wasn't Charlie. He wasn't sure that he *wanted* it to be him, for that matter. After all of the time they'd spent apart, it just didn't seem possible.

Then the figure turned around briefly, and Jared's heart caught in his throat, because he knew right then that it was Charlie. Against all of the odds, he'd come back.

*Well?* He asked himself. *Are you just going to sit here and wait for him to leave again, or are you going to go out there and see him?*

That was all it took for him to get out of his chair and start making his way through the house. He still wasn't sure that he'd seen what he thought he'd seen, and he certainly wasn't sure that he was doing the right thing, but all he knew at that moment was that he had to get to Charlie as quickly as possible, had to let him know how sorry he was that things had turned out the way they had. Every other thought but that flew out of his head as he almost ran through the house.

Just before he got to the back door, however, his dad's voice stopped him.

"Jared."

He turned to face his dad, who stood there in the kitchen, one eyebrow raised.

"Did you know he was here?" Jared asked.

His dad just shrugged.

"He came to the door about fifteen minutes ago. I figured you'd see him walking up the hill sooner or later." He gave a little laugh. I"m very glad that it was sooner rather than later. Charlie's a very patient man, but I think he's waited for you long enough."

Jared wanted to argue with him and tell him all the reasons that he was, in fact, worth waiting for, but his dad had a point. When it came right down to it, Charlie *had* driven all the way across the country to be here or...at least...Jared hoped that he'd driven. He'd hate to think about how much fuel it would take for yet another flight from California to West Virginia...

"Jared, stop stalling," his dad interrupted his thoughts. "Because I know that's what you're doing."

Jared grinned sheepishly.

"It's just that...now that he's here, I'm not sure what he's going to say, y'know? We didn't part on the best of terms before. What if he hasn't forgiven me?"

"Jared," his father said with exaggerated patience. "Do you really think that Charlie Garrett would drive all the way across the country just so that he could tell you he doesn't want to be with you? Now, for the last time, stop stalling and get out there!"

Jared suddenly felt such a rush of feeling and love for his father that he ran over and gave him a hug, which the other man eagerly returned.

"I love you, dad," he said, surprised at his own rush of feeling.

"I love you too, son. Now, for the last time: go!"

This time Jared actually did what his father said and went to the door, pushing it open. His eye was drawn inevitably to the top of the hill, where the sun was, unsurprisingly, bathing Charlie in its glow.

*Jeez,* Jared thought, *does he have to be perfect now, too? I bet by the time that I get up there I'm going to be drenched with sweat and huffing and wheezing, and he's going to be practically perfect Charlie Garrett.*

The whole time he climbed he kept Charlie in his sights, still not quite believing that he was here, that he was waiting for him, Jared Russell.

"W...what are you doing here?" he managed to stammer out, once he got to the top. "I just saw you on the TV the other day ago, and you looked so happy."

"I was," Charlie replied. "Because I knew that I was going

to be coming back here, to West Virginia. To home. To...to you."

A hard knot inside of Jared that he hadn't really known was there suddenly let loose, and the next thing he knew he was in Charlie's arms, which reached out to welcome him.

"I was so afraid I'd lost you," he said, nuzzling this man that he loved, savoring the mix of sweat and sun and cologne and all of those special things that made Charlie what he was. He wanted to stay like this forever, so that he would know how much he meant to Jared and how he was never going to let him go now that they were together again.

At last, though, they did have to pull apart, but that was only so Charlie could kiss him. This was a kiss that was somehow both tender and passionate, as if each of them were desperate to tell the other how they felt with their bodies rather than their words. Only the awareness that his parents were almost certainly watching from down at the house kept Jared from taking this even further.

Finally, he pulled away and asked the question that was burning on the edge of his tongue.

"Why did you come back?"

Charlie just raised an eyebrow.

"What?" he asked, raising his hands defensively. "I just want to know what brought you back here. I mean, I did act like kind of a jerk, you know."

"Believe me, I know that better than anyone," Charlie said, the faintest bit of bitterness in his voice. "But I guess the answer to your question is simple enough. I love you, Jared. I love you for your stubbornness and your creativity and all of the things that make you, you. I love you for how you make me feel and for how you make me want to be a better and more engaged person. I love you for being prickly and prone to offense." He finally seemed to run out of breath and words, and so he just shrugged and said. "I just love you, okay?"

At first Jared couldn't think of anything to say. This wasn't the first time that someone had said they'd loved him, of course, and it wasn't even the first time that he'd believed them. It *was* the first time, though, that someone was willing to point out all of his flaws and talk about them like they were things to be loved in their own right rather than just fixed.

*You don't deserve him,* that mean little voice in the back of his head said. *You're just going to hurt him again, and you're going to prove that he was right to have left you in the first place.*

Just a short time ago, this would have caused Jared to withdraw, but this time, buoyed up and given strength by Charlie's incandescent smile, he punted those thoughts away. It was almost like he could see them disappear over the crest of the next hill, and he smiled.

He took a deep breath. "You know what? I love you, too. I love the way that you always make me feel like I'm a good and decent person, even when I have trouble seeing it. I love the way that you have a smile that can light up a room. I love the way that you love my family and my friends and the way you want to be a part of my life." He paused, and then went on. "And, to be honest, I love that you're from West Virginia, and that you stood up to Councilman Rhodes and all of the other homophobes in Huntington."

"I'm starting to think I should make a movie called *Ten Things I Love About You,*" Charlie said, but there was a twinkle in his eye.

"Oh, just shut up and kiss me," Jared said, because that's the only thing he wanted in the world right then.

And Charlie did.

# EPILOGUE

*And they lived, if not happily ever after, at least happily enough.*

Jared sighed as his fingers left the keys. It was an ending, that was for sure, even if it wasn't quite what he'd wanted when he set out to write his memoir. A few agents had expressed some interest in it, and he was hoping that at least one of them would be willing to put in the time and effort to make it a better product.

*Heaven knows it could use it,* he thought wryly. *But hey, it's done, and that's the most important thing. The best manuscript is a done manuscript, as the old saying goes.*

He had no idea whether that was actually an old saying, let alone whether it was actually true, but he was going to go with it because it's what he needed to tell himself right now.

Jared yawned and stretched, his joints popping pleasantly. He'd lost count of the number of times that Charlie had told him that he needed to get up and move around more often. He'd told him that that might be how they did things in California, but here in West Virginia it was more common to just sit until the job was done.

*I'm starting to think that Charlie might have a point, though,* he thought, and then he smiled.

There were times that he couldn't quite believe that Charlie had actually put his money where his mouth was and moved back to the Mountain State. They both knew there would be challenges ahead, both in terms of their relationship and in terms of the future they were trying to build. After all, it wasn't as if Charlie's speech at the film festival had really moved the needle that much in terms of state politics for queer folks, even if it had helped his career.

*Rome wasn't built in a day,* Jared reminded himself. *These things take time. I'm just glad that he decided to move back here so that we could be together.*

Of course, he knew that wasn't the only reason that Charlie came back, though he liked to think that it was a big part of it. The golden boy of the Romance Network had come back to his home state to do good work, first by pouring a lot of money into forming a new film production company head-quartered in Huntington and then by setting up a foundation to develop Annamoriah as an artist colony, just as he'd said he would.

*That man,* Jared thought, as he looked around their shared bedroom, *he really is something special. I'm just glad that I had the good sense to see it before it was too late.*

Smiling, he headed out the door and down the stairs. Even now, after they'd been living together for quite a while, he still found it surprising how much lighter his steps felt, almost like he was walking on air, as cliche as that sounded.

He walked into the kitchen, drawn by the smell of freshly-brewed coffee. No matter how busy he was or what he was doing, Charlie always found time to make sure that Jared had his little pick-me-up ready. He'd even gone the extra mile and gotten an old-fashioned percolator, because he knew that was the kind of coffee that Jared preferred.

*What did I do to deserve this?* He thought to himself, but then quickly reminded himself that he was worthy of love. That was one of the things that Charlie had taken a great deal of trouble to remind him of again and again: that, no matter how much other people might have tried to convince otherwise, he was worthy of love and respect. It was a lesson that Jared still wasn't entirely sure that he'd ever learn, but he was going to keep trying, both for Charlie's sake and his own.

Jared grabbed his coffee cup and padded out to the living room, making sure not to stumble over Lorelei on the way out. The fluffy polydactyl cat was the very first thing that the two of them had gotten once they settled on the house, and she'd immediately made it clear that the house was hers and that she let them live there on her sufferance.

Charlie sat on the couch looking out the windows at the valley spread below, Jasmine their golden retriever curled up next to him. There was something almost too ironic about the fact that they'd adopted the very dog that so many people compared Charlie to, but Jared supposed there was a certain kind of symmetry in that. He'd learned, the hard way, that sometimes it was okay to just lean in and enjoy the little joys that life gives you, even when it seemed as if they were too good to be true.

He stood there for a few seconds, just hovering in the doorway, gazing at the man he loved.

"Are you just going to stand there and stare at me all day or are you actually going to come in and sit down?"

Charlie turned and gave him one of those smiles that were his speciality. No matter how many times it happened, no matter how many smiles he received, Jared always felt like he was going to melt into the floor whenever he saw that flash of white teeth and that gleam of pure love shining in Charlie's eyes.

This time was no exception.

"How did you know I was standing here?"

Charlie gave him a knowing look. "For one thing I heard it when you put your foot on that creaky floorboard that you refuse to fix because you think it gives the house character. For another, you can never hide when this one is always aware of what you're doing." He pointed meaningfully at Jasmine, who looked up at both of them with nothing but adoration in her eyes.

Jared huffed.

"I suppose that's true. I'm going to have to get better at moving stealthily, I guess."

"I don't think you need to go that far," Charlie said, patting the couch next to him. "I kind of like knowing where you are in the house. I don't like having people sneak up on me. I'm a romance movie star, not a horror movie star."

Jared smiled and walked over. Charlie was selling himself short, because he was much more than just a Romance Network star, now. *The Gentleman Usher*, along with the good press from all of his philanthropy, had done wonders for his career. He had more offers than he knew what to do with, so many that he could be selective about which ones he took.

Wedging himself between Jasmine and Charlie—which earned him a disgruntled side-eye from the former and a sigh of relief from the latter—Jared snuggled into his boyfriend's shoulder.

"Are you happy?" Charlie asked.

It was such a simple question, if also a loaded one. It took Jared a few minutes to put his thoughts together, but he didn't take too long, because he knew Charlie might get the wrong idea. Their love was strong, but Jared didn't like to tempt fate.

"I am, yes," he said finally, meaning every word. He snuggled closer to Charlie, who put his arm around him and pulled him close. "I'm happy because you're here. I'm happy because we've built this life together." He took a deep breath, bracing himself for what he had to say. "And I'm happy just being me. I know that might not seem like a lot to you, but it's something I've struggled with my whole life. Thanks to you, though, I'm really, truly happy with myself."

There. The words were out. Charlie, in that way that only he had, kissed Jared gently on the top of his head.

"I'm really glad to hear that. I knew from the moment I met you that you were something special. I'm glad you can finally see that."

Jared felt the warm flush of joy moving over him.

"What about you?" he asked. "Are you happy, Charlie?"

Charlie laughed.

"I'm happier than I've ever been in my life. I'm with the man I love. My relationship with my mom is better than it's ever been. I have a cat and a dog that both love me, most of the time. And I'm doing what I love and doing good in the world. Yes, I'm happy."

Jared was glad to hear that. He'd been unsure that moving Charlie's mom back to West Virginia would be a good idea, but she'd never been happier. They made a point of visiting her every week and, while she was sometimes a bit uncomfortable seeing them together, she'd always been polite. It wasn't everything. It was a beginning, though.

Even though Jared knew there were still a lot of things they had to figure out, he also knew they could do it together. They'd built a life for themselves, they were together, and they were in love.

And, most importantly of all, they were home.

# ACKNOWLEDGMENTS

This book was inspired by the Appalachian Queer Film Festival, and so I want to thank Jon Matthews and J. Gallienne, my fellow members of the board who've done so much to keep the festival going. Y'all inspire me so much, and I can't wait to keep working with you to make the festival great, showing the world just how queer Appalachia is, has been, and always will be.

I also want to give a shout-out to the Queer Romance Book Club, hosted by the Buzzed Word in Ocean City, and to the PFAG Book Club of Salisbury. Both groups have taught me so much about queer community and the enduring power of queer literature. I can't wait to see what we read next!

The enormously talented A.J. Norris of Delicious Nights Design deserves so much credit for the amazing cover for this book. She captured Jared and Charlie so well, and her artistry brought my vision to life even better than I thought possible.

Kelly, we've been through so much together since we first became close back in 2005, and there's not a day of my life where I'm not grateful that you're in it. You're more than a friend; you're family. You're my brother, and I love you (even if you give me a hard time and are a bit too ruthless when it comes to "de-TJifying" my writing).

Abby, you're the sister I never had. I feel like you *get* me in ways that almost no one else does. I hope you know that my picking on you is a sign of my love. I respect the *hell* out of you, and I love you to pieces.

Ben, as I never tire of saying, you're an absolute gem.

Meeting you in 2021 was a bit of serendipity, and I'm so very grateful that our friendship has endured and flourished. You also give the best haircuts in the world.

Roger, you're my oldest friend. We've been through a lot together, but somehow we make it work. I'm sure you'll see more than a little of Cameron in Annamoriah. See? I told you I didn't really hate our hometown as much as I like to pretend.

Jarrell, you may drive me crazy at times, but I love you to pieces. You've been a steadfast cheerleader through every step of this process, for which I am so very thankful.

Steve, despite the fact that you can't pronounce "Appalachian" correctly to save your life, you've been a key part of this novel from the beginning. You have a knack for being supportive while asking probing, insightful questions, something I continue to appreciate. I value our late-night conversations, and I look forward to many more.

Melissa...where do I even start? Since you burst into my life in 2009 you've been my rock and, in some ways, my platonic soulmate. We're two country kids who made good, and I thank you so much for the joy and the light that you bring into my life.

Jilly, this novel wouldn't be what it is if you hadn't been there and provided your keen eyes, insight, and romantic sensibility. You were there at the beginning of Jared and Charlie's romance, and you've been there every step of the way, offering generous critique and encouragement. This book is only as good as it is thanks to you.

Bridget, what can I say? You're one of my favorite people in the world, and though we exasperate each other, what we have is real and deep. I admire you so much as a writer, a scholar, and a friend. Thank you for coming along for this crazy indie publishing ride.

Lindsay, I'm so glad we got to meet each other through Aaron. We Pisces just understand one another on a deep level.

Thank you so much for helping to make this book a success. You're a genius.

Julie, of all of my cousins, we've always understood one another better than anyone else in our family. You've always loved me and welcomed me into your home. You're a treasure.

Zach, I'm so very glad that we reconnected. Found family means so much to queer folk, but so does birth family. We queer Appalachian kids gotta stick together and, as you say so often, being close to you makes me feel complete. I love you.

To all of my friends and professors at Marshall University and in Huntington—where so much of this story takes place—thank you so much for being such a key part of one of the formative times of my life. You helped to make me who I am today. Thank you from the bottom of my heart. Thank you as well to my professors and colleagues at Syracuse University, who made my time there such a joy.

Tiggy (because I'm the type of person who thanks their cat), you're an absolute asshole and a jerk, but I love you to bits. I'll give you an extra can of Fancy Feast on release day.

Aaron, somehow I never run out of words to talk about how happy you make me and how much you make me a better person. I cherish each and every day that we have together. The world might be crazy sometimes, but you make it better and infinitely more bearable.

Even though she passed away in 2020 and thus never got to see this novel come into the world, I want to thank my grandma, Evelyn Dague, for being the best grandparent any kid could ask for. Much like Marla, I suspect you knew I was gay, but we never talked about it. Still, I never doubted you loved me, and I miss you every day.

Last, and certainly not least, I want to thank my parents, Kathy and Tom West. There's more than a little of you in Doug and Joyce. You've shown me the sort of unconditional love that every queer Appalachian kid should have, and as long as I live I will always be so very thankful that I get to call you mom and dad.

If you're a queer Appalachian and you happen to be reading this book, know that I'm pulling for you. Those hills and hollers are our home just as much as they are anyone's. Never forget that, and never stop fighting!

And to anyone I've missed in this set of acknowledgments, rest assured that I'll get you in the next one!

# ABOUT THE AUTHOR

The proud son and grandson of farmers and coal miners, TJ West is a queer writer and culture critic. He holds a Bachelor's degree from Marshall University and a Master's and Doctorate from Syracuse University. Though he is based in Maryland's Eastern Shore–where he lives with his partner and their cat–the Mountain State will always have a piece of his heart.